THE BLITZ
DETECTIVE

By Mike Hollow

THE BLITZ
DETECTIVE

Mike Hollow

Allison & Busby Limited
11 Wardour Mews
London W1F 8AN
allisonandbusby.com

First published by Lion Hudson as *Direct Hit* in 2015.
This edition published by Allison & Busby in 2020.

A CIP catalogue record for this book is available from
the British Library.

10 9 8 7 6 5 4 3

ISBN 978-0-7490-2672-1

Typeset in 11/16 pt Sabon LT Pro by
Allison & Busby Ltd.

The paper used for this Allison & Busby publication
has been produced from trees that have been legally sourced
from well-managed and credibly certified forests.

Printed and bound by
CPI Group (UK) Ltd, Croydon, CR0 4YY

For Catherine and David,
my great privilege

PROLOGUE

He was alone, and there was no one to help him. Trapped in the silent space between two rows of graves, he heard every rasp of the madman's breath. The reek of stale beer soured the air between them as the dark figure grabbed his lapels and pulled him close. The attacker's face was vicious, and the cap yanked down onto his forehead was shabby. No witness could have identified him, even if there had been one in this gloomy wilderness of the dead. But Hodgson knew him well enough, and wished they had never met.

It was absurd. There were houses just a hundred yards away. He could trace the outline of their roofs and chimneys against the night sky to his right. But in the depths of the blackout, with not a light showing anywhere, he might as well be on the moon. The only people out at this time of night would be the ARP wardens and the police, and he could hear no sound of them. They would have plenty of things to attend to.

He knew he was trembling but could not stop it. He was out of his depth, overwhelmed by a familiar surge of panic. His father used to say dogs and horses could smell fear, so maybe people did too. He remembered the two women who'd stopped him on Stratford High Street in the autumn of 1916 and given him a white feather. Perhaps they could smell cowardice on him. He could have made an excuse: he'd been officially ruled unfit for military service in the Great War because of his short-sightedness. But no, he just took the feather without complaint and went on his way. He knew they were right: he was a coward through and through.

Now he heard himself babbling some futile nonsense about reporting this to the police. The man released his hold on one lapel, but only to slap him in the face. The sting bit deep into Hodgson's cheek, and his glasses rammed painfully into the bridge of his nose. He wanted to cry. *It's just like the way gangsters slap hysterical women in the pictures*, he thought. *He knows that's all it takes with someone like me.*

'Not so high and mighty now, are we, Mr Hodgson?' his tormentor snarled. 'I think it's time you started putting a bit more effort into our little arrangement. Don't you?'

He flung Hodgson back against a gravestone. Its edge cracked into his spine and he slumped to the ground.

Humiliation. Again. All through his life. His wife might like to think he had some status because he worked for the Ministry of Labour and National Service, but he knew his post was shamingly junior for a man with twenty-four years' service. After all this time he still wondered if she knew what kind of man she had married. But *he* knew, only too well. He saw himself, eleven years old, and the gang that set about him on his way home from school, older boys looking for fun in their last term at Water Lane. His West Ham Grammar School uniform made him an easy target. When they snatched his cap and tossed it onto the roof of the nearest house, he understood for the first time in his life that he was a victim. They were just a bunch of fourteen-year-old boys, but he was outnumbered and powerless. Now he was outnumbered by one man.

'I will, I will,' he said. 'It's just difficult. You don't understand.'

'Oh, I understand all right,' said the man, hauling him back onto his feet.

Hodgson pushed his glasses back up his nose to straighten them. Now he could see the scar that ran three inches down the side of his assailant's face, just in front of his ear. The man didn't look old enough for it to be a wound from the last war, and not young enough to have been involved in the current one. He tried not to think how he might have got it.

'You just look here, Mr Hodgson. You're a nice man, so I'm going to give you one more chance.'

The sneer in his voice made his meaning clear. He pulled a crumpled piece of paper from his trouser pocket and stuffed it into the inside pocket of Hodgson's jacket, then patted him on the chest in mock reassurance.

'Right, Mr Hodgson, you just fix it for this little lot, and there's a pound in it for you for each one. Mind you do it right, though. If you don't, I'll shop you, or worse. Now you won't forget, will you?'

Hodgson hurried to give his assurance, relieved that the ordeal was over. Before the words were out of his mouth, he felt the first blow to his stomach, then a second full in his face, a third to the side of his head and another to his stomach. After that he lost count.

He became aware of a boot nudging his left leg.

'Been celebrating, have we, sir?'

He didn't know where he was or what time it was. His eyes stung as he strained them open. Two figures stood above him, silhouetted against the lightening sky. He couldn't see their faces, and took them at first for soldiers, or perhaps a Home Guard patrol, from the outline of their headgear. One of the men squatted down beside him, and now through a blur Hodgson could make out the word 'Police' stencilled in white on the front of his steel helmet.

'I think you'd better come along with us so we can get you tidied up before your missus sees you,' said the policeman.

Hodgson closed his eyes. He felt their grip on his arms, one either side, as they got him standing.

Every part of his body ached. He struggled to focus his mind and glanced down at his cheap black suit, crumpled and filthy. How was he going to persuade them he was a respectable civil servant when he must look like a common midnight brawler? Even worse, how was he going to explain all this to Ann?

He had to think of something. He had to find some way to stop that maniac destroying his life.

CHAPTER ONE

There were times when Jago wished he wasn't a policeman. Right now he'd like to go out, cross the street and rip the thing off the wall. It had been stuck up there for so long, he reckoned most people probably ignored it, but it still made him feel angry. Everything about it was pompous and patronising, he thought, like the government that had put it there.

He tried not to think about it. That wasn't why he'd come here. Apart from the view across West Ham Lane to that confounded poster, Rita's cafe was an oasis, a sanctuary of friendly welcome and good home cooking. Today, like time without number in the past, he'd come here for respite from the job, from crime, from the world.

He saw Rita approaching, cloth in hand and pencil behind her ear as usual. She wore her years well, he thought. A woman of a certain age, as the French put it – in other words fortyish, like himself, but already widowed for twenty-two years and with a daughter of twenty-three. In her floral-patterned apron and with her headscarf tied in a turban, she treated her customers as though they'd just popped round to her house for a cup of tea in the kitchen.

'Afternoon, Mr Jago,' she said. 'Enjoying the view?'

'No,' he said. 'Can't you get the council to take that poster down? It annoys me.'

She peered out of the window. The brown paper tape that criss-crossed the glass had been up for a year now and was beginning to peel away at the corners. She rubbed off a small smear with her cloth.

'I'm sorry about the state of these windows. I'll have to put some new tape up, I think, although why we bother I don't know. A year at war and we've never had a single bomb down this street. But what's wrong with the poster, dear? You mean that red one on the wall over there? It's in a bit of a state, isn't it?'

'Yes, but unfortunately you can still just about make out what it says. Look.'

Rita read the words slowly.

'"Your courage, your cheerfulness, your resolution will bring us victory." What's wrong with that, then?'

'Everything, I'd say. What idiot thinks you can win a war by being cheerful? They should try spending a

14

few weeks in a trench up to their knees in mud, blood and rats like your Walter and I did. Then we'd see how cheerful they were. And look: every time it says "your" they've put a line under it. They might as well put one under "us", too, and make it absolutely clear: we're the rulers and you're the ruled. It's a wonder one of those communists from the docks hasn't crept out in the night with a pot of paint and done it for them. What do these Whitehall pen-pushers use for brains?'

'Not your favourite poster then, Mr Jago? Honestly, I'm surprised at you. Coming out with things like that, and you a servant of the Crown. If people hear you talking like that you'll have to arrest yourself.'

'Don't worry, Rita: for your ears only. I don't go round saying that sort of thing to everyone, but I know I can let off a bit of steam with you.'

'I'll go up the road to the town hall if you like and ask them to scrape it off the wall, tell them it's annoying my customers and ruining my trade.'

'To be honest, Rita, it wouldn't surprise me if West Ham Borough Council had left it there on purpose. Think about it: you've got the world's worst propaganda poster, dreamt up by Chamberlain and his Tory government, and a council controlled by Labour for twenty years. They probably left it there deliberately to make a political point.'

'I think you're reading too much into it. And in any case, the weather's nearly done it for you – it'll be falling off the wall soon.'

She wiped the top of his table, then stood back and took a notepad from her apron pocket and the pencil from behind her ear.

'Now then, what can I get you? A spot of late lunch?'

'Just a pot of tea for two, please, and a couple of your delightful rock cakes. I'm waiting for my colleague to join me – he's just popped to the gents.'

'I'll bring the tea and cakes over when I see him come back. Is it the young man I saw you come in with? I don't think I've seen him in here before.'

'Yes, that's my assistant, Detective Constable Cradock. I'm taking him to the football this afternoon. Familiarising him with the local culture, you might say.'

'Well, you've got very good weather for it; I hope you win. This constable of yours, he looks a nice young man. Might suit my Emily. Is he spoken for?'

'Sorry, Rita, I have no idea – and if I had I wouldn't tell you.'

'I expect you miss your Sergeant Clark, don't you? He's back in the army, isn't he?'

'Yes, he was called up when war was declared, with all the other reserves. We're so short of manpower these days I can't get a detective sergeant to replace him, so I have to make do with a constable instead.'

'Same for me, dear,' said Rita. 'The last girl I had working here packed it in. Said she could get better money doing munitions work. Now I'm stuck with that Phyllis over there. Too slow to catch cold, if you ask me. Young people today don't know what hard work is, do they, Mr Jago?'

'It's not like it was when we were young, Rita, that's for sure. I look at Cradock sometimes and think I don't understand him. And it's not just a generation thing. It's the war: if you lived through it you see things differently, simple as that.'

'Too true,' said Rita with a sigh. 'Twenty-two years now since my Walter was killed, and it's with me every day. But to most people I'm just another war widow, and who wants to think about that? Present company excluded, of course: you've always been very understanding. Sometimes I think I should have gone away, lived somewhere else, started all over again, but somehow I never did. Don't know why.'

'Because people like you and me belong here, Rita, that's why.'

'I suppose so. No place like home, eh? Still, there's no point getting miserable, is there? That doesn't help anyone. Look, I've brought you the paper to look at while you're waiting. Yesterday's *Express*. I know you like to see it.'

She handed him that week's *Stratford Express* with a smile, then pointed at the wall behind him.

'Is that a new hat you've got there?'

'That's very observant of you, Rita. You should have been a detective.'

She laughed.

'Not me, dear. I'm not clever enough. It's just that

you're always so nicely turned out, not like most of the men round here, so I notice what you're wearing.'

Jago took the hat down from the hook on the wall and smoothed it with his jacket sleeve.

'You're right. I got it last week. It's the first I've bought for five years, and I plan to wear it for the next five at least.'

The hat was a charcoal grey fedora with the brim snapped down at the front. He didn't like to think what the men at the station would say if they knew what he'd paid for it. Even a detective inspector's salary didn't give much room for self-indulgence. If he'd been a family man they might call it scandalous, but he had neither wife nor children, and his conscience was clear.

'Very nice too,' said Rita. 'You always look a proper gentleman.'

She set off back to the kitchen, and Jago replaced his hat on the hook. He was peckish, and Cradock had not yet appeared. *Get a move on, boy*, he thought: *I want my cup of tea.*

Most of the Saturday lunchers had gone by now, but the cafe was still busy. Rita had the wireless on as usual, and beneath the customers' chatter he could make out the mellow voice of Hutch, crooning that it would be a lovely day tomorrow. All part of the national drive for cheerfulness, no doubt, he thought. But on a day like this it was almost possible to believe it. A week into September already, and still unseasonably warm: real seaside weather. Not that anyone was allowed within miles of the coast any more.

Cradock came into view at last.

'Come along, lad, I'm starving,' said Jago. 'What were you doing in there? I thought you'd set up camp for the duration.'

'Sorry, guv'nor,' said Cradock.

'Well, sit down. Your tea's on its way.'

Moments later Rita arrived with their order and carefully set out the cups and saucers, teapot, and strainer on the table, followed by two large rock cakes, each on a white china plate.

'There you are, gentlemen,' she said. 'Give me a shout if there's anything else you need.'

She gave Jago a theatrical wink and departed. Jago saw the look of alarm on Cradock's face.

'Don't worry, she's only joking. Rita and I go back a long way.'

He poured the two cups of tea and pushed one across to Cradock, then spooned sugar into his own from the chipped glass bowl in the middle of the table. He'd cut down from two sugars to one in January, when the rationing came in – doing his bit for the war effort – but his first taste of the drink was still agreeably sweet. He smacked his lips and gave a satisfied sigh.

'So how's your cheerfulness today, Peter?' he said, with a sideways nod towards the window.

Cradock followed his gaze and spotted the offending slogan.

'Reckon I'd feel cheerful if I was in the poster business, sir,' he said. 'Whoever prints them must make a packet.

There's always some who do in a war, though, isn't there? It's an ill wind that blows no one a silver lining.'

Jago inclined his head and stared into Cradock's face. 'And in English?'

'Sir?'

'Never mind: I got the gist.'

Cradock took a bite of his cake.

'You were right about these rock cakes, sir,' he said. 'Very tasty, very sweet.'

Jago rolled his eyes. 'Leave the catchphrases to the comedians,' he said. 'You're a police officer, not a music hall act. Do try to remember that. Too much time listening to the wireless, that's your trouble.'

Cradock seemed to be concentrating too hard on pushing cake into his mouth to notice what his boss was saying. Jago picked up the *Express* and studied the front page. A couple of minutes later he tutted and lowered the paper to address Cradock again.

'Have you seen what the local rag has to say about those air raids last weekend?'

Cradock shook his head, his mouth still full.

'They make it sound like an entertainment. Listen: "On Saturday and Monday afternoons many people had the thrilling experience of witnessing aerial combats in the district." Thrilling experience? They won't find it so entertaining if the Germans start bombing us properly. And here: it says, "An Anderson shelter in which five people were sheltering was blown to pieces." Very nicely put. What it means is that five people were blown to pieces in their own back garden, but they don't say that. What are they going to say when it's five hundred people a night being blown to bits?'

'You don't think that'll really happen, do you, guv'nor?' said Cradock, trying to catch the crumbs that fell from his mouth as he spoke. 'I heard something on the news yesterday about Mr Churchill saying the air raids haven't been half as bad as expected and the sirens don't actually mean anyone's in real danger. Something like that, anyway.'

'So you think we're past the worst of it, do you?' said Jago.

'Well, I'm not sure, sir, but it sounds quite positive.'

'Yes,' said Jago, 'like that Ministry of Information advert they had in the papers. Do you remember it? "I keep a cool head, I take cover, and I remember the odds are thousands to one against my being hurt." So all we need to do is keep a cool head, and everything will be fine. And be cheerful, of course. It'll be some other poor soul who cops it, not me.'

He gave a contemptuous snort and leant closer across the table, lowering his voice.

'All I'm saying is I think things might get worse before they get better. Churchill may be right, the raids may not have been as bad as the government expected – I mean, before the war some people reckoned we'd have fifty thousand dead on the first day. But that doesn't mean they won't get worse in the future, especially now Hitler's only twenty miles away across the Channel.'

'Well, best to look on the bright side, wouldn't you say, sir?'

'Oh, undoubtedly,' said Jago. 'Undoubtedly.'

He folded the *Express* and laid it on the table. It was hard work educating Cradock. The boy wasn't a patch on Clark, but then everyone had to start somewhere. He blew onto his tea to cool it and took a sip, gazing thoughtfully up at his new purchase on the wall.

Definitely a good investment, he thought. Being able to choose what he wore was still one of the best things about plain-clothes work. Two years in the army and then more as a PC on the beat was enough uniform for a lifetime, as far as he was concerned. It took a bit of effort, of course. A hat, for example, could either work for a man or against him. The fedora, he was sure, worked for him.

The same couldn't be said, he thought, of the man who caught his eye across Cradock's right shoulder. He was a broad-shouldered type, hunched in conversation over a table a few yards away. Jago only had a back view of him, but he could see that the man's hat, a trilby of sorts, was a very poor choice. Too narrow in the brim for his ears, the only effect it achieved was to draw attention to the way they stuck out on either side of his head. Like handles on a vase, thought Jago.

To compound the offence, the man was wearing his hat while sitting at a table and eating. Rita's might not be the Ritz, but even so, that sort of behaviour marked him out as someone with a severe deficiency in taste, or perhaps in upbringing. Jago began to watch him, and noticed the aggressive gestures he was making towards the man sitting across the table from him. Whoever he was, the trilby man was no shrinking violet.

The other man presented a very different picture. He was facing Jago, so his expression was clearly visible. This one seemed to have better manners. He'd removed his cheap-looking black bowler, but he clutched it to his chest, both hands gripping the brim. It made him look as though he were praying, thought Jago. He was chubby, with blotched skin, and he looked uncomfortable in his very ordinary-looking dark suit and stiff collar. A junior bank clerk, perhaps, not far into his twenties. His face was that of a scared rabbit.

Cradock's voice cut through Jago's observations, curtailing them.

'What time's the kick-off, sir? For the football, I mean.'

Jago shifted his gaze from the two strangers back to Cradock.

'Quarter past three,' he said. 'No need to rush your tea. We'll be there in good time. The crowds are so small these days they probably won't start till we get there.'

Cradock looked relieved: he was still busy with his cake.

'And that reminds me, Peter. Here's another tip for you,' said Jago.

'Yes, sir? What's that?'

'It's this: always take the lady's seat, unless there's a lady with you.'

He was amused to see the puzzled look that crossed Cradock's broad face.

'I'm not sure I follow you, guv'nor. You don't get seats at a football ground, not unless you own the club.' He thought for a moment. 'You don't get ladies either, for that matter.'

Jago gave him a patient smile. 'Not at the match: I mean here. It's something my father told me. If ever you take a lady out to dinner, give her the seat facing into the restaurant. Or the cafe, of course.'

'Why's that, sir?'

'To give her the view of the room. I think it's what he regarded as gentlemanly. Mind you, I don't think he ever had enough money to take ladies out to dinner, certainly not his wife. What I mean is, if you want to know what's going on in a place like this, take the lady's seat. That's how I know everything that's happening behind your back and you don't know anything.'

Cradock was about to turn round, but the inspector motioned him to stay put.

Jago was focused again on the timid rabbit-face, who now looked even more agitated. The trilby man was moving to rise from his chair. Jago did the same.

'Stay where you are; I'll be back in a moment,' he said to Cradock, and slid out from behind the table. He timed his move so that he crossed the man's path and brushed against his shoulder.

'Very sorry,' he said to the stranger. 'Wasn't looking where I was going.'

The man turned for a moment and uttered an indecipherable grunt that Jago took to be an acknowledgement of the apology, then walked on. Apart from the ears, and a scar on the left side of the man's face, there was nothing particularly conspicuous about him. But Jago took a mental photograph of his face nonetheless. Old copper's habit, he supposed.

He walked on past the agitated rabbit. Left alone at his table, the young man was staring straight ahead, still clutching his hat, but now as if it were the steering wheel of a car, out of control and heading for a smash.

CHAPTER TWO

Not so long ago she'd have given him a clip round the ear for talking back. But not now: working down the docks had changed him. She edged through the gap between the back of his chair and the kitchen wall and picked up the bottle, then wiped away the circle of milk with her dishcloth.

'Not on the table, Robert,' she said. 'You know I don't like it on the table.'

He looked at her as though she had just landed from another planet.

'What's the matter with you, Mum? Who cares where it goes?'

'It's manners,' she said. 'Putting the milk bottle on the table like that is common.'

'So? What's wrong with being common? That's what we are. We're working people, Mum, not a bunch of idle toffs putting our feet up in a palace.'

Irene pulled a chair back from the table and sat down.

'I do wish you wouldn't snap at me like that, Robert,' she said. 'If your father were here—'

'Yes, well he's not, is he?' said Robert. 'Perhaps if he had more sense he would be.'

'Don't talk about your dad like that. He's risking his life out there, serving his country.'

'No, he's not, Mum. He's just doing what he's told, so some fat capitalists can get richer, that's what it is. They're the ones feathering their nests out of this war, not the likes of us.'

'You think you know it all, don't you? Is that what you really think? You sound like one of those leaflets you bring home. It's not right. It's not respectful. How can you talk like that when you've got your dad at sea and Joe in the army? They're doing their duty.'

'More fool them, if you ask me,' said Robert. 'It's just one bunch of imperialists fighting another, and the sooner we get rid of the lot of them the better. I'll have no part in it.'

'You won't say that if you get called up.'

'But I won't get called up, will I? Reserved occupation. They need people like me to keep the docks working.'

Irene wiped the edge of the table. He had an answer for everything.

'So what about this evening: are you in?'

'No.'

'Where are you going?'

'Never you mind, Mum: just out with some friends.'

'I wish you wouldn't,' she said. 'They're not the sort of people you should be mixing with. They're trouble, and they'll get you in trouble.'

'If there's any trouble it won't be me who comes off worst.'

He pushed his plate away and stood up to go. Irene felt a familiar ache in her legs: she'd been on her feet too long.

'Get Billy in, will you, love?' she said. 'He's out in the backyard fiddling with his bike.'

Robert went to the back door and summoned his younger brother. Billy came into the kitchen, wiping his hands on a rag.

'Yes, Mum, what is it?'

'Just want to know whether you're in for tea tonight, love, that's all,' said Irene.

'No, I'm going out as soon as I've got the bike fixed. I'm on duty tonight too.'

Irene looked at him but said nothing. There was no point saying she was worried: that was something mothers did and boys didn't understand. But she was. In different ways, she was worried about all her boys. She ruffled his hair. He was sixteen now, but he still let her do that.

'OK, love. Thanks,' she said finally. Billy went back to his bike.

She cleared the table and took the dishes through to the scullery to wash them. The sun was glaring through the open window, and the afternoon was getting hot. She felt tired. She missed Jim, and it wasn't easy, what with work and the boys to look after and everything else.

From the scullery she heard a loud knock at the front door. She walked back the length of their cramped terraced house to see who it was. The windowless passage was gloomy but refreshingly cooler.

She opened the door. Like all the others in Westfield Street, the house opened straight onto the narrow street.

'Oh, hello, Edna,' she said. She was surprised to see her neighbour there. If Edna wanted her she'd normally call over the back fence, not knock on the front door. 'What are you—'

Her voice faded as she saw the expression on Edna's face. It was strained. As though she were about to cry.

Irene thought Edna must be in some kind of difficulty, in need of help.

'Is everything all right?' she said. Her neighbour made no reply.

Then Irene saw the boy standing behind Edna on the street. Younger than Robert, not even shaving yet, but wearing a uniform. Not in the forces, though. She saw the letters 'GPO' on his badge: a post office telegram boy. He was holding an envelope and looked scared.

Edna forced herself to speak.

'I'm ever so sorry, dear,' she said gently, stepping forward. 'This lad knocked on my door and asked if I'd come round with him – he was worried you might be on your own. He's got a telegram for you.'

Irene let out a soft gasp and bit her lip. She felt faint, and steadied herself with her left hand on the door frame as her head began to spin.

She was aware of Edna reaching for her as her knees gave way, and then nothing.

CHAPTER THREE

A camel trying to get through the eye of a needle. DC Peter Cradock had always thought this an odd expression. He had never had occasion to use it himself, but it came to mind now.

Jago had led the way from the cafe, threading through a maze of side streets until they reached the Barking Road, and then turning off it into Priory Road, where a terrace of small Victorian houses stared bleakly at the back of the football ground. The afternoon sunshine did little to enliven the rust-pocked sheets of corrugated iron that perched on drab concrete to form the back wall of the east stand.

The two men joined the crowd of spectators edging towards the entrance gates, slots in the wall just wide enough to allow one person through. The eye of the needle. Cradock followed Jago into one of the slots. It was dark and dank inside, like a prison. They shuffled through the restricted space in single file until they reached the turnstile. Jago paid for both of them, handing the money into a gloomy booth. The turnstile clanked as they pushed through, and they were into the ground.

'Welcome to the Chicken Run,' said Jago.

Cradock could see why people called it that. The stand was decidedly unimpressive: a flimsy-looking timber structure, just one storey, roofed with more of the same corrugated iron. Over on the far side of the pitch, however, he could see a grander affair: a two-tier stand that towered over the rest of the ground, with an overhanging roof to protect those standing below from the rain. It looked as though that was where the money had been spent, and it seemed to Cradock that it was like the whole of London. The west side was all wealth and fancy accommodation, where you could look down on the rest, but over in the east people had to make do with a run-down old shack that looked as though it would collapse if you sneezed at it.

They found a place to stand on the wooden terracing where they could get a good view of the pitch. It wasn't difficult: the place was almost deserted. Down at the front, boys draped their arms over the low wall that bounded the stand a few feet from the touchline, impatient for the match to begin. Here and there a younger one stood on an upturned wooden orange box, a relic of the days when greengrocers still had oranges to sell, thought Cradock. The detective constable had little interest in football, but even he knew this was nothing like the number of people who would have been at a match before the war, even in the second division. Everything had been cut back now, with the country split into northern and southern leagues so the teams didn't have to travel so far, which was how West Ham came to be playing Tottenham for the second week running. Even the football was rationed now, he thought.

He turned round and looked at the patchy crowd behind him: flat caps and frayed clothes in all directions, the uniform of the hard-faced men who worked in the maze of grimy docks and factories that sprawled north from the Thames. He wondered whether it was the risk of air raids or the lure of overtime in these difficult days that was keeping the rest away.

The match kicked off on time at a quarter past three, and the crowd, such as it was, soon unleashed its raucous vocal accompaniment to the ebb and flow of play. Cradock watched dutifully. He'd identified himself as a Tottenham supporter back in June, but that was just to show interest when Jago seemed so pleased that West Ham had won the War Cup. Now, though, he wasn't sure whether his guv'nor was passionate about football at all. Even here at a match he was just standing there, watching thoughtfully. At one point Cradock even fancied he'd detected a hint of sadness in Jago's expression. However, when West Ham took the lead in the first half he noticed a quiet smile of satisfaction crossing Jago's lips. Cradock wondered why he didn't jump and shout like some of the men around them, but he felt it wasn't his place to ask.

The referee blew his whistle to mark half-time.

'Good game so far, eh?' said Jago, a little more animated now as he turned to face Cradock. 'We might beat you again – that'd be a turn-up for the books.'

'Oh, definitely, guv'nor,' said Cradock. He couldn't think of an intelligent comment to make on the game, but hoped Jago would take this as the subdued silence of a fan watching his side losing.

By the time play resumed for the second half he was already looking forward to going home. But then Tottenham equalised, and contrary to his expectations he felt a faint stirring of interest. Before long, the tables were turned, with a hat-trick for Tottenham's Burgess. The score was now West Ham 1, Tottenham 4.

Cradock checked his watch. It was ten to five: only about ten minutes to go.

'Looks like your prediction might have been a bit premature, sir,' he said. The West Ham supporters in the east stand had gone quiet. On the South Bank terraces to their left, however, he could see Spurs fans celebrating, doing their best to make a creditable noise with their shouting and their rattles, despite their depleted numbers.

He was beginning to think he might finally enjoy the occasion, when the roar of the supporters suddenly trailed off into silence.

A murmur of sound seemed to come from below their shouting and melt it away, like news of a death spreading through a room. It was the eerie moan of an air-raid siren.

Cradock turned to Jago.

'Another false alarm, do you think?'

Before Jago could answer, the referee blew three blasts on his whistle: he was stopping the game. There would be no more football today, and the evacuation of the stadium began.

Cradock and Jago found themselves back on Priory Road, along with several hundred other spectators who had left the football ground with them. The way the crowd behaved seemed to be consistent with what they'd seen and heard reported over recent days and weeks. Many of those who spilt out of the exit gates started running immediately, fathers keeping a firm grip on sons as they sought safety. Others moved away into the neighbouring streets with less haste. Jago assumed these were the ones who had developed a more relaxed attitude over so many months of hearing alerts that proved harmless, and who hadn't been shaken from it by the intermittent bombing of recent days. Just yesterday there had been a raid, but it hadn't come as far north of the docks as this, so they probably thought there was no immediate danger.

'Back to the station, sir?' said Cradock.

'Yes, I think so,' said Jago. 'There'll be no buses running now the alert's sounded, so we'll have to go on foot, but we can cut through the back streets and take the shortest route possible. With any luck it'll just be another false alarm.'

They turned right into Castle Street, where uniformed constables and ARP wardens were directing the visiting Tottenham supporters to the nearest public shelters, then headed north past the main entrance to the football ground. Eventually they came to the turning Jago was looking for.

'Right, follow me,' he said, turning left into St George's Road. Cradock stayed close behind him: he knew the general direction in which they must head, but he didn't know these streets as well as Jago did. He was glad it wasn't dark yet.

It was quieter now: most people here seemed to have taken shelter. They hurried along the deserted street and soon they were in Ham Park Road. As they entered it Cradock hesitated. A sound he had not heard before was filling the air. It was coming from behind him, from the south, down by the river and the docks. He turned to face it. In the first second there was nothing to explain the noise, but in the next he saw it. A swarm of aeroplanes was approaching, tiny shapes in the sky, too many to count. The low, pulsing drone of their engines grew steadily louder as they got nearer.

He stepped into the road to get a better view. He knew his aircraft recognition skills weren't up to much, but he recognised the distinctive outline of the Dornier bomber, the one they called the flying pencil, and he saw other large planes that he assumed must be bombers too. Scores of smaller, silvery shapes roamed the sky above them: fighters, he thought.

'I don't believe it,' he said. 'There's hundreds of them. Germans. How did they get through?'

Jago looked up just as the first black dots began to tumble from the bombers and make their rushing descent to the earth. Then came the crump of explosions, and smoke billowing from somewhere in the region of the docks, a couple of miles away. It was bigger than the previous day's raid, bigger than any they'd seen since the war started. And this time it wasn't stopping at the docks. The planes were heading inland from the river, straight for them, leaving a trail of blasts that crept rapidly northwards. Before they could move, the dark shapes were above them.

A deafening noise broke out immediately behind them. The two anti-aircraft guns in West Ham Park had opened fire. Shrapnel began to rain down on the road and the roofs of the nearby houses.

'Watch out!' yelled Jago, dragging Cradock away by the arm. He glimpsed an archway over a pair of gates a few yards away and hauled Cradock into it. He pushed him down to the ground and dropped beside him.

They heard the scream of the falling bombs and felt the ground shake as they landed on nearby streets. Cradock peered out from the minimal shelter of the archway, then shrank back as the jagged blast of high explosives ripped through the evening air. A bomb had landed just a hundred yards or so down the road.

'Should we try to get under cover, sir?' he shouted above the din. 'There was a surface shelter back there.'

'Not likely. I saw them being built. Death traps: just brick walls and a dirty great concrete roof on top, ready to crush you. You'll never get me in one of them.'

As the words left Jago's lips he felt suddenly cold. There was a tension in his stomach that he recognised and fought to suppress.

He shouted at Cradock.

'Keep your head down, you fool.'

'Yes, sir,' said Cradock, pressing himself deeper into the archway and wishing he had a tin helmet with him.

The roar of the planes began to recede. Now the loudest sound they could hear was the clanging bells of fire engines. Acrid smoke began to drift across the street.

Jago got to his feet, followed by Cradock. His heart was thumping in his chest. He breathed deeply to calm himself down, not daring to speak lest Cradock hear a tremor in his voice. He made a play of brushing the dust from his suit and wiping his shoes clean on the back of his trouser legs as he composed himself.

'Is that yours, sir?' said Cradock.

Jago followed his pointing finger and spotted a sad-looking object that was lying in the road at his feet. It was a hat. His hat, lost and crushed as he dived for cover. He picked it up and examined it with a brief sigh, then stuffed it onto his head. The fortunes of war, he thought. Now it would just have to be a battered survivor, like him. He turned to Cradock.

'Right, my lad, it looks like they're going, so we'd better hop it too. And next time you see the Luftwaffe coming for you, don't stand gawping at them: hit the deck.'

'Yes, sir,' said Cradock. He hadn't been bombed before, and he hoped to make a better impression on the inspector if it happened again.

'Where to now?' he added.

'Back to the station. Looks like you can say goodbye to your evening off.'

With a quick backward glance the men stumbled from the shelter of the archway and continued on their way to the police station. The war was now in their backyard. A long-buried anxiety began to claw its way back to the surface of Jago's mind at the thought of what the night might bring. He felt haunted, and he recognised the ghosts.

CHAPTER FOUR

The pedals were heavy, and Billy could already feel sweat trickling down the small of his back. It was ten past nine, but the evening air was still holding out against the chill of night. His calf muscles tightened as he forced the juddering contraption forward.

He was still struggling to cope with the shock. He felt ashamed and angry with himself for leaving his mum like that, for using his ARP duty as an excuse to abandon her, but he couldn't face it. He didn't know what to say or do to help her.

He kicked down with one foot, then with the other, with rhythmic force, the only way he could find to quell the confusion in his head. Sorting that out would have to wait. He'd left the Boy Scouts when he started work two years ago, but their values were still engrained in him. He knew his duty must come first, and that was to get the message through to the control centre. He had to stay calm.

He tried to think about something else, about better times. About the bike project.

When they'd started, the idea had been exciting. Rob said he'd help him build one out of any old bits and pieces they could lay their hands on, and then they'd cycle down to Southend for days out. They would have done, too, if they hadn't run out of time. But that was a year ago: now everything had changed. Southend was a Defence Area, and he'd heard the whole coast was sealed off, right up to King's Lynn. No visitors allowed.

Rob had changed too. Not fun to be with any more, more like a lodger than a brother. Billy didn't understand why.

He pushed at the pedals, straining to build up more speed. He wished he could have got the three-speed gears working and found some drop handlebars: these old sit-up-and-beg ones were useless.

If it weren't for the terrifying noise it would have been like riding through a ghost town. Normally on a Saturday night there'd be people out on the street, especially after a warm day like today. You'd see them having a chat, rolling in and out of the pubs, having a good time. But not tonight. The air was full of those throbbing engines, just like this afternoon. More bombers.

He couldn't believe they were coming back for a

second go in the same day. The whistle of falling bombs that he could hear and the blasts that shook the ground as they landed seemed to be coming from everywhere between here and the river. Anyone with any sense would be in their shelters. He pictured his mum, huddled in the damp little Anderson shelter in their backyard where he'd left her, and muttered a hasty prayer for her towards the sky. He wasn't sure it would be heard through this racket, even if there was someone there to hear it. The Luftwaffe certainly wouldn't take any notice.

Bombs were falling somewhere out of sight in the streets to his right, but Plaistow Road was clear, so he pressed on. The tall outline of the Railway Tavern loomed into view on his left. The pub and all the houses around it were dark, their blank, blacked-out windows like the closed eyes of a corpse. The whole street looked dead.

In another year and a bit, Billy would be eighteen, old enough to go into any pub he chose and buy a drink. But he'd be old enough to be called up too. And unlike Rob, he wouldn't be able to dodge it. The thought of going into the forces began to unsettle him again. He told himself to focus on the job in hand.

He turned right into Corporation Street and immediately lurched into the gutter as a grey-painted requisitioned taxicab with a ladder on its roof rattled past, hauling a trailer pump. In the same moment he saw why it was here: just down the street there were buildings blazing. The Auxiliary Fire Service men were already out of the cab and manhandling the pump into position.

It was clear that more than one bomb had hit the street. Twice he had to get off his bike and haul it through the obstacles. He could see the school was still standing, but across the road shops and houses he'd known all his life were now ragged heaps of bricks, slates, and unidentifiable debris, spiked with blackened timbers snapped like matchsticks.

He reached Manor Road and was able to cycle again until he was forced to make another detour, this time along the edge of the cemetery. In the shadows he could just make out the rows of gravestones. They all faced away from the road, as if finally turning their backs on the living. Billy remembered how it had felt when he was a kid, thinking of all those dead people lying just feet away. He tried to block the thought from his mind.

He turned right as soon as he could, but then had to stop again. The greengrocer's on the corner had taken a hit: it was just a slew of rubble spanning the road. Flames curled through the drifting smoke. He didn't fancy climbing over the top of that, but there was a turning ahead. Maybe he could bypass the obstruction.

Dragging the front wheel of his bike round, he headed off down a side street, then turned into another to try to find his way back. The street was darker than the one he'd just left: there were no fires here. He'd cycled half the length of it before he realised he was in Jasmine Street, and that was a dead end. He stopped. His shirt was soaked in sweat, and he felt so frustrated he wanted to kick something.

He was about to turn back the way he'd come when he saw someone standing in the shadows at the far end of the street. A man, wearing overalls. He was gesturing with his arm, beckoning. He stepped into the road, and Billy could make out the large white letter 'W' on the front of his black steel helmet: an air-raid warden.

'Come over here, lad,' the man shouted. 'What are you doing out in this?'

Billy approached and pushed his arm forward so that the warden could see his armband.

'ARP messenger,' he said. 'I've got to get to Rainford Lane, to the control centre. I've got a message to deliver.'

'Perfect,' said the warden. 'Then you can take one for me too. Come over here.'

He turned away and headed for a small black vehicle parked at the side of the road. Billy propped his bike with one pedal on the kerb and followed. It looked like a tradesman's van, but there was no writing on the side. He thought maybe someone had abandoned it because of the raid, but then he made out the figure of the driver sitting in the cab.

'You squeamish, son?' said the warden.

'Course not,' said Billy.

'Then take a quick look at this. It needs reporting.'

The warden opened the offside cab door and motioned Billy towards it. The driver didn't look up. *Surely he can't be sleeping through this racket*, thought Billy. Perhaps

44

he'd been caught by a blast and knocked out, or worse. He might need help. But the van looked undamaged: even the windscreen was intact. It definitely wasn't a bomb that had stopped it.

He peered into the cab. The warden switched on his hooded lamp and directed a little light over Billy's shoulder.

Now he could see the man clearly. He looked about fifty, and was dressed in a suit, so perhaps not a tradesman after all. He was sitting at the steering wheel, his head slumped forward slightly onto his chest. His hands hung limply in his lap.

The next thing Billy saw made him gasp. It was the blood: on the man's wrists, on his clothes, glistening in the lamplight.

He turned back to the warden.

'Is he . . . ?'

'As a doornail,' said the warden. 'And I fancy it wasn't the Germans' work. We need to get the police here. As soon as you get down to the control centre, ring them up and tell them there's been a suspicious death. Give them my name: Ron Davies. Now get on your way.'

Billy returned to his bike, his mind running through what he'd just witnessed. It was the first time he'd seen a dead body. The first time he'd had to call the police. He knew that was what you did if you found a body, but at the same time something about it didn't make sense.

There was no time to puzzle it out. He got on his bike and went back the way he'd come, away from the dead end. He still had to find a way round the blocked road. He tried another turning, and this time the road looked clear. He forced the bike up to what passed for speed again. The dead man's face was fixed in his mind. Then, as if of its own will, his dad's face seemed to float in and take its place. He tried to get them both out of his head, but they just got mixed up together.

In the sky over East London the searchlights criss-crossed in search of the enemy. Billy glanced up at them, but couldn't see any planes. He felt powerless, frustrated. It was then that the anger crept up on him again, grabbing at his throat, choking him. Inside his head he was raging at his dad for being a fool. He hated him. He hated the Germans. He hated the government. He hated the whole world. As he neared the control centre he was grateful for the smoke that cut into his eyes. It would give a reason for the tears that blurred his sight.

CHAPTER FIVE

Detective Inspector Jago peered ahead through the windscreen, scanning the road for hazards as best he could. It was past ten o'clock at night, but with so many buildings ablaze the darkness wasn't the problem: it was the smoke swirling around the car like fog, erasing familiar landmarks, that was giving him trouble. At times the vehicle's masked headlamps could barely make out the white safety markings painted on the kerb. There were fire engines everywhere, their hoses snaking across the roads in all directions, further impeding progress for anyone else trying to get through. He leant forward, his hand gripping the dashboard. He was beginning to regret letting Cradock drive, but he'd decided the boy needed the experience. He might have to do a journey like this on his own any time soon, and Jago wouldn't trust him to find his way round the back streets of Plaistow in these conditions, especially when any landmarks he might know could be wiped off the map by a bomb at any moment.

'Watch where you're going, lad,' he snapped. 'Look at the size of that hole in the road there.'

Cradock sat hunched over the steering wheel, nosing the car forward.

'Doing my best, guv'nor. It's a bit tricky with all this going on.'

'You can say that again,' said Jago. 'But I don't want my car going down a bomb crater.'

He wished he still had Clark to work with. There had always been something solid about Clark. Cradock was willing enough, and might make a decent detective one day, but Jago missed Clark's experience. He had good judgement too. The kind of man you could rely on, especially at times like this. Jago hadn't seen him since November, when the detective sergeant had been recalled to the colours, but he'd celebrated with a small whisky on hearing in June that Clark was one of the lucky ones who'd got back safely from Dunkirk.

The car bumped over a fire hose and snapped him back to the present.

'So couldn't this have waited, sir?' said Cradock. 'At least until after the raid?'

'Don't be silly,' said Jago. 'We can't leave bodies lying around in the street.'

Cradock wasn't sure whether this was some kind of joke, so said nothing. He glanced to his left. Jago was staring ahead at the road, his face expressionless.

'Left here,' said Jago.

They turned into Crompton Street. Before they had gone fifty yards they found the road blocked by a collapsed building.

'Turn back, sir?' said Cradock.

'No,' said Jago. 'We're only round the corner from where the boy said. We'll walk.'

Cradock stopped the car and got out. Jago reached for the door to open it, but as his fingers touched it the crash of bombs landing somewhere out of sight pounded his ears. His body seemed to freeze, suddenly detached from his will. It was happening again. He could feel a familiar silent panic creeping through him. It was irrational, but he recognised it. The helpless terror of the artillery barrage.

Cradock was crouching beside a wall. 'Everything all right, sir?' he shouted over the noise.

'Yes, fine,' said Jago. He forced himself out of the car and onto the street, then turned and refocused on Cradock's face.

'I just wondered why you'd stopped, sir,' said Cradock. 'We're a bit exposed here, aren't we?'

'I'm sorry,' said Jago. 'I was somewhere else. Let's go.'

They set off down the road as fast as they could, skirting the random debris of high-explosive destruction. The noise of the bombing receded into the distance. They turned left into Jasmine Street, a narrow lane lined with small houses. It was darker than the streets they had just left, and deserted. From what they could see, it hadn't been hit yet.

The van was parked halfway down the street. Jago saw a figure pressed into a shop doorway, a bicycle lying on the pavement beside him. It was a young lad, and he looked anxious. Not surprising, thought Jago.

The boy showed no inclination to move as the two men approached. He stared at their faces, saying nothing.

'Police,' said Cradock. 'What's your name?'

'Carson – Billy Carson.'

'Address?'

'Eighteen Westfield Street, just off Plaistow Road.'

'Let's see your identity card.'

The boy got to his feet and brought the card out of his pocket. Cradock perused it and handed it back.

'So it was you who reported this incident, was it, son?' said Jago.

'Yes,' said Billy. 'I told the people at the ARP control centre. They phoned the police, then told me to get back here and wait for you.'

'Tell us what happened.'

'Well, I was on my way to the control centre. I had this urgent message to deliver. A warden stopped me just over there and told me to look at this van. There was a man in the driver's seat, blood all over him. The warden said he was dead and told me to report it to you lot.'

'And what time was this?'

'Well, I was only here long enough to see what had happened, then went straight to the control centre. I was there by a quarter to ten, so I must have got here at about five-and-twenty to ten and left at twenty to.'

Jago checked his watch. It was coming up to half past ten.

'Right, my lad, you can go now,' he said. 'We'll be in touch later. Mind how you go.'

Billy looked relieved to be released. They watched him wobble off on his bike until he turned the corner and disappeared.

'Time for a closer look at that van,' said Jago.

They crossed back to the other side of the street, and Cradock opened the cab door. He pulled his flashlight from his pocket, then faltered.

'Don't tell me you're worried about the blackout,' said Jago. 'The whole borough's lit up like a Christmas tree. They don't need your torch for a target. Now, get some more light onto that body. I want to see everything.'

'Yes, sir,' said Cradock. He leant into the cab and shone his torch on the man at the wheel.

'Well, what do you see?' said Jago.

'Lots of blood, like the boy said. Cuts to the wrists too.'

'That's interesting. What do you reckon?'

'Well, sir, the windscreen's intact, no broken glass, no other damage to the vehicle. Nothing I can see to make it an accident. So either someone's slashed him, or he did himself in.'

He turned back to Jago, grinning. 'Mind you, too

late to arrest him for attempted self-murder now, sir. If he did try, he's got away with it.'

Jago gave him a look of disdain.

'You'll drive me to it one day, my boy. And I don't think knowing I was breaking the law would deter me, any more than it deterred this poor fellow, if you're right.'

'We'll never know now, will we, guv'nor?' said Cradock. 'About him, I mean, not you.'

'If you get on with your job we might,' said Jago. 'Now out of the way and let me have a look.'

He took the torch from Cradock.

'You'd better get busy with your notebook. I can't see us fetching the police surgeon out in the middle of all this, let alone a photographer, so get as much detail down as you can.'

Cradock stepped back and began to make his notes. Jago reached his arm into the cab and touched the man's face.

'No sign of rigor mortis yet, and he's still as warm as I am, so he can't have been dead for long.'

He bent down and studied the man's wrists for a few moments with the torch.

'Right,' he said, 'look at these wrists again, Detective Constable. How many cuts do you see?'

Cradock squeezed in beside Jago and looked over his shoulder. 'Two, sir: one on each wrist. That's all it needs.'

'Yes,' said Jago, 'but that's the point: just two. No scars, so it looks like he's never tried before. But if he's a first-timer, where are the other cuts? They usually do a few smaller ones first, don't they? To make sure the blade's sharp enough and to work themselves up to it. They don't normally just make two big cuts like this straight away.'

'You're right, sir,' said Cradock. 'But on the other hand, a man with strong will and self-control could do it with one cut, couldn't he?'

'Yes,' said Jago. 'I saw men in the war who wounded themselves just to get out of the front line. It's surprising what a man can do to himself if he's under enough stress.'

'Wait a minute, sir,' said Cradock. 'Can you shine the torch on his jacket for a moment?'

Jago directed the light onto the dead man's chest.

'Now that's interesting,' he said. 'That slightly complicates the idea of suicide.'

He carefully opened the man's jacket. Both detectives could see that the white shirt beneath was covered with blood.

'A wound to the chest too,' said Jago. 'So did he slit his wrists and then stab himself in the chest, or was it the other way round?'

'Sounds a bit difficult either way,' said Cradock. 'Does that mean someone else killed him? But if it's murder, why cut the man's wrists? It's a slow way to die, so you'd have to restrain him, and that'd mean hanging around in a public place. Too risky, surely. If you wanted to kill him, stabbing's a much better bet, but then why cut his wrists too?'

'Indeed,' said Jago.

He played the torch round the blood-soaked seat and floor of the cab. A small object lying just in front of the driver's seat glinted in the light.

'Aha,' he said. 'This looks interesting.'

He took a clean handkerchief from his pocket and reached down to the floor to pick up what he'd seen. It was a pocketknife. The blade, about three inches long, was open, as was a short spike.

'The weapon, do you suppose?' he said, showing it to Cradock. 'Looks like some blood still on the blade. Curious spike too: I wonder what that's for.'

Cradock inspected the knife.

'So why's it still here?' he said. 'I mean, if this is a suicide it makes sense: he does the deed and the knife falls where he drops it. But if it's murder, why would the killer leave it here? Unless someone came along and he had to clear off in a hurry, of course.'

'Or maybe he heard a bomb landing close by and decided to leg it,' said Jago. 'Or she, of course,' he added. 'If there was a killer, we can't rule out the possibility that it was a woman.'

'Or maybe he – or she – left it here because they wanted to make it look like suicide,' said Cradock. 'But surely if they'd stabbed him in the chest too they'd know it wouldn't look like that? They can't have thought we wouldn't find the other wound.'

'So,' said Jago, 'what we're saying is it could be suicide, but on balance it looks more like a murder.'

'Yes.'

'But there is another possibility. It could be an attempted suicide and a murder.'

'How's that?'

'Well, theoretically, I suppose, it's possible that he did slit his own wrists but then somebody else came along – or was already here with him – and decided to finish him off with a stab to the chest. Or indeed that he did inflict both wounds on himself: slit his wrists and then stabbed himself in the chest. Stranger things happen in Japan, from what I've heard. Seems a bit unlikely in West Ham, though.'

'So where do we go from here?'

'Out of all those possibilities, I think the most likely is that someone else killed him and made a rather poor attempt to make it look like suicide, so we're going to treat it as murder until and unless we find evidence to suggest another explanation. But I'd like to find out whether anyone who was close to him thinks the idea of suicide is viable – not just so we know whether he could have done it, but to see whether anyone would like us to believe that and tries to encourage us in that direction. We need to know more about him.'

'Shall I check his pockets, sir? See if we can find out who he is?'

'Yes, of course,' said Jago. 'That's probably the only thing about this blasted war that's made the job easier. Identity cards, I mean. As long as any poor blighter who's unfortunate enough to get murdered has the decency to make sure he's carrying it when he dies.'

He shone the torch on the man's face. 'Mind you, I think I can save you the trouble. If you'd been on K Division a bit longer you'd know who this is.'

'What, you mean he's got previous?' asked Cradock.

'On the contrary,' said Jago, 'you'd have seen him on the bench in Stratford magistrates' court. Unless I'm very much mistaken, this is Mr Charles Villiers JP. When he's not getting murdered in the back streets of Plaistow, he's a Justice of the Peace.'

CHAPTER SIX

'Oi! What do you think you're doing out in this? Get to the shelter.'

The two detectives turned to see a stout middle-aged woman striding briskly towards them along the pavement. She was wearing the black steel helmet of an ARP warden and looked as if she would tolerate no nonsense.

Jago pulled his warrant card and National Registration identity card from his pocket and showed them to her. 'We're police officers,' he said. 'I'm Detective Inspector Jago and this is Detective Constable Cradock, West Ham CID.'

The woman switched to a less peremptory tone.

'Very sorry, Officers. With you not being in uniform I thought maybe you were up to no good, or just out in a raid when you had no business to be.'

'Don't worry,' said Jago. 'Are you responsible for this area?'

'Yes,' she replied, 'I'm the post warden, Mrs Gordon.'

'Right,' said Jago. 'We've got a body here, and we think it may be a suspicious death. One of your colleagues found it earlier this evening: Mr Davies. Do you know about it already?'

'No,' she said. 'But that doesn't surprise me. Generally people don't tell me anything. Some of the old ARP men round here don't seem to think women count. Don't suppose they'd complain if I pulled them out if a roof fell on their head, though.'

She smoothed her coat down, as if restoring her dignity.

'Well, Mrs Gordon, DC Cradock and I need to get the body removed, and this vehicle too, but with all this mayhem going on it's going to be a while before we can organise it.'

'Do you want some help? We're using the municipal baths over on Romford Road as a temporary mortuary. I could try and get one of the light rescue parties to take the body over there.'

'No. I need to get the police surgeon and a photographer down here before the body's moved, and I can't do that till this raid's finished. In any case, the rescue squads'll have more than enough to do getting people out who're still alive.'

'Right you are,' said the warden. 'Between you

and me, I've heard we're pulling out so many dead tonight, the mortuary's already getting pretty full. There's a rumour going round that the council's ordered three thousand canvas coffins, you know. Grim business, this.'

'Indeed,' said Jago. 'Now, all I need you to do is give your details to the detective constable here, in case we need to talk to you in the next day or two.'

'In that case,' said the warden, 'I'll get back to work.' She gave Cradock her name and address, then bade them goodnight and made her way back down the street.

'Shall we try to get a PC down to guard the scene?' said Cradock.

'I don't think we're going to find one tonight who's not already doing something more important. No, we'll stay here until the raid's over. We can keep an eye on it from over there,' said Jago, gesturing to where Billy had been sheltering when they arrived.

Cradock looked sceptical about the protection the doorway would offer, but could see there was nowhere more suitable if they were to keep an eye on the van and its grisly contents.

'But first,' Jago continued, 'let's see if there's anything else of interest in the cab, and check the back of the van too.'

They searched quickly. The inside pocket of the dead man's jacket yielded his identity card, which confirmed that he was indeed Charles Villiers and provided his address. His wallet contained nothing of interest, and their check of the cab was equally fruitless. Cradock walked round to the back of the van and opened the unlocked doors. 'Nothing to help us here, sir,' he shouted back. 'It's completely empty: clean as a whistle.'

The two men crossed the street and stood in the shop doorway. Like every other building in the street the shop appeared to be deserted.

'Seems strange, doesn't it, sir, to be investigating a death in the middle of an air raid?' said Cradock. 'I mean, who knows how many people have been killed tonight? It could be hundreds.'

'I wouldn't be surprised if it were thousands,' said Jago. 'But a crime's still a crime, even if there's an air raid going on. We seem to have a local magistrate out in an empty van on a Saturday night in the middle of an air raid and getting himself murdered. So what was he doing? Where was he going? Why would he go out on a night like this?'

'Right now, sir, I don't think I've got any answers,' said Cradock. He squeezed himself further in. This doorway wasn't going to be of much help if a bomb came anywhere near, he thought. He felt exposed and vulnerable.

He looked down the street. The rooftops on all sides stood out against the red and orange glow of the sky. Acrid smoke from burning timber was still billowing across the area, mingled with the pungent odour of soot and brick dust from the demolished houses.

His nostrils were stinging, but he began to detect another strange, sweet smell in the air, like caramel. He wondered whether the sugar refinery down by the river had been hit. That'll mean more rationing, he thought. The guv'nor might even have to give up sugar in his tea completely.

He looked at Jago. The inspector was gazing up at the night sky. The searchlights did little more than illuminate the mountainous plumes of smoke that spread as they rose and drifted towards central London.

'They've given us a real kicking tonight, haven't they, sir?' said Cradock. 'We don't seem to be shooting any of them down. Surely there should be more ack-ack fire than this: where are all the other anti-aircraft guns? Why aren't we fighting back?'

'The usual problem, I expect,' said Jago. 'When I was in the army the troops had a number of colourful expressions for it, but in polite terms you might call it "shortcomings in military administrative efficiency".'

Cradock could feel his legs going to sleep. He shifted his position, careful not to kick his boss.

'I suppose you've seen a lot of this sort of thing, sir. Being in France, I mean, with people shelling you and trying to kill you.'

'Every day and every night. I suppose that counts as a lot.'

'Sounds like a nightmare.'

'It was. But you just had to get on with your job. A bit like tonight, really.'

'It must have been awful for your family at home, knowing you were out there.'

'I didn't have any family: my parents were both dead by then. Perhaps it's a mercy that there was no one to worry about me.'

'Not even a sweetheart, sir?'

'Never you mind, Constable.'

Cradock thought he saw a flicker of a smile cross Jago's face, but he couldn't be sure in the peculiar light. His curiosity was beginning to get the better of him, but he didn't want to overstep the mark.

Before he could make up his mind whether to ask another question, the decision was made for him. He heard the chilling scream of a bomb descending, then the loudest blast he had heard all evening. It was followed swiftly by another. Jago was already on his feet.

'Quick!' he shouted. 'They're getting a bit close – run for it! Follow me!'

Jago began to dash for the end of the street, with Cradock hot on his heels. They reached the junction, turned right and flung themselves behind a wall. An ear-splitting explosion from the street they'd just left showered them with soil and fragments of debris. The noise stopped, and they hauled themselves to their feet.

Cradock was first back to the turning they'd just left. He looked down the street where they had been sheltering and saw it immediately. Where the van had been standing there was now nothing – just a gaping crater.

'Mrs Muriel Villiers?' said Jago.

'Yes.'

'I'm Detective Inspector Jago and this is my colleague, Detective Constable Cradock. Please allow me to express my condolences. I gather you've been informed of what happened.'

'Yes,' she replied. 'The constable said my husband had been found dead during the air raid, and that then he—'

She broke off. The composed expression on her face gave way to one of distress.

'Yes, I'm sorry, Mrs Villiers. Shortly after he was found, a bomb landed very close by.' Now it was Jago's turn to hesitate as he sought the right words. 'There are no identifiable remains.'

'But you're sure it was my husband?'

'We'd seen his identity card before the bomb fell, and I recognised him from seeing him on the bench at the magistrates' court.'

'I see. Won't you come through to the drawing room?'

They followed her into a room with large windows and comfortable-looking soft chairs. A young man was sitting there, whom she introduced as Edward, her son. They accepted her invitation to sit.

'I'm sorry to disturb you on a Sunday morning, but I'm afraid I have to ask you a few questions,' said Jago.

'Yes, of course.'

'You see, we're not convinced it was an accident.'

'What's that supposed to mean?'

'It means we're exploring other possible causes

of death. Please forgive me for asking what may be a painful question, but can you think of any reason why Mr Villiers might want to take his own life?'

From the corner of his eye Jago saw a look of surprise on Cradock's face, but he commanded silence with a glance. Mrs Villiers seemed not to have noticed it, and her own face maintained its composure.

'I'm sure I couldn't say. My husband was not in the habit of confiding in me about his plans for the day, let alone his inner torments.'

'Did he have any?'

'Torments? If he did, I wouldn't know about it. My husband was what you might call an officer and gentleman of the old school. He didn't talk to me about his business or about his feelings. I think he felt the weaker sex was not to be troubled by such things.'

'Would you mind telling me what your husband's business was?' said Jago. 'I'm aware of him as a magistrate, but I've never known what he did with the rest of his week.'

'He owned a printing business,' said Mrs Villiers. 'I think he used to manage to sit as a magistrate once a week, or once a fortnight. It's easier for people who've retired or have a private income and don't have to work, but he was still very busy with the business – yesterday he was at work all day and didn't come home. I don't think he was able to give the court as much time as he would have liked to.'

'And are you aware of any business difficulties or

other pressures in his life that could have driven him to take his own life?'

'I'm not aware of any, but that doesn't mean there couldn't have been any. He certainly wasn't himself in the last few weeks. As far as I know he was still making plenty of money, but he definitely seemed preoccupied: something on his mind.'

'Worried?'

'I think you could say that, yes.'

'So your husband ran a printing business. Can you tell me more about it?'

'Not much. The print works isn't very big, but I think things had picked up with the war. Government contracts for leaflets, that sort of thing. I'm sure Edward knows more about it than I do, though: he works there.'

Jago turned to her son.

'Mr Villiers, do you have any reason to think your father might have taken his own life?'

'I think he would have despised the idea,' said Edward. 'My father seemed to have rather a gift for despising.'

'What do you mean?'

'Three months or so ago some poor soul was fished out of the river. Left a note. Well, it happens from time to time, doesn't it? I don't need to tell you that. But in this case it turned out he was related to one of our employees. I remember my father saying at the time that suicide was a form of cowardice. That was one of many things he despised. Cowards should be shot: you know, *pour encourager les autres*, that kind of thing. He was an old soldier, you see, and I suppose it was something to do with that. I can't imagine him doing something he despised so heartily.'

'But is it possible that for some reason he found himself under such pressure or threat that he began to detect precisely that in himself? Might that not have driven him to contemplate suicide?'

'You're playing with words, Inspector. I cannot speculate on what my father might have been thinking. All I can say is I find it difficult to believe he would take his own life.'

Jago rose from his chair and walked across the room to the French windows. He studied the view of the garden for a moment, then turned round to face into the room and addressed the mother and son.

'In that case, can either of you think of any reason why someone might want to murder Mr Villiers?'

He looked first at Edward. The young man shrugged his shoulders and shook his head slowly.

'I suppose he might have had enemies,' he said, 'and someone might have wanted to, but I can't imagine who. He didn't confide in me either.'

Jago turned to Mrs Villiers and raised his eyebrows enquiringly.

'Murder?' she said. 'The idea's absurd. Why would anyone want to murder him?'

'That's what I was rather hoping you could tell me,' said Jago.

'I told you, I know nothing of my husband's affairs, business or private. He led his life and I mine.'

'Would you describe yourselves as a close married couple?'

'I'm not sure what you mean by that. If you mean did we live in each other's pockets, then no, it wasn't like that.'

Edward got to his feet and stood facing Jago with his chin angled slightly upwards. Striking a pose, thought Jago.

'What my mother means is that he was married to the business first, and to her second.'

'Edward,' said Mrs Villiers, 'how could you? Mr Jago, my husband's business affairs were very demanding. He had to work long hours, and we didn't spend a lot of time together.'

'Had to, or chose to?' said Edward.

She gave Jago a beseeching look. 'Inspector, please pay no attention to my son. He and his father didn't always see eye to eye, and I'm afraid he sometimes says things he doesn't mean.'

'I'm sure Mr Villiers can speak for himself,' said Jago, turning to the young man. 'Do you live here with your mother, sir?'

'Yes, I do,' said Edward.

'And may I ask your age?'

'Twenty.'

'Had your call-up papers yet?'

'No.'

'But you've registered?'

'Yes, I registered a month or so ago, but I was found medically unfit.'

'I see. And you're employed in the family business?'

'Yes, I work for my father. Or I suppose I should say worked, now.'

'And how would you describe your relationship with your father?'

'Well, he wasn't the sort of chap to do me any favours at work, just because I was his son.'

'And you know of no one who might have wished your father harm?'

'Yes, that's what I said. But if the way he treated his own son is anything to go by, I imagine he could have left a whole host of resentful people in his wake.'

'What does that mean?'

'It means he drove a hard bargain. Devil take the hindmost, that sort of thing. Perhaps it just means he was a good businessman. How would I know? He didn't take me into his confidence. I think I was rather a disappointment to my father. Not quite the son he wanted.'

'Nonsense,' said Mrs Villiers. 'You were the apple of his eye.'

Jago turned back to her.

'Who inherits the business?'

'I do.'

'And what will become of it now?'

'God knows. I suppose Edward and I will end up running it. I doubt very much that we'd be able to sell it in the present circumstances. But I really know nothing about it.'

'So if I have any questions about the business, who should I talk to?'

Edward stepped forward.

'I don't think my mother is in a position to advise you on that, Inspector. I would suggest you talk to Johnson. He was my father's right-hand man in the business, or something close to it. The *éminence grise* of the print shop. He knew a lot more than my father about printing, that's for sure. But I don't know whether anyone knew anything about my father's business affairs, not even Johnson. As you've probably gathered, my father was a rather private man, at least as far as we were concerned.'

Mrs Villiers picked up a silver cigarette case from a small table.

'Inspector, I didn't offer you or your colleague a cigarette. Will you have one?'

'Not for me, thank you,' said Jago. 'Nor for my colleague. We're almost finished.'

'You'll excuse me if I do. This has all been rather demanding.' She took a cigarette and offered the case to Edward, who also took one. Jago observed the way she smoked it. He might have expected her to be tense, but as he watched her the word that came to mind was 'languid'.

He took an envelope from his pocket and produced the knife they had found in the van.

'Has either of you seen this before?'

Mrs Villiers looked at it and shook her head.

'Could it have belonged to Mr Villiers?'

'It's possible,' she replied, 'but I've never seen it, so I really can't say.'

'And you, sir?'

'I don't know either,' said Edward, turning away.

'Take a close look, please,' said Jago.

Edward approached and bent to examine the knife.

'Actually, yes, I believe it was his. It looks very similar to one he used to carry at work. I couldn't swear to it, but I'd say it looks like his to me.'

Jago replaced the knife in the envelope.

'Thank you. Now I must ask you both where you were last night between the hours of seven and ten,' he said.

Mrs Villiers moved to the window, holding her cigarette to one side.

'We were both in the Anderson shelter,' said Edward, 'weren't we, Mother? There was the air raid.'

'Yes,' she said, not looking round.

'Can anyone else confirm that?'

'Well, it wasn't a cocktail party.'

'I'll take that as no. Just one last question, Mrs Villiers,' said Jago. 'Is there any more family?'

She turned to face him.

'Edward was our only child. My husband's parents are both deceased, as are mine. There's just one relative, my husband's brother. He's called Arthur Villiers, a retired solicitor, unmarried. He lives out at Brentwood, where I believe he amuses himself by commanding the local Home Guard. I don't think you need to add him to your list of suspects.'

'Thank you, Mrs Villiers. That will be all for now.'

She showed them to the door and closed it behind them. As the sound of their feet trudging across the gravel drive faded, she leant back against the door and exhaled a stream of cigarette smoke towards the ceiling.

'Why didn't you tell them the truth about him?' said Edward. 'He was an unscrupulous bully.'

'How can you say such a thing?' said Muriel.

'It's true, and you know it,' he replied, raising his voice. 'And as far as I'm concerned, the world's a better place without him.'

CHAPTER EIGHT

'Come.'

The divisional detective inspector's voice sounded faintly through the heavy wooden door. Like a duke summoning his butler, thought Jago. Only one rank between them, but it wasn't the first time Jago had seen what happened when a bit of promotion went to a man's head. Perhaps he was jumping to conclusions, though. He tried to be more generous: Soper might be thinking it was one of the constables at the door, not him. He turned the handle and stepped into the office, followed by Cradock. The DDI was at his desk, studying a file.

'Ah, good morning, John,' he said, looking up. 'Take a seat.'

Jago hung his coat, hat, and gas mask on the coat stand in the corner of the office, then positioned himself carefully on the flimsy-looking upright wooden chair that stood before the desk. It offered a marked contrast to the more ample leather-padded swivelling affair on the other side.

Cradock remained standing at the side of the room. It was eight o'clock on Monday morning, and after two nights of air raids and the beginnings of a murder enquiry he was anxious not to nod off.

Soper snapped the file shut.

'What's this about a murder, then?'

'Suspected murder, sir. The body was found on Saturday evening, about nine-thirty. We couldn't get a doctor to him, but my guess is that he wasn't long dead.'

'And do we know who the deceased is?'

'Yes, sir. It's Charles Villiers, who was a magistrate, and we believe the killer tried to make it look like suicide.'

'Villiers of the Stratford bench?'

'That's right, sir.'

'Lord help us. And where's the body?'

'Unfortunately, sir, destroyed by enemy action.'

'Destroyed by enemy action? Well, you know what they say: no body, no murder. You'll have a job convincing the court there was a murder if you can't produce a body.'

'In this case, sir, there *was* one, at least long enough for two witnesses to see it, in addition to Cradock and myself. I established the deceased's identity and suspicion of murder to my satisfaction before the body was lost.'

'To your satisfaction, eh? And what about a jury's satisfaction? And a magistrate, of all people. It'll probably turn out he played golf with the divisional superintendent.'

'I'm sure we'll be able to rely on the discretion of the press, sir, especially at a time like this. They don't have as much space to print such reports as they used to.'

'Yes, but you know what people are like: no smoke without fire. I don't know anything about this man's private life, but if someone killed him and tried to make it look like suicide, there must have been grounds for them to think people would believe it.'

'That's a very good point, sir. We'll follow that up.'

'Well, carry on then. I suppose it's too much to ask for a quiet life when the whole division's being blown to pieces. Just clear it up as quickly as you can. What else do you have to go on?'

Jago beckoned Cradock, who pulled out his notebook and flicked through to the relevant page.

'Well, sir, the body was reported by a local lad, name of Carson, sixteen, an ARP bicycle messenger. But as far as we know at the moment there's nothing to suggest any involvement on his part in the death of the deceased.'

'Anyone else you're aware of who might have done it?' said Soper.

'He was a businessman as well as a magistrate,' said Jago. 'It could have been a business rival, someone he'd cheated maybe, although we should perhaps assume he was as honest as the next magistrate.'

Soper gave him a quizzical look, but Jago continued.

'Or it could have been someone who'd been up before him in the police court. In that case, every villain in East London could be a suspect. The only people we've spoken to so far, though, are his wife, Mrs Muriel Villiers, and his son, Edward Villiers.'

'Do you think one of them could have done it?' said Soper.

Jago turned to Cradock.

'What did they say, Constable?'

Cradock consulted his notes again.

'Mrs Villiers couldn't think of anyone wanting to kill him, sir, and her son said he couldn't imagine him committing suicide, so that doesn't get us very far.'

'She didn't rule out the possibility of suicide, though, did she?' said Jago. 'Said he hadn't been himself recently, was preoccupied, something on his mind.'

Soper's eyes strayed to the files waiting on his desk.

'Anything else?'

'Well, sir,' said Cradock, 'there didn't seem to be much love lost between the three of them. Not what you might call the perfect family – or the perfect marriage, for that matter. She wasn't exactly grief-stricken either. If she was trying to encourage us in thinking it was suicide, it might suggest she had something to do with his death.'

Soper looked up from his desk.

'But you've already said you think it was murder.'

'Yes,' said Jago, 'but we didn't tell her that.'

Soper scratched his head.

'Now you're losing me. But what about the son?'

Keep up, thought Jago. This was the man in charge of all criminal investigation on K Division of the Metropolitan Police. He'd been good in his day, but if it hadn't been for the war and the manpower shortages he'd probably have been tending his roses by now.

'He didn't get on with his father, sir, that's for sure,' said Cradock. 'There was quite a bit of bad feeling there. I could imagine him snapping and doing something violent.'

'So there's a possibility that either he or his mother could be involved,' said Jago. 'Neither of them seems to have had much time for him. Or they could be in it together. Or for that matter one or both of them could have got someone else to do it. They might be covering up for each other: they've only got each other for an alibi at the time of death. But it could be someone quite unconnected with them. If whoever killed him wanted it to look like suicide, they may have known of something going on in his life that would make that plausible.'

'Sounds like you need to do some more digging,' said Soper. 'Just keep your noses clean. Don't go digging a hole for yourselves. Is my meaning clear?'

'Yes, sir,' said Jago. 'No need for you to worry. We won't tread on any toes.'

Soper leant back into his chair and scrutinised him across the desk. Jago couldn't tell whether the DDI was pondering his words or had simply run out of things to say.

The silence was broken by a creak from the older man's chair as he returned it to an upright position.

'One more thing before you go, John,' said Soper. 'You've got an appointment this afternoon with a man from the Ministry of Information. He's called Mitchell and he's bringing a newspaper journalist down here to meet you. An American, if you please.'

'American? What does the American press want with me?'

'Don't ask me. Seems they want to do a report on East End morale under the Nazi onslaught – you can imagine the kind of thing – and someone thinks a bit of local police liaison would be a good idea. Your name came out of the hat. Or to be more precise, you were specifically requested by the man from the ministry.'

'How strange,' said Jago. 'Any idea why?'

'Ours but to do . . .' said Soper. 'Perhaps it was that medal you got.'

'Plenty of police officers have medals, sir.'

'But they don't all get their picture in the papers, do they?'

'That wasn't my fault, sir.'

'I'm not suggesting it was. But it seems you've caught someone's eye. Anyway, I've said you'll meet them here at three o'clock. And I gather the Ministry of Information thinks it's crucial that the American public read the right thing about what's going on here, so watch what you say.'

Soper picked up the file again and motioned with his

hand to indicate Jago was free to go. Jago rose from his chair and made for the door, collecting his hat and coat on the way. Before he got his hand to the doorknob he heard Soper's voice behind him.

'Gas mask, John.'

He looked back at the coat stand. His gas mask was still hanging there. He grabbed it and slung it over his shoulder.

'Sorry, sir.'

'Regulations, you know. We can't have police personnel going about without their gas mask. Got to set a good example to the public. Even police officers with medals aren't gas-proof.'

'How's his lordship this morning?'

Jago recognised the hoarse tone coming from the front desk. The station wouldn't be the same without it.

'Respect, Tompkins, respect,' he said, suppressing a smile.

'Sorry, sir,' said the station sergeant. 'I mean how's Mr Soper, of course.'

'That's better,' said Jago. 'He's in fine form.'

Sergeant Tompkins gave Jago a weary look over the top of his half-moon reading glasses.

'More's the pity. Before we know it he'll start having ideas. And we know where that gets us, don't we? Just like the old days in France. You remember: the footsloggers up to their wossnames in mud at the front, and all those red-tab staff officers in their chateaux miles behind the lines, coming up with ideas.'

'But you weren't in the infantry, were you, Tompkins?'

'No, sir, not exactly, but near enough. Ally Sloper's Cavalry, that was me.'

'Come now, where's your regimental pride?' said Jago teasingly. 'You make the Army Service Corps sound like a bunch of loafers and ne'er-do-wells. Didn't it get turned into the Royal Army Service Corps at the end of the war? You can't all have been scoundrels.'

'That's as may be, sir, but as far as I was concerned it was just horse transport, driving ammunition wagons up to the front line for four years with the occasional distraction of getting shelled and shot at. And what did I get for it?' He fingered the medal ribbons on his tunic. 'Pip, Squeak and Wilfred here, two pounds in my pocket, and a third-class railway warrant home.'

'But you came through,' said Jago.

'Yes, and don't think I'm not grateful for that. But here we are now and it's happening all over again, going from bad to worse.'

He paused, lost in thought.

'Anyway, sir, I've got something for you here. There was a bloke brought in early Saturday morning, found in the cemetery, all roughed up. Turned out he was quite a respectable type, though, if you know what I mean: not the sort to get mixed up in a brawl in a graveyard. Didn't want to make a complaint, though. When we asked him who'd done it he clammed up. Looked frightened. If you ask me, there's some funny business going on. Thought you might like to know.'

'Thanks,' said Jago. 'I'll get Cradock to follow it up.'

He walked back to his office in search of Cradock and a cup of tea. It was nine o'clock. He thought of what the last two days had brought, and what might yet come. Old Frank Tompkins was right: it was all going from bad to worse.

CHAPTER NINE

Jago and Cradock took the number 697 trolleybus from the police station down to Plaistow High Street and walked the short distance from the stop to Westfield Street. They knocked on the front door of number 18 and heard the sound of feet padding down the passage. The door opened a little and they saw a short, trim woman in a black dress covered with a sleeveless wrap-around apron made from blue and white floral-print cotton. She peered round the door at them.

'Detective Inspector Jago and Detective Constable Cradock, West Ham CID,' said Jago. 'Mrs Carson?'

'Yes, that's me.'

'We've come to see your son Billy, Mrs Carson. I

expect you know he reported finding a body to us on Saturday evening.'

'Yes, he's here. Come in. Please excuse my pinny.' She slipped off the apron and rolled it into a ball, clutching it nervously to her waist.

'He was expecting you to call today,' she said, 'and Sainsbury's said he could stay at home until you'd finished with him. Come this way.'

They followed her down the narrow passage into the rear part of the house.

'You don't mind the kitchen, do you?' said Irene. 'I would offer you the parlour, only there's a touch of damp in there at the moment, and what with everything that's been happening I haven't had a chance to do anything about it.'

They seated themselves at the table. Cradock noticed that Jago, true to his precept, took the chair that faced into the room. Irene kept her pinny rolled up in her lap.

'Cup of tea?' she said, half getting up.

'No, thank you. We don't want to put you to any trouble. We shan't be long.'

'OK, then.' She sat down again and looked up warily.

'Could we see Billy? Is he here?'

'Yes, of course; I'll call him.'

She went to the foot of the stairs and called his name. Billy came down and walked slowly into the room. He took a seat without meeting their gaze.

'It's all right, Billy, there's nothing to worry about. We just want to ask you a few questions.'

'Nothing to worry about?' He turned to Irene. 'Mum, haven't you told them?'

Irene dabbed at her eyes with the edge of her crumpled apron. 'No,' she said.

Jago leant closer and spoke quietly.

'Has something happened?'

She shook her head silently, holding the pinny to her face.

'I'd better explain, then.' Billy turned to the two policemen. 'It's about my dad.'

He looked at his mother, but she did not raise her head.

'He's in the merchant navy. Able seaman, on freighters, on the Atlantic run as far as we know. On Saturday afternoon my mum got a telegram. It was from the shipping line, and it said his ship had been sunk, with no known survivors. Then we got a letter from them that said the same.'

'Billy,' said Irene, 'it said we weren't allowed to tell anyone.'

'But these are policemen, Mum. Surely it's all right to tell them?'

'Yes,' said Jago, 'you're allowed to tell us, but apart from us it's just your immediate family.'

'The telegram said he's reported missing.' He turned to Jago with pain in his eyes. 'That means he's dead, doesn't it?'

'It means you must be prepared for the worst,' said Jago.

Irene sobbed, then wiped her face firmly.

'I'm sorry, Inspector, it's just too hard to bear. But you

carry on; I'll be all right.' She sat up straight in her chair and pushed the apron to one side.

'Thank you, Mrs Carson,' said Jago. 'I'm very sorry.'

He turned to Billy.

'I gather you work for Sainsbury's. Is that right?'

'Yes, up in Angel Lane, in Stratford. I went there straight from school and I've been there two years now. I work on the dairy counter.'

'Are you one of the young assistants who pat the butter with those wooden paddles?'

'Yes, that's my favourite thing.'

'I used to love watching it when I was a boy. And what do you do with the rest of your time?'

'I'm one of Gillman's Daredevils. Have you heard of us?'

'I don't think I have. Is that anything to do with Councillor Gillman?'

'Yes, he started the Daredevils last year, when the war started. It's a team of ARP messengers, about two dozen of us, mostly boys. At first we didn't have much to do, but just lately it's got really busy. That's how I came to find that bloke in the van – but then you know that already.'

The sound of the front door creaking open and then loudly slamming was followed by a heavier set of footsteps in the passage. Robert Carson entered the room and stopped short.

'Oh, it's you lot,' he said, with a dismissive look. 'I'd forgotten you were going to be here.'

'And you are . . . ?' said Jago.

Irene jumped to her feet.

'This is my other son, Robert,' she said. 'My other one who's still at home, that is. My oldest, Joe, is in the army.'

'And before you ask,' said Robert, 'I'm in a reserved occupation. Electrician in the docks. Vital war work.'

He tossed his cap onto a chair and sat down.

'I'm Detective Inspector Jago and this is Detective Constable Cradock. We're here because your brother reported finding a dead body on Saturday evening,' said Jago.

'Do you know who he was yet?' said Billy.

'We do,' said Jago. 'He was Mr Charles Villiers, a local businessman and magistrate.'

He studied the faces of the mother and her two sons, ranged before him. Robert looked indifferent; Billy's expression was blank. Irene reacted with a barely perceptible but startled intake of breath.

'Did you know him?' asked Jago.

'Never heard of him,' said Robert.

'Are you sure?'

'I don't mix with magistrates. I'm a working man.'

'Billy?'

'I know the name, but I'd never seen him before.'

'Mrs Carson?'

'Well, yes,' she began slowly. 'I worked for him. I do some cleaning at his company, Invicta Printing.'

'And what kind of man was he?'

'I don't know as I can say, really. I didn't really have anything to do with him.'

'Nothing at all?'

'Well, he was the boss, wasn't he? I'm just a cleaner.'

'Two different worlds, Mr Jago,' said Robert, staring him in the eye. 'The bosses and the workers. One lives off the backs of the others, and never the twain shall meet. I'm not surprised if someone's done him in: a man like that probably had lots of enemies. Probably got his comeuppance. His sort all will one day.'

'A man like what?' said Jago. 'You said you'd never heard of him.'

'I haven't. But they're all the same. Bosses, capitalists, they're all oppressors of the working class. All they want is profit, and they'll cut any corner to get it. All I'm saying is people who play rough like that sometimes get it back.'

'I don't think I said anything about him having been killed by someone either,' said Jago.

'Well, I was just assuming, wasn't I? Why else would you coppers be here?'

Irene interrupted. 'Mr Jago, don't take any notice of what Robert says. He's a bit passionate about his beliefs, that's all. I don't hold with everything he says, but if it turns out that Mr Villiers was killed because he was up to no good, one of those war profiteers or something, I'd say good riddance.'

'Calm down, Mum,' said Billy. 'Don't get in a state.'

'I won't calm down. I've just lost my husband, Mr Jago, and I don't know what I'm going to do. He risked his life to bring food and everything we need into this country, and all they paid him was three pounds eleven and six a week. And now he's dead. I've heard stories about thieving in the docks that would make your hair stand on end. As soon as the stuff's unloaded, there's someone out there stealing it and making a fortune out of people like me and my husband. There's no justice in this world, no justice.'

She began weeping, and Billy put his arm round her.

'We'll be on our way now, Mrs Carson,' said Jago.

He turned as he reached the door and heard Irene's sobbing voice.

'People like that deserve everything they get.'

CHAPTER TEN

'Griggs,' said the man in the brown warehouse coat and cloth cap. 'Goods in and out, gatekeeper, caretaker and general dogsbody, that's me.' He eyed them up and down like an undertaker estimating for a coffin. 'Nothing gets in or out of Invicta Printing without me knowing. So how can I help you two gentlemen?'

There was barely room for Jago and Cradock to squeeze into the dilapidated wooden shack in which Griggs mounted guard over the entrance to the print works. Jago nudged a box to one side with his foot to make a little more space to stand in.

'We're investigating the death of Mr Villiers,' he said. 'Were you here on Saturday when he left the premises?'

'That I was,' said Griggs. 'On duty, as usual.'

'Can you tell us what time he left?'

Griggs pulled a grubby book from under the wooden desk and thumbed through the pages.

'Here we are,' he said, bending back the spine of the book and placing it on the desk in front of them. He stabbed at an entry with a dirt-engrained forefinger. 'He left at a quarter to eight in the evening, in the van, with Mr Johnson – he's one of the bosses here.'

'And who was driving?'

'It was Mr Johnson. I remember because the window was open and I had to bend down close to say goodnight to Mr Villiers, and Mr Johnson pulled a face, as if I was smelly or something.'

'Did they say where they were going?'

'No, but then again that's none of my business. I just have to clock people in and out, and write it in this book of mine,' said Griggs. 'I assumed Mr Johnson was driving Mr Villiers home. I was off yesterday, and then when I came in this morning I wondered why the van wasn't back, but then I heard that Mr V had been killed and all in that air raid.'

'Thank you, Mr Griggs,' said Jago. 'We spoke to Mr Edward Villiers yesterday, and he recommended that we speak to Mr Johnson.'

'Ah, yes, young Mr Villiers,' said Griggs, with a smirk that suggested he was sharing a private joke with himself.

'Is Mr Johnson here today?' said Jago.

'Yes.'

'In that case we'd like to see him.'

'Very well, gentlemen, if you'd care to follow me, I'll take you to his office.'

He took a last drag on his cigarette, stubbed it out in an ashtray overflowing with dog-ends, and rose from the cluttered desk. At the door he paused and reflected for a moment. 'I suppose that'll be just "Mr Villiers" now,' he said, and led Jago and Cradock out of the hut.

They followed him as he plodded across the cobbled yard of Invicta Printing Ltd. Griggs noticed that Cradock was holding his nose, and laughed.

'Sorry about the smell,' he said. 'That'll be the chemical works down the road. It makes an almighty stink, especially if the wind's blowing the wrong way. You get used to it in the end. Doesn't seem like the kind of place a man like Mr Villiers would choose for his business, does it? But I reckon it's probably cheap here and helps to keep his profits up.'

The yard was enclosed on three sides by buildings that looked as though they might date back to early Victorian times, with worn bricks and sagging roofs. Cheap or not, they were certainly showing their age, thought Cradock.

'This used to be a silk-printing works back in the old days,' said Griggs, 'or so they say. But they packed that in years ago. It just does what I'd call normal stuff now.'

He pointed to the first building on their left, a two-storey structure with a slate roof, large wooden double doors and two small windows.

'That there's the main store, where we keep the stock.'

'Stock?' said Cradock.

'That'll be paper to you, sonny,' said Griggs. 'We're printers, and paper's the stuff what we print on.'

Cradock cast a wondering look at Jago but said nothing.

'Then we've got the garage, where we keep the van; used to be a stable, as you can probably tell. The bit next to it, that's where we keep all the old junk: a couple of presses that we don't use any more, and that sort of thing. I reckon that's where they'll be chucking me before too long.'

He laughed, but there was a bitterness in his tone that struck both the men with him. He wheezed and began to cough. Pausing until he could speak again, he gestured towards the building directly in front of them, the largest. A repetitive clunking and hissing of machinery pounded through its partly opened windows and echoed round the yard.

'Over there's the main print shop with the newer machines: that's where all the work gets done these days. You'll find it a bit noisy in there. Mr Johnson'll be up them stairs there, in the office.'

Griggs stumped up the steel staircase that ran along the outside wall of the building to a door on the first floor, with the two detectives in his wake. He knocked on the door and showed them in.

'Some visitors for you, Mr Johnson. Policemen. They'd like to have a word with you about poor Mr Villiers.'

'Thank you,' said the man sitting before them. He rose to greet them, removing a cigarette from the corner of his mouth and placing it carefully in an ashtray on the desk. He was tall and heavily built, and wearing a dark suit with a white shirt and a black tie. As he extended his right arm to shake hands, Jago noted the worn cuff and the ink stains on his fingers. Johnson caught his eye and smiled.

'Please excuse the state of my hands, Mr . . . ?'

'Jago, Detective Inspector. And this is Detective Constable Cradock.'

'Albert Johnson. As I was saying, please excuse the state of my hands. I help Mr Villiers – or I suppose I should say *helped* him – to run the company, but in this line of work you have to be willing to get your hands dirty. And that was my side of the business rather than his.'

'How do you mean?'

'I mean I've worked in print all my life. Mr Villiers got the orders in and dealt with the clients, but I'm the one who runs the practical side. I don't think he would ever have described himself as an expert in printing.'

'How long have you worked here?'

Johnson retrieved the cigarette from the ashtray and drew deeply on it, blowing a stream of smoke towards the ceiling.

'Just over two years. I joined the company in 1938.'

'And how would you describe Mr Villiers?'

'Well, I can't say I knew him well. He was the boss, if

you know what I mean. We didn't socialise outside the job. He moved in different circles to me.'

'And what kind of circles would they be?'

'Oh, you know: people with big houses and fancy wives, the Rotary Club probably, businessmen, wheelers and dealers. Senior policemen too, I shouldn't wonder, what with him being a magistrate.'

'Do you have any idea of how the business was going?'

'I don't see all the figures, but to be honest, I think the war saved him. When I first came it all seemed a bit hand to mouth, but then we started getting government work, information leaflets and suchlike, and since then we've been working at full capacity most of the time. Mind you, even in the bad old days when the machines were idle, it didn't seem to cramp his style. Always had a new car, that kind of thing.'

'And how would you suppose he managed that?'

'I don't know. Perhaps he had a private income. Like I said, I'm not privy to all the financial ins and outs in this place.'

'Would you describe Mr Villiers as a trustworthy sort of man?'

Johnson stubbed out the remains of his cigarette in the ashtray.

'I'm not sure I can say. I think to trust someone you've got to know them. And I never really knew Mr Villiers – not that well, anyway.'

'Thank you, Mr Johnson. Now tell me, please, what happened on Saturday. What time did you leave here?'

Johnson looked thoughtful.

'Oh, that must have been sometime after half past seven, I think. I'd been working with Mr Villiers on some estimates for jobs we were bidding for. He said he had to visit someone down Plaistow way and asked if I'd drive him in the van, so of course I said yes. We set off, but then after a bit he said he'd changed his mind. I should drive to my place, then he'd drop me off and drive himself over to Plaistow and then home to Forest Gate.'

'Where is your place?'

'I live in Greengate Street, number 22. It's a flat over a newsagent's, just past the old tramways depot, where they keep the trolleybuses now.'

'And do you know why Mr Villiers changed his mind?'

'No. But then it's not my place to ask the boss why.'

'Do you know who he was visiting? Was it a customer?'

'Don't know, I'm afraid. He didn't say. I'm not aware of any current customers down there, but as I said, that was more his side of the business.'

'What time did he drop you off?'

'I didn't really notice, to be honest, but it must have been about twenty past eight. We'd been held up on the way, because one of the roads was blocked after the air raid, so I had to get out and walk the last bit. It would have been about ten minutes' walk, and I remember the sirens went off again when I was nearly home. I looked at my watch and it said half past eight, so yes, I must have left him at about twenty past or so.'

'And can you tell us where you were for the rest of the evening?'

'Yes, that's easy. When the sirens went off I was right by a friend's place, so I stopped and took shelter there. He's got an Anderson shelter and I haven't. We took a bottle of Scotch down into the shelter and I spent the rest of the night there until the all-clear went.'

Jago nodded thoughtfully.

'Thank you. Just a couple more questions before I go, Mr Johnson.' He pulled a buff envelope from his pocket and carefully removed the knife he and Cradock had found in the van. 'Do you recognise this?'

'Yes,' said Johnson, 'it's an old printer's knife. It's got a special spike called a typesetting pick. If I'm not mistaken it's the one Mr Villiers had. Not that he ever did any typesetting himself, of course, but I think he liked it because it suited the part, what with him having a printing business, and as far as I know he used to carry it with him all the time.'

'Thank you. And finally, were you aware of any worries Mr Villiers might have had?'

'No. Nothing he told me about, anyway.'

'Do you think Mr Villiers was the kind of man who might take his own life?'

Johnson paused for thought again.

'I don't know. He was a bit cagey about his private life. But on the other hand, with someone like him I think anything would be possible.'

* * *

Jago and Cradock made their way back to Griggs's shabby hut by the entrance to the yard. Griggs was sitting inside it, sipping tea from a chipped white mug.

'Care for a cuppa?' he said.

'Thank you, but no,' said Jago. 'I'd just like to ask you a couple of questions.'

'Fire away.'

'What kind of man was Mr Villiers?'

Griggs put on a thoughtful expression. 'Well, he paid my wages, so he wasn't all bad.'

'A decent employer, then?'

'I'd say so, yes. Bit posh, of course. I think he was a major or something in the war, obviously used to giving orders. Bit of a ladies' man too, I reckon.'

'What do you mean by that?'

'Well, he used to chase after some of the women who worked here. You know the sort of thing.'

'Is that just hearsay?'

'What does that mean?'

'I mean is that just what people say, or did you actually see him do it?'

'Yes, of course. Just the other night. Most people had gone home and the cleaner was here. I came round the corner and found him talking to her. But it wasn't just like he was talking to her. It looked like he'd got her cornered and was standing really close, like. I could see she was trying to get away: she was pushing him with her hands. So I made a bit of a noise to show I was there, and he jumped off her like a scalded cat.

I acted like I hadn't seen anything, but I saw her slip away pretty quick, and she wouldn't look up at me.'

'Did you recognise her?'

'Oh yes, straight off. It was that Mrs Carson. Irene Carson, she's called.'

CHAPTER ELEVEN

Jago strode briskly up West Ham Lane. Dignity required that he should walk, not run, but he was going to be late. He ran a finger round his collar to let some air in.

Overhead, the afternoon sky was turning the same silver-grey as the barrage balloons that swayed placidly on their tethering cables in the faint breeze. There was rain coming.

By the time he got to the police station it was five to three. He was hot and annoyed. He slipped in between the stacks of sandbags that flanked the front door and nodded a quick greeting to Tompkins. This wasn't the time to get into conversation.

He reached the CID office by two minutes to three. It was empty, and he leant against the wall for a few moments to calm himself before the visitors arrived. He wondered what kind of man the American would be. Probably some suave Clark Gable type who would make him feel like an inadequate Englishman.

The door opened and Soper ushered in the two visitors. Jago gave them a cursory glance as they entered, but to his surprise, the sight that greeted him did not remotely match his expectations. Not least because one of the two strangers was a woman.

Before he could compose himself, the meeting was under way.

'Allow me to introduce you,' said Soper. 'Detective Inspector Jago, this is Mr A. J. Mitchell from the Ministry of Information, and this is Miss Dorothy Appleton, who is a journalist from the United States.'

'Mr Jago,' said the woman, 'how nice to meet you. You look a little surprised. Perhaps you weren't expecting a woman?'

'Not at all,' said Jago, still unsettled. 'Do take a seat. And you too, Mr Mitchell.'

'I shan't stay, actually,' said Mitchell, airily. 'I have matters to attend to, and if I might just have a word with you before I leave, Mr Soper, I shall then be on my way.'

A minute later Jago was alone in the room with the reporter. He gave her a chair and sat behind the desk, facing her.

'Miss, er, Miss Appleton,' he said, then hesitated. 'It was Miss Appleton, wasn't it, not Mrs? I'm afraid I didn't entirely take in what Mr Soper said.'

He could hear the awkwardness in his own voice. There was no ring on her left hand, but he realised he had no idea what the American practice was.

'Yes, it's Miss, Inspector. And I must apologise for what I said just now. There was no reason for me to suppose you weren't expecting a woman.'

'Well, actually,' Jago began. 'That is to say, I—'

'Don't worry about it. We tend to think of you British as being a little old-fashioned, but I'm sure you have women journalists here too. Maybe it's just more common in the States. And I guess police work is still pretty much a man's world over here, yes?'

'Well, we do have some women police.'

'Oh really? How many?'

'In the Metropolitan Police, about a hundred and fifty, I believe.'

'And how many men?'

'About thirty-three thousand.'

She paused.

'So that's about half a per cent, then?'

'Yes.'

'And what do they do?'

'They're mainly responsible for looking after vulnerable women and children, that kind of thing.'

'So no detectives, then?'

'No.' Jago felt as though he were being cross-examined in court.

'You know, five years ago my paper had me write a story about a woman in New York City who was our

102

first female police detective. She's a detective sergeant now, I believe.'

'Well, perhaps things move a little more slowly over here.'

'I guess so. It's a good thing the same can't be said of your fighter planes,' she said. Jago took it as a conciliatory remark and decided to try to change the subject.

'So, Miss Appleton, what brings you here today?'

'Well, as you know, I'm a journalist. I work for the *Boston Post* as a foreign correspondent, based here in London, and I'm covering the war from the British angle. I'm interested in how ordinary people are coping with it.'

'I see. So you asked to meet some ordinary people and they came up with me?'

She laughed.

'Not at all, Inspector. I'm accredited to your Ministry of Information, of course, and some time ago I told them I'd like to write some pieces about public morale. I wanted to focus on the East End of London, because it's where the poorer people are, the ones who were maybe having a rougher time of the rationing and what have you. And as it happens, of course, with these terrible air raids we've been having since Saturday, right now this is exactly where the story is.'

'Glad we could oblige,' said Jago. 'But where do I come into this?'

'I just figured it would be good to have a contact who could explain life here to me, someone who knows everything that goes on in a place like West Ham. And a policeman is that kind of person.'

'But why me?'

She leant closer and lowered her voice conspiratorially.

'I'll let you into a little secret,' she said. 'I saw your picture in the newspaper. You'd been to Buckingham Palace to get some medal. The King's Medal, was it?'

'The King's Police Medal.'

'The paper said you'd disarmed a man with a gun, and I thought that was interesting. I didn't know if I'd be able to write about my policeman, but I thought if I did, it would help if he were some kind of hero. So I made a note of your name, and when I went to the ministry I asked for you. Simple as that.'

Jago considered her words for a moment and then stood.

'Well, Miss Appleton, I'm under instructions to assist you, so assist you I shall. But I must make one thing clear: I am currently engaged in a suspected murder investigation and my time is limited, so if you think you can tag along with me as I go about my duties I'm afraid you're mistaken. I'll be happy to meet you when time allows, answer your questions and help you in any way I can, but you must understand that there are some difficult areas in this borough, and I'd advise you not to go running round everywhere without consulting me. On top of that, now we've got these air raids. Frankly, it's no place for a . . .'

He hesitated. She was looking him straight in the

eye, both her eyebrows raised in an expression of innocent enquiry.

'It's no place for a person who's a stranger to the area to be wandering round on their own.'

'Exactly,' she said. 'I appreciate your concern and gladly accept your offer to escort me as and when the need arises. Now perhaps you could have someone call a cab for me and I'll be on my way. I'll leave you my card.'

Jago felt outmanoeuvred and had the uncomfortable sense that she was making fun of him. He took the card, noting her address: the Savoy Hotel, Strand, London. Only the best for the *Boston Post*, he thought.

He walked her back to the front desk and left Tompkins with the challenge of assisting her with her transport arrangements.

On returning to his office, Jago sat at his desk and reflected briefly on their conversation. He wasn't entirely convinced. Surely she could have found someone else to explain life in the East End to her. Why did she need a detective inspector? He knew from experience that journalists could be a devious bunch. She might see him as a useful contact, but he had a feeling she wasn't telling him the whole story.

CHAPTER TWELVE

'What really happened on Friday night, Sidney?'

He could not bear to look at her. She clearly knew he was lying, and her voice was stern. He tried again.

'It was an accident. There was nothing I could do about it. I'd been out for a drink with that old friend of mine, as I said, and I was on my way home. It was dark, and I couldn't see a thing – you know what it's like in the blackout. Suddenly a bike came round the corner, and the next thing I knew I was flying through the air and landing in the gutter. I don't know how long I was lying there. I might even have been knocked out, I think, because it was so late when I got home.'

His voice trailed off, and he forced himself to face her, hoping she wouldn't ask any more questions. It seemed quite plausible to blame his cuts and bruises and the state of his clothes on a collision with a cyclist in the dark: everyone knew that blackout accidents had caused more injuries over the past year than enemy action. But beyond that point he was struggling to connect his story with the facts of the matter in a way that was even half convincing.

'Who was the friend you were with?'

'It was an old school friend. He's called John.'

She said nothing, but fixed him with a sceptical gaze.

Inside he felt a mixture of guilt and fear. *When have I ever mentioned old school friends before? She probably knows I don't have any. She must think I was with another woman. She'll be thinking I'm having an affair with someone, and her husband's caught up with me.*

He knew he had a choice: he could either tell her now or attempt to keep lying to her for the rest of his life. The second option did not seem viable.

'I'm sorry, Ann,' he said hesitantly, 'that's not right: it wasn't an old friend. You see, something's happened. I didn't want to worry you, but I'm in trouble and I don't know what to do.'

'What is it?' she said. Her voice was impatient, as if she were talking to a naughty child. He looked around their sitting room: a picture of lower-middle-class respectability, everything neatly in its place. Even that made him feel false. A white-collar job meant he wasn't working class, but he wasn't sure he qualified for even the lowest ranks of the middle class.

'I-I don't think I can tell you everything, and it might be best for you not to know.'

'Don't be silly. Tell me.'

'It's to do with work. I've got mixed up with a man who's making me do things that are against the rules, illegal things.'

'Can't you report him?'

'He's not someone I work with. He's from outside, a criminal. And he's violent: he's the one who did this to me.'

'Let's take it to the police, then. We have to stand up to people like that.'

'Oh, Ann, you sound like my father. It's not as easy as that. He told me to stand up to bullies when I was a boy, so I tried, and all I got was another beating. It doesn't work with people like that. He's just vicious.'

'But you can't have someone attack you on the street and do nothing about it.'

'You don't understand. I've taken money from him. If I report him, they'll find out what I've done and send me to prison.'

Ann could see he was afraid. She had always known Sidney was weak, and the idea that some unscrupulous person had got their claws into him by offering him easy money was no surprise. She thought for a moment, then spoke.

'Sidney, we need to get help with this.'

'But I've already told you, if I go to the police I'll end up in more trouble than he does.'

'I'm not talking about the police. There must be ways of dealing with people like this that don't involve the police.'

'But people like us don't get mixed up in things like that.'

'No, but if the alternative is you being ruined, we may need to.'

'So what do you have in mind?'

'I don't know, Sidney. This isn't exactly a situation I've dealt with before. But I do know this: you need to tell me exactly what's been going on, and we have to find some way to get free of this man, or maybe find someone who can do it for us.'

Sidney was shocked to hear his wife speaking like this. But she had always been the strength in their marriage, the strength that held it, and him, together. If she had decided that action was needed to rescue them from the mess he'd got them into, he had no doubt she would take it.

Billy let himself into the house with his latchkey. He'd walked home from work, pushing his bike instead of riding it, because he knew his mum would be out this evening and the house would probably be empty. The shop had been busy all day, and it had kept his mind off things, but all the way home he'd found himself thinking of his dad. He imagined him on a blazing deck, wild-eyed as the shells landed, his only choice to stay on the ship and burn with it or to leap to certain death in the raging sea. Or even worse, trapped below in the engine room as the torpedo struck, seeing the steel bulkhead breached and the water cascading in, knowing that within minutes it would engulf him, ending his life in a desperate, panic-filled struggle for breath.

'That you, Billy?'

He heard the familiar rough voice of his brother calling from the kitchen. He ran down the passage and threw himself at him, his eyes brimming with tears.

'I need you, Rob. I don't know what to do.'

Robert put his arms round him and held him, awkwardly trying to comfort him.

'Come on, mate, it'll be all right. Come and sit down. Look, Mum's left us some grub in the oven.'

They ate together in subdued silence. The only sound was the comforting bubbling of water and the gentle hiss of steam coming from the kettle on the kitchen range. There wasn't as much meat in the stew as there would have been before the war started, but it was bulked out with carrots, onions and cabbage, and it was hot. Billy began to feel better. He was glad Rob was at home.

The light outside was fading: the sun was going down. They put up the blackout curtains and made a start on washing the dishes. Before the job was half done the air-raid siren cut through the quiet of the evening.

'Come on, down the shelter,' said Robert. 'We'll finish them later.'

They picked up the blankets and lantern their mum had got into the habit of leaving by the back door since the bombing started, then made their way across the backyard to the Anderson shelter. They had helped their dad dig the hole for it and assemble the corrugated steel panels last year, when he was on leave. Even half buried in the ground and with a covering of soil over the top it looked flimsy.

They stepped down into the shelter and made sure the blackout curtain was in place before lighting the lantern. The smell of paraffin mixed with the stale odour of damp that filled their cramped refuge.

'What a dump,' said Robert. 'It smells like old fish down here.'

'Damp enough for fish too,' said Billy, carefully moving his blanket to avoid the patch of water on the floor.

'It's just typical, though, isn't it?' said Robert. 'Round here, people think they're lucky if they've got one of these down the end of their garden, and if they haven't they have to go to one of the public shelters that are probably even worse.'

'How's that?' said Billy.

'Haven't you heard? That raid we had on Saturday night – when the bombs got close some of those brick ones in the street just fell down.'

'Blimey,' said Billy, 'I didn't know that.'

'And some of them surface shelters haven't even got roofs. What's the good of that?'

Robert leant forward, becoming animated.

'But then you go up the West End and you'll find all the rich types in their luxury apartments and hotels have got a lovely shelter in the basement, reinforced, blast-proof, air conditioning and everything. Suppose a few charabanc-loads of people from here turned up and said they wanted to share: what would happen then, eh?'

Billy laughed. 'Yeah, that would be a sight to see.'

'And that's just the ones who haven't moved out to their country mansions for the duration,' Robert continued. 'And meanwhile the government won't even let people like us use the Tube stations for shelter. They want us to fight this war for them but they don't care how many ordinary working people die.'

'We can't just give in to Germany, though, can we?'

'Look, Billy, all I'm saying is it's not our war. People like you and me didn't start it, did we? It's just like the last time: it's all about kings and empires and money.'

'I suppose you think we should stay out of it, like Russia.'

'Yes, I do. It's different there. They got rid of the toffs, and now it's the workers that run the country. Everything belongs to the people, so everyone gets a job, a decent place to live, food to eat. They've got rid of the people who start wars, too. You know what that Churchill's like: a right warmonger. But Stalin's not interested in imperialist wars; he wants to build socialism in one country, so then other countries can do it too. I tell you, when the workers are in charge all over the world we'll all live together in peace.'

'Sounds nice,' said Billy.

'It's time for us to take control,' said Robert. 'We're going to start changing things – you'll see.'

'Right,' said Billy, thoughtfully. He looked up. 'That

reminds me, Rob. Talking of toffs and the like, I've been meaning to ask you. When those coppers were round here this morning asking about that dead bloke Villiers, why did you say you didn't know him?'

'Cos I don't, that's why.'

'But you—'

Robert raised a warning finger before Billy's face.

'No names, no pack drill, all right? You take my advice, Billy: never give a copper the time of day. If they want to know something, let them find out for themselves. I'm giving them nothing. Strike breakers and bully boys the lot of them, in the pay of the ruling class. You keep your mouth shut, Billy, and you won't go far wrong.'

CHAPTER THIRTEEN

At a little after seven-thirty on Tuesday morning Jago was in Rita's cafe, ordering bacon and eggs and a large mug of tea. There was something very pleasant about having your breakfast cooked for you. It was somehow comforting, and made him feel he could cope with whatever the day might throw at him.

He usually had breakfast in the police canteen – lunch too, if he wasn't out somewhere on a case. Cooking at home took too much time, so when he was off duty he preferred to eat out as often as possible. He'd never felt guilty about this before the war, but when the government brought in food rationing at the beginning of the year it had made him think twice. The fact that meals in restaurants and cafes weren't subject to rationing undoubtedly made his life easier, but he knew the trouble most working people had eking out their food ration through the week, especially those with families. And after the recent air raids you only had to walk down the street to see people's lives bombed into chaos. The best compromise he could make with his conscience was to eat modestly. At least then he knew he wasn't abusing the privilege of having enough money to eat out.

This morning, though, he had forsaken the police canteen. He wanted some time alone, to think.

There were fewer people in the cafe than there had been on Saturday. Most of them were men, eating alone, probably on their way to work. There wasn't the background jumble of animated conversation that there'd been on Saturday either, but then that was before the shock of the air raids. Now the atmosphere seemed sombre. A fanciful image floated into his mind, of plump, jolly housewives in aprons serving up a cooked breakfast by the kitchen range to appreciative husbands in working-men's clothes. Probably something he'd seen in a film, he thought: not likely to be a reality in many homes around East London today.

He had sometimes envied married colleagues who had wives to look after them. When he came home from the war, so many men had been killed that people were saying there would be a generation of spinsters. Any man who wanted a wife could take his pick. But what was the point of that if you didn't find someone you could love? You had to meet the right person, and at the right time.

Life wasn't always like that, and it hadn't been like that for Jago. He'd never set out to be a bachelor, but he'd rather pay to have his shirts washed and ironed and his house cleaned, and eat his breakfast in a cafe, than spend his life in a miserable marriage.

The smell of frying was making him feel hungry. He looked at his watch: no rush yet. He thought of Muriel Villiers and her late husband. That didn't seem like a marriage made in heaven either. What had been going on between them? It was beginning to look as though the man Jago had seen on the bench at Stratford magistrates' court dispensing justice to all and sundry had feet of clay. People might have their own reasons for wanting to tarnish his name now he was dead, but the fact remained that so far no one had had a good word to say about him. The more Jago heard about Villiers, the more unsavoury a character he seemed. But unsavoury enough for someone to murder him?

He thought about Cradock. It wasn't long since the young lad had transferred into the CID, and in peacetime he'd probably have had to serve longer before he got the chance. Jago had given him a long list of tasks yesterday; *it'll be interesting to see how he's coped with them*, he thought.

He was interrupted by the arrival of Rita. She set a plate of eggs and bacon before him, with toast, a small dish of jam and a steaming mug of tea.

'There you are, love: just what the doctor ordered,' she said. 'Enjoy your breakfast, but watch the plate: it's hot.'

She smiled and turned away to attend to her next order. Jolly and plump, thought Jago, and good at cooking breakfast, but not a woman he could ever imagine being married to. There had to be more to it than that.

He poured a little HP sauce onto his plate from the bottle on the table and tucked into his food. The thought of Rita brought another and very different woman to his mind: the American.

Definitely a modern woman, he thought. Certainly not lacking in confidence, although he supposed you didn't get to be a newspaper reporter in America by being a shrinking violet. A tad too confident for his liking, though. Their meeting yesterday afternoon had felt like a tennis match in which she had taken the first two sets. He needed to fight back and gain the upper hand, but he fancied he'd have his work cut out for him.

He drained the last of his tea, put on his coat and hat, slung his gas mask over his shoulder and set off for the police station. His destination was a three-storey brick building that stood rather imposingly on the corner of West Ham Lane and Barnby Street, overlooking the green space of the recreation ground. It had been built at the end of the last century and exuded late-Victorian confidence. Jago had always found it quite an attractive building, although he supposed that depended on which side of the law you found yourself.

He entered the station, and the fresh air of the

outside world gave way to the smell of disinfectant that always seemed to pervade its corridors. Tompkins was at his counter.

'Morning, sir. Mr Soper would like to see you immediately.'

Jago signalled receipt of the message as he passed and headed for the DDI's door. This time it was ajar when he reached it. He tapped twice on the polished wood.

'Come in,' said a voice from inside the room. Jago went in.

'Shan't keep you a moment, John,' said Soper. 'I just want to fill you in a bit. I couldn't say anything at yesterday's meeting with that American woman, but I want you to know what that fellow Mitchell from the MoI said to me after we'd left the room. To put it briefly, he wants you to manage her. Damned if I understand why, but apparently the ministry is happy for foreign reporters like her to see what's happening and report the truth to the outside world. Of course, she has to operate under the same restrictions as our own reporters, so no straying into military areas or giving away precise details of what's been bombed and where, that sort of thing, but apart from that she can go where she likes and say what she likes. Not the way I'd run a war, but then I'm not the Ministry of Information.'

'What does he mean by "manage her", sir?'

'As far as I can tell, he just means point her in the right direction when you can, and try to chat with her about what she sees, let her know what we think. The way

Britain is presented in the American press is of critical significance to the war effort.'

'But how do I know whether what I think is the same as what "we" think? I don't necessarily agree with everything the government says or does, nor am I required to.'

'You're a policeman, John. Just do your duty. I know I can rely on you.'

He paced across to the window and looked out.

'Another bad night last night. You may not have heard yet, but a school was bombed in Canning Town. Agate Street. It was being used as a rest centre. Apparently it was full of people who'd been bombed out and were waiting for transport to evacuate them when it was hit. Very nasty business, by all accounts. You might like to take her down that way. Show her a bit of Silvertown too. It's had a pasting – not surprising with the docks at the end of the street.'

He turned back to his desk and reached for a piece of paper.

'Just one other thing, John. That American woman wants you to call her at her hotel this morning. Here's the number.' He looked at the paper. 'Temple Bar 4343.'

Jago took the paper and hurried off to his next meeting, with Cradock.

'Right, what have you got for me?' he asked.

'Some interesting information, sir,' said Cradock. 'I went back to see the ARP warden who found the van with the body in it. He says he was in Whitwell Road earlier that evening, about a quarter past eight, and saw a van that looked just like that one backing into some small commercial premises. And Whitwell Road's just round the corner from where we saw the body. He says there were two men in the van. He couldn't see their faces from that distance; all he could say was the driver looked a good half a head taller than the bloke in the passenger seat.'

'Right,' said Jago, 'you need to find out who those premises belong to.'

'Already done that, guv'nor,' said Cradock. He looked pleased with himself. 'They belong to one Frederick Cooper, known as Fred to his friends.'

'Can't say I know him.'

'No, sir. But I spoke to the PC whose beat that is – where Cooper's premises are, I mean. He said Cooper doesn't have any convictions, but he's reckoned to be a bit of a slippery character locally, probably up to no good on the quiet.'

'So what was our Mr Villiers doing visiting him, if that's where he was? And who was with him? Johnson says Villiers didn't drop him off until about twenty past eight, when they were still on their way to Greengate Street, and he remembers because it was just before the sirens went off too. He can't have been in two places at the same time.'

'Johnson's got some explaining to do, then.'

'He certainly has. What else have you got?'

'Well, yesterday evening I went to see that man they found roughed up in the cemetery, the one you asked

120

me to follow up. Definitely something funny going on there. His name's Hodgson: Sidney Hodgson. Says he got knocked over by a bike in the blackout, but he looked really nervous and obviously didn't want to talk to me. All on edge, he was. His wife was as cool as a cucumber, mind. Quite a looker too, if you know what I mean.'

'All right, Constable. Keep your mind on the job.'

'Yes, sir, sorry. Anyway, she didn't bat an eyelid. You'd think it'd be the other way round, wife all worked up, worried about her poor injured hubby, crying all over the place. Maybe it wasn't a bike at all. Maybe she'd been knocking him about.'

'I think you'd better restrain your imagination unless some evidence turns up,' said Jago. 'But you're saying you think he's hiding something?'

'Yes. I asked him why he was saying it was some unknown cyclist who'd knocked him over when our PCs said they'd found him in the middle of the cemetery and he looked as though he'd been beaten up. He just looked worried, as if he didn't know what to say, and then his wife stepped in and she explained it: said it was easy to get into the cemetery now the railings had been cut down for making into Spitfires or whatever it is, and they reckoned it must have been someone taking a shortcut in the dark.'

'And what do you make of that?'

'Just seems odd to me that he's the one who was there but she's the one who knows what happened. He looked to me as though he'd had a fright. I think there's more to it than meets the eye, but if he doesn't tell us, we're not likely to find out what.'

'I agree,' said Jago. 'Good work.'

'Thanks, guv'nor,' said Cradock, with a smile and a hint of surprise in his voice.

'And now we'd better be on our way,' said Jago. 'I need to go back to Invicta Printing Ltd and talk to Mr Edward Villiers again, see what he says when his mother's not there. I want you to go and find this fellow Cooper and find out what he's up to.'

He was about to open the door when there was a knock on the other side and Sergeant Tompkins came in.

'Excuse me, sir, but I've got a message for you. A lady phoned, said you hadn't called her. Asked me to give you this message. Said she didn't need a reply.' He handed a piece of paper to Jago and left.

Jago read it silently, folded it and put it in his pocket.

'Anything important, sir?' said Cradock.

'I don't think so,' said Jago. 'I shall be out this evening. I've been summoned to dine with that American reporter.'

'Somewhere nice, sir?'

'That I shall have to tell you tomorrow. It's not one of my regular haunts.'

'Where is it, then?' said Cradock. 'Just in case I need to contact you, of course.'

'Of course. It's a little place called the Savoy Hotel.'

CHAPTER FOURTEEN

Griggs was on duty at the entrance to the Invicta Printing premises when Jago arrived.

'Morning, squire,' he said, touching the front of his cap in a gesture that Jago might have taken as obsequious if he hadn't already had dealings with the man. 'Come to do a bit more digging? I reckon you'll find more dirt than diamonds here.'

'I've come to see Mr Edward Villiers,' said Jago.

'Righto. He'll be up the stairs over there in his dad's old office, next to where I took you to see Mr Johnson. Do you want me to take you over?'

'I can find my own way, thank you, if you've no objection.'

'Suit yourself.'

Jago mounted the steps again and found Villiers in an office that was roomier than Johnson's and noticeably better fitted.

'Come in,' said Villiers, shaking him by the hand. 'Sit down. Make yourself comfortable. Are you any nearer to finding out what happened to my father?'

Jago settled into an expensive-looking sofa.

'Not yet, I'm afraid.'

'Do you still think it might have been suicide?'

'To be honest, Mr Villiers, I think it was not. I suspect your father was murdered, and that someone – for whatever reason – wanted to make it look like suicide.'

Villiers sat down too, in an armchair that matched the sofa.

'Well, that rather changes the picture. Does my mother know this?'

'No, not yet,' said Jago.

'Is it all right for me to tell her? I think it will come as a shock.'

'Yes, please do.'

'Very well. But murder – who would do a thing like that?'

'That's what I was hoping you might be able to help me with. When I visited you and your mother on Sunday morning, I asked you both if you could think of any reason why someone might want to murder him. My recollection is that your answer suggested you didn't, but you thought it possible he had enemies. Could you expand on that?'

Villiers lit a cigarette and blew smoke towards the ceiling, then leant forward in his chair towards Jago, his face adopting a serious expression.

'Look, Inspector, I'm going to be perfectly frank with you. I think my father was a hypocrite, in the original Greek sense of the word – you know, play-acting. He liked people to think of him as a decent chap, *bien soigné*, a pillar of the community – distinguished retired officer, gentleman, successful businessman, magistrate keeping the streets safe. That's the picture he liked to paint. Whether it convinced anyone, I don't know. I told you he was a private man, and he was. Maybe that was so no one would get close enough to know him as he really was, rather than the image he presented to the world. My mother and I were the closest to him in that sense, but I didn't feel I knew him. I don't think I've ever felt that since I was a boy.'

'What about your mother?'

'I've always felt much closer to her.'

'No, I mean was she close enough to him to see beneath the surface?'

'I don't think I could say. She was always very loyal to him, but she may have had her own reasons for that. You'll have to ask her.'

'So what grounds do you have to say your father was not the man he claimed to be?'

'Well, nothing very specific, but for one thing I didn't like the way he treated my mother. He could be very suave and sophisticated when he wanted to be, but with her I think he was patronising at best, and at worst he was cruel. He was definitely king of the castle in our home, and in his marriage too – a bit Victorian in that way, I suppose.'

'Can you give me an example?'

'I don't think she was allowed to know anything about the money side of things. He gave her the housekeeping, but she had to ask him for money for clothes; I've heard her doing it. It's certainly no surprise that she knew nothing about the state of the business. I work here and I realised some time ago that I don't know the half of it either.'

'Do you mean the business was in trouble?'

'No, I mean I think there were jobs that weren't going through the books.'

'Do you have any evidence for that?'

'No, I don't think I do. Nothing on paper that you could make a case with. It's just one or two odd goings-on I've seen at the works, when I've had to stay late after the staff have gone home, odd snippets of conversation I've overheard. I don't have any specific evidence, but I've wondered for a long time whether he was doing jobs on the side, for cash – what you might call "informal enterprise".'

'So nothing you can put your finger on?'

'No. For all I know he could have been smuggling tinned peaches out of the docks and selling them on the black market. I've really no idea. All I know is this: he may have been stingy with my mother, but he never seemed short of cash. If you're wondering who might have killed him, maybe you should be looking to see if he had any murky underworld connections. Not the sort of thing you'd expect of a magistrate, but then as I've said, I think my father spent a lot of time putting on an act.'

'Thank you, Mr Villiers,' said Jago. 'You've been very helpful. Now if you'll excuse me, I'd like to have a few words with Mr Johnson.'

Jago tapped on the door of the neighbouring office and opened it. Johnson looked up from his desk. He was talking on the phone, the handset propped between his left shoulder and his ear as he searched with both hands through a mess of papers. He lowered his voice in what Jago assumed was a rapid curtailment of the conversation and put the phone down.

'Good morning, Inspector,' said Johnson. 'Do take a seat. You must excuse me: with Mr Villiers unfortunately no longer with us I'm having to deal with some of the customers, and the paperwork isn't all as tidy as one might wish.'

He took a pack of cigarettes from his pocket, opened it and extended it towards Jago.

'Cigarette?'

'No thanks.'

Johnson took one out for himself and lit it.

'How can I help you?'

'I won't take long,' said Jago. 'I'm just trying to

tidy up a few loose ends of my own. Can you tell me how tall you are?'

Johnson looked surprised.

'I'm six foot two.'

'And Mr Villiers?'

'I'd say he was about five foot eight. But what's that got to do with anything? I'm very busy, Mr Jago.'

'I want you to think back to Saturday evening. You told me that you'd driven Mr Villiers in the van and that he dropped you off at about twenty past eight and you walked home. Is that correct?'

'Yes, it was about then.'

'But I have a witness who says he saw that same van backing into some premises in Plaistow at about a quarter past eight, with two men in the front, the driver taller than the passenger. Even allowing for the fact that you and the witness weren't using the same watch, it would be quite a coincidence for Mr Villiers to drop you off, have time to pick up a new driver who was the same height as you, or a passenger who happened to be as much shorter than him as he was than you, and arrive at those premises at the same time as he was dropping you off somewhere else. Would you agree?'

Johnson paused for a moment, then said, 'I'm sorry, Inspector, I'm afraid what I said to you wasn't entirely accurate. I've had a lot on my mind recently.'

'In that case I must ask you to answer my questions more carefully, Mr Johnson. I'm sure you know that if you were to make a false statement under oath in court you would be committing a criminal offence. This is a murder enquiry, and it is most important that you answer truthfully and accurately.'

Johnson looked shocked.

'Murder? But yesterday you said Mr Villiers had committed suicide.'

'I asked you if he was the kind of man who might take his own life. That's not quite the same thing.'

Johnson was silent for a few moments, as though thinking, before he spoke again.

'I understand. The truth is Mr Villiers didn't drop me off. I drove all the way to that place, following his directions.'

'What time did you arrive?'

'I would have said it was twenty past eight, but if your witness says a quarter past it's quite possible it was then. I didn't check my watch at that point.'

'And what happened when you got there?'

'Mr Villiers went in, but he told me to wait outside.'

'So do you have any idea what he was doing, why he'd gone there?'

'No, I don't. I thought it was a bit strange, though. I assumed it must be something private, not normal business, otherwise he wouldn't have kept me outside.'

'If it wasn't normal business, what did you think it was?'

'To be honest, I thought it was possibly something a bit irregular. You know, something he didn't want me or anyone else to know about. But I didn't see or hear anything to prove that; it was just the feeling I had.'

'Do you know whose premises they were?'

'No, I'm afraid I haven't the faintest idea, and it struck me at the time that Mr Villiers clearly didn't want to tell me.'

'So what happened next?'

'I was beginning to think maybe there was some funny business going on, when the door opened. Mr Villiers stuck his head out and said he was going to be busy, and so I'd better find my own way home on foot.'

'Funny business? You didn't say anything about funny business when we spoke to you yesterday.'

A look of concern crossed Johnson's face. He hesitated, then answered.

'Look, Inspector, I hope you'll understand. I didn't know what Mr Villiers might be involved in, but whatever it was, I didn't want to get mixed up in it. If you want my honest answer, I've got an idea he was making some sort of delivery to that place.'

'Why's that?'

'It's just that he didn't normally take the van home. He must have had some reason for going in the van.'

'Did you look to see what was in the back of the van?'

'No. Why should I? When you're driving the man who owns the company, you don't check what he might be taking out. It's the staff you have to keep an eye on. You may find that strange, but that's the way it is. I thought he might be delivering something, but I didn't know what, and I didn't want to know. I try to keep my nose clean, Mr Jago.'

'Is that why you didn't tell me this yesterday: to keep your nose clean?'

'I'm sorry. I just wanted to keep out of the whole business. I don't know what he was doing there; it was something private between him and his customer.'

Jago tried to read Johnson's face, but it was impassive.

'So, when Mr Villiers opened the door, did you see anyone else?'

'No, he only opened it a fraction, on one of those chains, and it was dark: everything was blacked out by then.'

'So what did you do?'

'I walked home, as I said to you yesterday. In fact I ran part of the way when I heard the sirens go off, and I spent the rest of the night in my friend's shelter. I went home when the all-clear sounded.'

'Could you give me the name and address of this friend of yours?'

'Yes. His name's Bob Gray and he lives at 9 Prince Regent Lane; he's got the upstairs flat there.'

Jago added the details to his notebook.

'So why did you give me a different version of events yesterday?'

'I'm truly sorry, Inspector. I didn't mention being there because I really didn't know what Mr Villiers was doing, and I thought it might be something fishy. I've never been in any sort of trouble, and I didn't want to get mixed up in anything like that, so when I heard he'd been found dead I suppose I panicked. I'm sorry, it was a stupid thing to do, but I thought it would just be easier to say I wasn't there.'

'Thank you, Mr Johnson,' said Jago. 'And next time I ask you a question, I would advise you to think carefully and give me an accurate answer.'

When Cradock got to Whitwell Road there was no sign of Cooper, but plenty of evidence of the previous night's work by the Luftwaffe. On one side of the road, where a house, or probably two, had stood for generations until yesterday, there was now only wreckage, and half of the adjoining property had been torn away by the blast. Cradock had seen demolition sites before, but never anything with this air of crazy randomness. Before him lay a tangle of smashed bricks, tiles and timber, mingled with the twisted remains of everything that had once made this someone's home. The shade of a standard lamp was perched incongruously on top of an unhinged door, and what looked like a zinc washtub, dented and battered but still miraculously holding a pair of washing tongs, lay on its side on a pile of rubble, mocked by the sooty filth that covered everything.

He looked at the exposed carcase of the house next door. An iron bedstead was hanging over the edge of what remained of a bedroom floor, and a delicate floral pattern was still visible on the strips of wallpaper that fluttered behind it. He felt as though he were intruding on someone's privacy. He wondered if anyone had been in when the houses were hit. Any bodies would have been removed by the rescue units during the night, or might still lie buried in the basement if there was one. The proximity of death was disturbing. He had woken this morning in the shelter. Not much sleep, but at least he had survived. He began to feel guilty that he was alive while others with just as strong a claim to life as his were dead. People would be wandering through debris like this today in agonies of grief. His own work for the day seemed trivial in comparison.

He turned away from the scene of destruction. He needed to find Cooper, if his place was still standing. He checked his notebook for the address the warden had given him. Number 58 was a dingy, three-storey building in the style of many in the area, with a parapet facade concealing a low-pitched roof. Perhaps the people who built them seventy or eighty years ago had thought the style smart, but whenever Cradock saw a row of these bleak, brick rectangles he found the effect depressing.

The ground floor looked as though it might once have been a shop, but now the windows were boarded up and the paint on the masonry around them was peeling. Above them the brickwork had been gnawed by something toxic in the air, and to one side of the front door a pair of heavy wooden doors were rotting at the bottom. They were closed, but he guessed this was where Villiers' van had been seen backing into the yard or whatever space lay behind them.

He knocked on the front door, but there was no answer. He banged on the double doors, then grabbed a round doorknob and rattled them as hard as he could until he heard a voice.

'All right, all right, I'm coming.'

He heard the sound of a heavy bolt being shot on the other side. The door was pulled back a little and an elderly, stooping man in a greasy jacket and with a dirty muffler round his neck poked his head out.

'Yes?' he said.

'I'm looking for Mr Cooper,' said Cradock. 'Do you work for him?'

'I do. He's not here.'

'Can you tell me where I can find him?'

The man looked him up and down. To Cradock it seemed as though he were deciding whether this specimen was a suitable visitor for his employer. The man must have concluded that he was.

'He's at home. Go down there, to the end of this road, and you'll come out opposite the Plaistow Baths on Balaam Street. Turn right there, then left into Barking Road, and his house is down on the left, number 467.'

Cradock was glad to get away from Whitwell Road. He strode along briskly, and within little more than five minutes he was ringing the bell beside Cooper's front door. The contrast with where he had just come from was striking. Cooper's residence was a three-storey Victorian house, somewhat more substantial than most others in the area. It had a porch, sash windows, and a small front garden with steps down to a basement, and it looked well maintained. Not the kind of place Cradock could aspire to on what he earned.

The door opened, and he saw a large figure scowling down at him from the doorstep.

'Mr Frederick Cooper?'

'What if it is?' growled the man.

Cradock produced his warrant card and identity card.

'I'm Detective Constable Cradock. I'd like to have a brief word with you.'

'Would you, indeed? You'd better come in, then,' said the man, opening the door wide and motioning Cradock in. Halfway down the light and spacious hallway he stopped and turned round to face Cradock; this was clearly as far as his hospitality extended. He was a young man, about the same age as Cradock himself, if not younger. He was wearing an expensive-looking suit, generously cut in the pre-war style, with turn-ups on the trousers and wide lapels. Judging by first impressions, thought Cradock, the man's manner was not as refined as his dress.

'So you are Mr Frederick Cooper?'

'Course I am. Who did you expect?'

Cradock decided to ignore the sarcasm.

'I'm making enquiries in connection with the death of Mr Charles Villiers last Saturday evening. Did you know Mr Villiers?'

'Never heard of him.'

'The reason why I'm here is that on Saturday evening an air-raid warden saw Mr Villiers backing his van into your premises on Whitwell Road. Perhaps that might help you to remember.'

Cooper stroked his jaw.

'Ah, yes, I think I recall now. Must have slipped my

memory. He was the bloke from the printer's, wasn't he? I couldn't remember his name when you first said it. You say he's dead?'

'That's correct.'

'Well, he wasn't dead when he left me. I can assure you of that. Got caught in the air raid, did he?'

Cradock ignored the question.

'Can you tell me what Mr Villiers was doing at your premises?'

'Yes, he came over to talk to me.'

'About what?'

'He was going to print some stationery for me, wasn't he? For my business. He said he'd come and discuss it. Probably because I was a new customer, I suppose.'

'So he wasn't delivering anything to you?'

'No, just visiting.'

'And yet he backed his van into your yard rather than leaving it on the street. Why would he do that?'

'I don't know. Perhaps he thought it was a rough area. Maybe he thought your lot would immobilise it, nick the rotor arm so the Germans couldn't use it to invade East Ham or something. Who knows? I didn't ask him.'

'And what is your business, Mr Cooper?'

'I'm a trader. I buy and sell. You know, a bit of this and a bit of that.'

'Can you be more precise?'

'Well, clothes mainly. Gents' and ladies', but mostly ladies'.'

'You have a shop?'

'No, that's too complicated for my liking. I buy most of it in from workshops down in Whitechapel and Mile End and I sell them mainly in Queen's Road Market. You know the place? Off Green Street, just by Upton Park station. Maybe I could fix you up with something for the missus.'

'Thank you, but no.'

'Single man, eh?'

Again Cradock forced himself to ignore the remark. The man seemed to be getting pleasure from trying to provoke him.

Cooper flashed him an unconvincing smile.

'Don't worry, it's all legit. A public service, really. People still need clothes, even in a war, especially the ladies. And there's rumours going round that we might be getting clothes rationing, same as with the food, so business is booming – air raids permitting, of course. High quality for low prices, that's my motto.'

'What do you use the place in Whitwell Road for?'

'Storing stuff, mainly. All the clothes and suchlike, anything else I might be selling. You got a problem with that?'

'No, Mr Cooper. As I said, I'm investigating the death of Mr Villiers, not your market stall. You may be the last person who saw him alive. You said he left your premises; what time was that?'

'I couldn't say precisely, but I reckon it was about a quarter to nine, something like that. I remember thinking he was stupid to chance it.'

'What do you mean?'

'Well, the sirens had gone off a bit before, and I was all for sitting tight, but he said something like he'd been through a lot of shellfire in his time and he wasn't going to let an air raid stop him. I reckon he was an old soldier – he certainly talked like a major-general. Probably just a jumped-up corporal with ideas above his station.'

'So you didn't go with him?'

'Not a chance, mate. Heroics is for fools, if you ask me.'

'Can anyone confirm that you stayed there?'

'No such luck. I was on my own all night.'

A cold expression formed on Cooper's face.

'Now, is that enough for you? I think that's all I've got to say on the subject, so if you don't mind, I shall bid you good day, Officer.'

'That will be all for now, thank you,' said Cradock, folding away his notebook. 'If there's anything else I need to know, I'll be back.'

'Any time, my son, any time,' said Cooper, and steered him towards the door.

CHAPTER FIFTEEN

The wheels clicked rhythmically across the rail joints as the train swayed and rattled its way eastwards from Stratford through the dense housing of East London. Jago leant his shoulder against the window and watched as terrace after terrace of drab, soot-blackened dwellings slipped past. He was feeling drowsy after three nights of interrupted sleep. The sight of a hoarding on the side of a pub advertising Johnnie Walker whisky reminded him to tell Cradock to check up on Gray in the morning, and then within seconds he dozed off. The next thing he knew, the train was lurching violently as it crossed a set of points, banging his head against the glass. He awoke to hear the sound of someone speaking, and realised it was Cradock. He sat up straight and alert.

'I'm sorry. What did you say?'

'My fault, sir,' said Cradock. 'I didn't realise you'd nodded off. I was just asking whether you'd found out anything useful at Villiers' place.'

'Ah, yes, Invicta Printing Ltd,' Jago replied. 'The answer's yes and no, I suppose.'

'How's that, sir?'

'Well, young Edward Villiers wasn't much help. He seemed to think his father might have been doing some shady deals on the side, but he didn't have any evidence. There may be something in what he says, but on the other hand the dead can't defend themselves, can they? If Edward's mixed up in something that's not above board himself, it would be in his interests to set us off chasing hares in the wrong direction.'

Jago wriggled into a more comfortable position on his seat.

'I had more luck with Johnson, though,' he continued. 'It was strange, really. When I challenged his account of what happened on Saturday night he seemed to cave in very quickly and admitted he did go to those premises in Plaistow. And yet all I could throw at him was the fact that he was tall and the witness's statement would suggest it was him in the van with Villiers. I was on very thin ice, but he admitted he'd been spinning me a yarn immediately. It was almost too easy.'

'Guilty conscience, perhaps?' said Cradock. 'Maybe he was expecting to be found out, and as soon as you challenged his account, he thought you'd rumbled him. He seemed quite a straightforward fellow.'

'He did, didn't he? But even so I don't trust him. He keeps changing his tune, and I still think there's something he's not telling us. He said the reason why he didn't want to own up to being there was that he thought there was something fishy going on. He didn't want to get mixed up in it. I asked him who the place belonged to, and he said he didn't know. If nothing else, all this bears out what Edward said: Mr Charles Villiers JP seems to have had another side to his life. And here's another thing: Johnson said he reckoned Villiers was making some sort of delivery, although he didn't know what it was.'

Cradock interrupted him.

'That's interesting, guv'nor. I asked Cooper if Villiers was delivering something, and he said no.'

'One of them's lying, then,' said Jago. 'I'm inclined to think Cooper's a bigger liar than Johnson is, and if I'm right, it suggests Villiers wasn't visiting Cooper for a simple chat. Johnson can't or won't tell us what Villiers was up to, nor can Edward, but somebody can, and I'm beginning to think the finger's pointing at our Mr Cooper. What did he have to say for himself?'

Cradock got out his notebook and turned to the page where he'd written Cooper's address.

'I found him at home eventually,' he said. 'He lives in Barking Road, number 467, not far away from his place where he met Villiers. Nice house, but he's a nasty piece of work. Sarcastic, cocky – trying to put me in my place, and no mistake.'

'I hope you didn't rise to the bait.'

'No, sir.'

'Good lad. Carry on.'

'Thank you, sir. Cooper's a trader – says he sells clothes in Queen's Road Market. First of all he denied knowing Villiers, but when I pressed him he said Villiers had come to see him about a print job. Business stationery. He says Villiers left on his own in his van at about a quarter to nine.'

'So,' said Jago, 'he was probably the last person to see Villiers alive.'

'Yes, I told him that.'

'Do you think Cooper could have killed Villiers?'

'I only had a short time with him, but I got the impression he wouldn't stop short of anything if someone got in his way. He certainly had the opportunity. He doesn't have anyone who can confirm he stayed behind when Villiers left. He could've gone with him in the van, or even followed him down the road: the van was only round the corner when we found it.'

'So he's got the opportunity but no alibi, and he could easily have had the means, but did he have a motive?' said Jago. 'Why would he want to kill Villiers?'

Cradock paused, trying to get his thoughts into order.

'That's what I can't work out, sir. Cooper definitely seems to be a dodgy character, and I wouldn't be surprised if half the stuff in his store turned out to be nicked. You wouldn't expect Villiers to be up to no good with his sort, what with Villiers being a JP and all, but perhaps he was, and perhaps they fell out over something. After all, young Edward and Johnson have both let on that Villiers was involved in some funny business.'

'Yes,' said Jago, 'although they might just be trying to blacken Villiers' name for some reason we don't know. We can't rule out that possibility. But to get back to Cooper: if Villiers was delivering something to him, as Johnson says he was, why did Cooper deny it, and why did he even deny knowing Villiers?'

'Cooper's trying to hide something from us,' said Cradock. 'That much we do know. Whatever it is, it's probably something criminal, and it looks like Villiers was involved in some way. What about you, sir? Do you think it could be Cooper that killed Villiers?'

'I'm not sure,' said Jago, 'but he's got some explaining to do, that's for sure. I think it's time I met Mr Frederick Cooper. Let's see him wriggle out of this.'

The train slowed a little, and he glanced out of the window as a brief interval of green fields appeared beside the track, with a view of open countryside beyond. Minutes later the train crawled into the station and laboured to a halt in a screeching and squealing of brakes. A few people got off, leaving the carriage almost deserted. Jago stood up, pulled down the window and breathed in deeply to clear his head. He chuckled to himself.

'A penny for them, guv'nor?' said Cradock, as Jago settled back into his seat.

'What's that?'

'Your thoughts, sir. A penny for your thoughts.'

'Oh, I see. I was just thinking. It's nearly three months now since the government said all the signposts had to be removed.'

'So the Germans wouldn't know where they were when they landed?'

'Yes. So here we are: we've arrived at the station, but no signs anywhere. There's no Germans here, but it means we've got no idea where we are either.'

'Very confusing.'

'An ingenious idea, no doubt, but you've only got to stick your nose out of the window to know exactly where we are. We must be in Romford.'

'How's that then, sir?'

'Because the air stinks of hops and malt. The brewery's only a quarter of a mile down the road, in the middle of the town, and they're always doing something there that makes that smell. We just have to hope the Germans don't know that.'

Cradock went to the window and sampled the air. Jago was right: the town did have a very distinctive odour.

'But back to the job in hand,' said Jago. 'We need to find out a bit about the dead man's brother, see if he can tell us anything useful about the deceased. He may be one of those Colonel Blimp types, so when we get there, I'll do the talking. You just listen and watch.'

'Very good, guv'nor,' said Cradock.

The sound of doors slamming along the length of the train signalled that it was about to depart, so he pushed the window up again and sat down.

They were now only three stops from Brentwood. Within half an hour they were knocking on the door of Major Arthur Villiers.

Jago surveyed the garden as he waited for the knock to be answered. A straight path led from the wrought-iron gate, flanked on each side by a single neat rectangle of closely trimmed grass. He noted that he could see none of the moss or dandelions that bedevilled his own small patch. The lawns were separated from the path by beds of geometrically aligned ranks of plants and shrubs, and on one side the grass extended round the side of the house as far as a high fence that guarded access to the rear of the property. Jago suspected that it was money for a gardener rather than a consuming hobby that kept it all so thoroughly under control.

The door was opened by a middle-aged woman in a dark blue dress covered by a grey paisley-patterned apron. Before Jago could speak, a man in a green tweed suit and brown brogues appeared beside her, his right hand cupping the bowl of a briar pipe.

'Thank you, Mrs Wilson. I'm expecting these gentlemen.'

She gave a polite nod towards the two men on the doorstep and retired into the depths of the house.

'That's Mrs Wilson: she keeps house for me. Doesn't live in, just comes in three times a week to keep everything shipshape and Bristol fashion, as they say in the navy. Looks after the laundry and does a little cooking. Don't know what I'd do without her.'

At first glance the man at the door was rather as Jago had expected: fiftyish, about five foot nine, and a little overweight, he lacked only a walrus moustache to complete the likeness of Blimp that was so familiar from the newspaper cartoons. His manner was bluff and hearty, but there was something about it that struck Jago as not quite convincing.

'We appreciate your sparing this time to see us, Major Villiers,' he said.

'Not at all,' said the major, switching his pipe to his left hand in order to shake hands with the two policemen. He waved them in with a sweep of his pipe stem and led them to a sunny drawing room at the back of the house. The smell of aromatic tobacco smoke that filled the house reminded Jago of his father.

'First of all, may I express my condolences on the loss of your brother,' he said.

'That's most kind of you, Inspector,' said Villiers. 'My brother and I may not have seen eye to eye on everything, but he was nevertheless my brother, and it's a hard loss.'

'I understand,' said Jago. 'This is my colleague Detective Constable Cradock. We have just a few questions for you.'

Villiers turned to Cradock, drew himself up and looked him in the eye with a severe expression. 'Good afternoon, Constable. Very well, Inspector, carry on.'

'Thank you, sir,' Jago continued. 'Very nice place you have here, if I may say so. It's a pleasant change to be out in the country after all the bombing we've had down our way. I expect it's a bit quieter here.'

'We're all on the front line now, Detective Inspector.'

'Of course. Am I right in believing you're involved in the Home Guard?'

'Yes, that's correct. When I heard the announcement in May that the Local Defence Volunteers were to be set up, I thought it was an opportunity for me to be useful.' He crossed the room to the French windows and gazed out into the garden. 'I came out of the last war as a major, so I have some military experience, and I'm retired now, so I have the time.'

He turned back to face them, his hands clasped behind his back.

'Your brother's wife told us you command the Home Guard in Brentwood,' said Jago.

'Not exactly,' Villiers replied with a smile. 'I'm merely a company commander, responsible for part of the Brentwood volunteers. My sister-in-law probably thinks my role is more important than it is. She's very sweet like that, but you can't expect a woman to take an interest in the niceties of military command structures.'

'Happier in the kitchen, eh?' said Cradock.

Jago flashed Cradock a silencing glance, but Villiers' expression had already clouded. He stalked across the room and swung back to glare at Cradock as if he were inspecting a sloppily turned-out private on parade.

'Don't misunderstand me, Constable,' he said. 'That's not what I mean at all. Mrs Villiers is no fool. She's a very fine woman and I have the utmost respect for her. She's not had an easy life, and after what she's had to put up with, I wouldn't be surprised if military affairs were of no further interest to her at all.'

'Of course,' Jago interposed. 'I'm sure DC Cradock meant no disrespect to your sister-in-law. But her husband had a military background, didn't he? Are you saying that he was what she had to put up with?'

The major calmed a little before speaking again.

'All I'm saying is that I think my brother was a disappointment to her. If you want my honest opinion, I'd say I believe that when she married him, she thought she was getting an officer and a gentleman for a husband, but all she got was an officer.'

'So you're suggesting he wasn't all he appeared to be?'

'I'll be frank with you, Inspector. I didn't get on with my brother. I'm sorry that he's been killed, but he and I haven't been close since we were young men. I haven't seen him for several years, and I'm not sure there's a lot I can say to help you.'

'It would help me to know what caused the estrangement between you.'

'If you must know, it was to do with the war. The last one, I mean. My brother liked people to know that he'd been a captain in the army, and it's true that he was, but there were times when I couldn't agree with the way he conducted himself. As far as I was concerned, he simply wasn't playing the game.'

'How do you mean, sir?'

'Well, as it happened, the whole business came to a head over one particular incident. He hadn't broken King's Regulations or done anything illegal, but I could not condone what he'd done.'

'Could you explain a little more, sir?'

'I don't really want to go into details. Speaking ill of the dead and all that, you know.'

'I understand that, Major Villiers, but it would help us to know what kind of man he was.'

'Very well, if you insist. It came up in a conversation we had just after the war. My brother and I were together one evening, reminiscing about it all. We got onto the subject of discipline at the front. I'm sorry to say not all the men were everything we would have wanted them to be and it was sometimes the devil of a job to get them over the top under fire. He mentioned quite casually that he'd shot a man for cowardice, and I'm afraid we got into quite an argument about it.'

'Why was that?'

'As you may know,' said Villiers, 'military service at the front in the Great War was a very difficult business, and discipline had to be maintained. Perhaps you were there, Mr Jago?'

Jago nodded slowly in reply, and the major continued, now addressing his remarks to Cradock.

'In those days, a soldier convicted on a charge of

cowardice would be shot at dawn, with no right of appeal. But the fact is, many of these men were shell-shocked. They should have been in a hospital, not a trench. Some of them had volunteered for service under age and shouldn't even have been there.'

He turned to Jago again.

'You understand what I'm saying, don't you?'

'Yes,' said Jago. 'We all had to find our own ways of coping, and some of the men just couldn't.'

'Nowadays it wouldn't happen: they'd be imprisoned, not shot. But back then it was a different story.'

'It certainly was,' said Jago. 'And what was it you and your brother disagreed about?'

'In the case that he mentioned, the accused was still alive after the firing squad had done its work,' Villiers continued, his voice tense. 'My brother finished him off with his revolver. That was his duty. In any case he was a strict disciplinarian and would have had no qualms about it. But what I found repellent was that he seemed to have almost enjoyed it: he thought the man deserved his sentence and it was a jolly good show. We had quite a row about it, and after that we just didn't see each other. I thought he was cruel and proud of it, and that's why I broke with him.'

Major Villiers paused, and then spoke in a quieter voice.

'You know, Detective Inspector, I've often thought about the life that poor young soldier never had and the one my brother's enjoyed since then. And I've also wondered how many other lives he may have ruined since then, who else may have suffered at his hands. It's always seemed to me a great foolishness that a man with his temperament should have been appointed a magistrate.'

CHAPTER SIXTEEN

Albert Johnson knocked on Gray's door. There had been no daylight bombing today, and the air-raid sirens had remained silent as the light began to fade, so people were venturing out onto the street. A pair of women in coats and headscarves walked by, and he noticed one of them glancing up at the sky as if fearful of aeroplanes approaching. He heard the sound of feet stumping down the staircase behind the door, and then a fumbling with the lock on the inside. It opened, and there was Bob Gray.

He looked a little unsteady, and he held a glass tumbler in his hand.

'Come in,' he said, waving Albert in, and backed up against the wall to let him pass. Albert heard the front door slam behind him as he made his way up the narrow stairs, then a second sequence of creaks joined the ones his own feet were making on the worn wooden treads. Gray was making his way up the steps at his own pace.

Albert waited for him at the top, then followed him into the small sitting room at the front of the flat, overlooking the street. It struck him as a miserable place. The curtains were still open, and even by the residual daylight that managed to penetrate the grimy windows he could see the state the room was in.

'Come on, Bob,' he said. 'Where's your blackout curtains?'

'I can't afford blackout curtains,' said Gray. 'I've put a couple of nails in the top of the window frame there. Hang that old eiderdown on them.'

Albert picked up the eiderdown, cautiously keeping it away from his nose, and hooked it on the nails. He drew the cheap floral-pattern curtains over it.

'Will that keep the light in?' he said.

'I haven't had any complaints yet.'

Gray switched on the light.

'Take a seat, my friend,' he said, and slumped into an old armchair. Albert took the one facing it, on the other side of the small gas fire that sat in the hearth.

'You shouldn't be drinking so much, Bob,' said Albert. 'It won't do you any good.'

'Don't worry about me. I'm not as bad as I look. Things have been a bit difficult for me the last few months, that's all. I have a little drink to get me through the evenings, but I'm all right. Have one yourself.'

He gestured towards the table. Albert picked up the bottle of Gordon's gin that was standing in the middle of it and pulled out the cork stopper. There were several glasses too, but he couldn't tell which ones were clean. He chose one that looked as though it might be and poured himself a double measure.

'Got anything to go in it?' he asked. 'Tonic?'

'Water,' said Gray.

Albert took the jug of water from the table and added some to his glass.

'Cheers,' he said.

'Cheers.'

Bob wasn't very talkative tonight, thought Albert. He sat in silence himself. If Bob didn't want to speak, that was all right.

Eventually Bob opened his mouth.

'You've been a good friend to me, Albert,' he said, 'just like your George, and don't think I don't appreciate it. I'm sorry about the state of this place. I just don't seem to be able to keep on top of things these days. I wish you'd known me before, back in the good old days, before all this happened. I was a different man then.'

'War changes people, Bob. I know that as well as any other man.'

'Don't talk to me about war,' Bob snarled. He seemed to have become animated for the first time since Albert had arrived. He put his glass down and glared at his guest. 'This isn't a war, it's a shambles. You should've seen us. Retreat, retreat, nothing but retreat, till the Germans pushed us into the sea. What kind of country is this? Sending us into action with rifles against tanks. Those politicians should've taken a turn at sitting on the beach with us. That would've bucked their ideas up. Shoot the lot of them, I say.'

'But you're back now, Bob. You got away.'

'But George didn't, did he? And what about the rearguard? What about the Coldstreams, the East Lancs? They didn't get away, didn't stand a chance. All dead or captured now. And all those people waving at us on the trains when we got back, as if we'd just won the war or something. What were they thinking? You don't know what it was like over there.'

'I think I do.'

'Yes, I'm sorry, Albert, of course you do. I shouldn't go on like this. It's just that I can't get it out of my head. It was pitiless. Stuck on a beach waiting for a place on a boat that might never make it through, running for your life every time a Stuka came screaming down to bomb us. Men were trying to dig holes in the sand to get away from it all. Can you imagine it?'

'Don't go upsetting yourself now, Bob,' said Albert.

'But George was the best friend I'd ever had. Your George. You must feel it even worse than I do.'

'I do,' said Albert. 'I do.' He took a swig from his glass and sat in silence, watching the weak flame sputtering in the gas fire.

'I wish I'd had a mate like him when I was a kid,' said Bob. 'No one ever cared about me when I was a boy, but he always did, always watched my back. In the end it was so bad we didn't know what we were doing. Your George died right beside me. Maybe I am drinking too much, but I just can't stop thinking he took the bullet that was meant for me.'

'You're all right now – you're home. They won't get you back into uniform now.'

'If they find me I'll kill myself. I'm not going back.'

'But they won't find you, will they? You've got yourself a new identity card. Nobody even knows who you are now.'

'That's right,' said Bob, tipping the last of his own glass into his mouth and refilling it. He took the card from his pocket and passed it to Albert. 'Just like the real thing, isn't it? New name too: Bob Gray. I made sure it was something ordinary. Not Smith or Brown, of course, that would be too obvious, but something that wouldn't stand out.'

Albert studied the card and nodded approvingly. He handed it back.

'If the army come looking for me now,' said Bob, 'they'll only have my old name. They'll never find me. Besides, I reckon there's hundreds of men doing the same, maybe even thousands. Who wouldn't, after going through that? They're not sending me back, that's for sure.'

'And when the war's over you'll be able to settle down quietly and get on with life. No one's going to bother about a few deserters then; it'll all be old history. You'll see: everything's going to be all right.'

Bob sat up straight in his chair, holding his glass tight. Albert could see the intensity in his eyes.

'All right? I don't think so, Albert. I've gone too far now. You didn't know me before the war started. I wasn't like this then. I didn't drink much: just the odd pint, that's all. I was just an ordinary bloke, happy as Larry till all this kicked off and I got called up. It was the army that did this to me. They've ruined my life, chewed me up and spat me out. They turned me into a killer, and that's all that's left of me. Look at me now: hiding away here, drinking all night because I can't sleep. I tell you, Albert, there's no way back for me.'

CHAPTER SEVENTEEN

Jago was on the Central Line, approaching Holborn. Far above his head the war was beginning to leave ugly gashes on the city's streets, but here underground there was something comfortingly normal about the loud clattering of the train through the tunnel, and he found himself relaxing. He looked at his watch; he wasn't expected until seven, so there would be plenty of time to walk from Holborn.

He decided not to bother taking the branch line from there to Aldwych: it hardly seemed worth the trouble of changing, as it was only one stop. He'd never seen many people using it, and that was probably why. Rumour had it that the government was going to close Aldwych station and convert it into an air-raid shelter, but he hadn't seen any official announcement yet. It would make sense, he thought. Since Saturday's raids some East Enders had taken to buying a penny ha'penny Tube ticket and riding round for hours until the bombing stopped. Who could blame them?

He got off at Holborn and took the escalator to the surface. As he headed for the exit he could hear a strange commotion. A group of poorly dressed people, twenty or more, had gathered in the station's entrance hall and were yelling angrily. Some had children in tow, and all were clutching a variety of bags, blankets and pillows. They evidently wanted to get into the station, but were being blocked by a smaller number of uniformed railway staff. He moved a little closer so he could make out what was happening.

A stout woman in an ill-fitting brown coat and scuffed shoes pushed her way to the front.

'Get out of the way,' she shouted. 'We've got children here. Are you going to leave us out here to be blown to pieces?'

'I'm sorry, madam,' replied one of the uniformed men, his tone betraying the strain of the confrontation. 'We're not authorised to admit members of the public to use the station as a shelter. There's nothing I can do about it.'

Other women joined in the dispute. They looked tired and worn, and some were weeping. No doubt the Transport Police would be along very soon to disperse them, thought Jago, but he felt sympathy for them. He imagined they'd been under the bombing for the last few nights and were desperate for safety and shelter. But the authorities had a point too: if they let a few in, thousands more might follow them, stampeding the underground stations and putting life and limb at risk. He was glad it wasn't his problem to solve.

He edged past the disturbance and out onto the street. The noise faded behind him as he set off down Kingsway towards the grand portico of Bush House, which loomed solemnly at the far end. The tall, stone-faced buildings that lined both sides of the road looked strong and safe in the early evening light, a far cry from the flimsy hovels of London's docklands.

At the thought of the recent bombing he began to feel uneasy. People on the pavement around him were hurrying to get home from work before the blackout, yet here he was, looking for all the world like a man out for a carefree night on the town. He felt his shoulders tense. Even now there might be bombers droning their way across the Channel from northern France. It was the same feeling he'd had on Saturday night when the air raid started. It was irrational, and he knew he had to get to grips with it. There was surely no mystery to it: two years on the Western Front explained a lot. The relentless bombardment of German artillery had killed men in their thousands, but for every one who died there were probably ten walking the streets today bearing some kind of wound, visible or invisible, physical or mental.

He had long since come to terms with his own

experience, or so he thought. But perhaps he hadn't: maybe it was just that for the last twenty years or so no one had been shelling him. It was clear to him now that the air raids were touching a nerve deep inside him that he had simply tried to deaden over all these years. His mind might tell him he had recovered, but his body was saying something different. He was in a new battle, and this time it was a battle with himself.

He stopped in the doorway of the Stoll Theatre to calm himself. He couldn't arrive like this. The building was reassuringly solid, its expansive stone facade rivalling the grandeur of Whitehall or Buckingham Palace. It seemed to trumpet the pomp and wealth of London, the heart of an empire on which the sun never set – and which now for the second time since this theatre was built was sacrificing a generation on the altar of power.

'No!' he said to himself under his breath. He must not let his thoughts drag him back to the trenches. He rested against the wall and watched the scant passing traffic for a few moments. Within his own lifetime this part of London had changed out of all recognition. He remembered his father bringing him to a smaller, humbler theatre nearby when he was a boy and telling him about all the old playhouses that had stood here in the days before it was all swept away – not by bombs but by developers. At the turn of the century this whole area between Holborn and the Strand had been one of the last rookeries in London – a warren of stinking slums, narrow cobbled alleys, tumbledown jettied houses, and street-corner pubs. Now, he thought, probably the only thing that remained of those days was the Old Curiosity Shop, just round the corner in Portsmouth Street, a fitting monument to the great slum-hater Charles Dickens.

The people who'd lived in that maze of back alleys must have been astonished to see Kingsway emerge in its place, one of the widest and finest streets in London, and even more so when the underground subway was opened to take electric trams along the whole length of it. Double-decker trams were still running beneath his feet as he stood there.

This was now undoubtedly the world of the rich, and he was heading for one of that world's most celebrated bastions.

At the bottom end of Kingsway he walked round the curve of Aldwych and into the Strand. He crossed the road and saw before him Savoy Court and the hotel entrance he had passed a hundred times but never used. The only thing missing was the famous illuminated 'Savoy' sign above the entrance; he assumed it must have been taken down because of the blackout regulations.

Before coming out he had changed into his best suit, the one he didn't use for work: a double-breasted navy blue pinstripe bought just before the war. Over this he wore his grey gabardine trench coat. Since the weekend he had attempted to restore his new fedora to its original glory, with some success, but still he was careful to remove it before anyone in the hotel could see it.

He pushed the revolving doors and entered the hotel. The front hall was like something out of a palace, its walls clad in sombre mahogany and the floor a spotless chessboard of black and white marble. The moment he crossed the threshold he felt out of place. Back in West Ham he might be a respected detective inspector, but here he was just an East End boy who didn't belong. He was relieved to see Dorothy Appleton standing by the reception desk, waiting for him.

She strode over to greet him. Dressed in an elegant powder-blue suit and a white blouse, her skirt just skimming her knees, she looked disconcertingly at home in these imposing surroundings.

'Why, Mr Jago, how delightful to see you,' she said, shaking his hand. She steered him towards the cloakroom. 'Leave your coat and hat here and we'll go down to the restaurant. Oh, and before you start getting concerned, the dinner's on me. This is a business meeting, and my paper will pick up the tab.'

No sooner had Jago handed in his coat than the air-raid alert sounded. He looked at Dorothy questioningly.

'Does that mean dinner is postponed?'

'Not at all,' she said. 'This is the Savoy: nothing interrupts the service. We'll just be dining a little further down than usual, and sadly you won't have a view of the Thames.'

A member of staff appeared beside them and ushered them to the marble stairway leading down from the front hall. They descended the steps until they reached a large underground room.

'This is the air-raid shelter,' said Dorothy.

It took Jago some time to take in the scene. The fine decor of the large columned room was offset by an incongruous array of steel and timber props supporting the ceiling, and neatly stacked sandbags. Tables were laid with immaculate white damask tablecloths, and there was a tiny dance floor. To cap it all, a dance band in white jackets was playing 'A Nightingale Sang in Berkeley Square'.

A waiter led them to a table for two and brought them menus. Jago continued to survey the room. The number of dinner jackets he counted made him feel down at heel even in his best suit.

As if sensing his discomfort, his companion whispered, 'This is where the idle rich like to spend their evenings these days. You and I are probably the only honest workers in the room. I could do without all of them – except for him, of course.'

Jago turned his head to see who she was referring to. 'Who?'

'Just over there: don't you recognise him from the movies? It's Leslie Howard. I just love him. He's so English. In fact—but no, I won't bore you with that. Let's see what this place has to offer tonight.'

Dorothy began to study the menu. Jago picked up his and scanned the dishes listed, but then snapped it shut and threw it down onto the table.

'I'm sorry. I can't do this.'

'Whatever's the matter?'

'I don't belong here. People in my world never get to eat food like this, in a place like this, even in peacetime. Not five miles from here there are hundreds of people with no homes left, and they're grateful to get a cup of tea and a sandwich from the WVS. Eating here, it's like spitting in their faces.'

'Now don't get all sanctimonious on me, Mr Jago: this is my treat.'

'I'm not being sanctimonious,' said Jago, his voice betraying his rising anger. 'I'm just trying to bring a little reality into this fantasy world you and these stuffed shirts are living in.'

'Fantasy world? You don't know me at all, Mr Jago. You think just because my paper puts me up in a fancy hotel, that makes me some kind of empty-headed East Coast socialite? Credit me with enough sense to know what goes on outside a place like this.'

'I sometimes wonder whether you Americans know anything about what's going on anywhere outside your own country. It's always the same: isolationism, and making money while the world burns.'

'And have you ever considered there might be some Americans whose job is to make sure exactly the opposite happens? People who force a little reality onto their compatriots' breakfast tables? People like newspaper reporters, for example?'

Jago fell silent. She had a point, he conceded reluctantly.

'All right, then,' he said, 'I'll grant you that. But that still only makes you an exception to the rule.'

'I'll take that as a compliment,' she said. 'I don't object to being thought of as exceptional.'

'I'm sorry,' said Jago, regretting his outburst. 'I do apologise. You must think me a real misery. It's very kind of you to invite me here, and I appreciate it. I'm sorry about the way I spoke to you at the police station yesterday, too. There's no excuse for bad manners.'

'I must admit it wasn't my impression of an English gentleman, but I accept your apology in the spirit in which it's made. And I offer you my own in exchange: I was a little feisty in that meeting. My only excuse is that I've met too many men who think women are only there to make the coffee – or perhaps over here I should say the tea. But since we're not making excuses, I won't offer that in extenuation.'

'Accepted likewise,' said Jago.

'There,' she said, 'that's better. Shall we start again?'

'Yes. I shall accept your hospitality and eat with good grace. Just no champagne, please.'

'It's a deal. Now, first things first. No more "Miss Appleton": you must call me Dorothy. And I confess I already know that your first name is John, so do I have your permission to call you that?'

'Permission granted,' said Jago, 'but on one condition: that you never call me by my first name in the presence of Cradock or any other policeman, otherwise I shall become extremely grumpy again.'

Dorothy laughed.

'Just like that man who was on the front desk at your

police station yesterday. Boy, was he grumpy. And I couldn't understand half of what he was saying. It was like he was speaking in some kind of code.'

'You mean Frank Tompkins? He's the station sergeant, and he's what you might call an old-time copper, a local man. He's seen it all.'

'Well, he's certainly old. Don't your policemen ever retire?'

'He did, two years ago. He just didn't time it very well. The war started, the military reserves were called up, and even if they were police they had to go, so suddenly we had a shortage.'

'And Frank was the solution?'

'Yes, him and a few others. Last year the government brought all the old police pensioners back to plug the gaps. Just when poor old Frank was getting used to having a lie-in in the morning. He acts grumpy, but I think he's loving it. If nothing else it means he gets paid three pounds a week on top of his pension, and I think his wife's glad to get him out of the house again.'

'How long have you been a policeman?'

'Since 1919. Compared with Frank that makes me a new boy.'

'And before that?'

'Two years in the army.'

'And before that?'

'You'll probably laugh at this, but my first job when I left school was on the local paper, the *Stratford Express*. I wanted to be a reporter.'

'Aha, so that's why you stopped shooting when I played the press card.'

'Yes, I'm afraid I couldn't condemn you – you were simply being what I'd hoped I'd be one day. I just didn't make it.'

'So what happened to your career in journalism?'

'The Great War happened, that's what. After a couple of years with the paper I was called up and sent off to France. By the time I got out of the army there were no jobs going in that line and I needed to earn a living. Besides, the world had changed, and so had I. Looking back now, I think I needed to find something that had structure and discipline in it, and maybe I had the notion of doing something that was about making life safer for people. I suppose it was a reaction to everything I'd seen in France, all that chaos and destruction. On top of that, they were recruiting for the police. I tried it and discovered I liked it, and here I am, still a policeman.'

'Yesterday, today, and for ever.'

'That's about it. I don't suppose I'll ever be a journalist now, but I learnt some useful things. There was an old sub there who taught me how to write a news story properly. It's come in surprisingly useful ever since. You know, that stuff that Kipling said about his honest serving men, the questions you've got to answer in a story – what, why, when, how, where, and who. I expect you know all that.'

'My stock-in-trade, exactly.'

'But those are the kind of questions I have to ask as a detective too. And I've added another one of my own:

168

what if? When you don't know who's done what and you need to get to the bottom of it, that's a very important question to ask. I expect if he'd been a policeman instead of a writer he'd have worked that out for himself.'

'So you've put the world of newspapers far behind you.'

'Yes, but I still read the paper every day, and sometimes I wonder what might have been.'

'Well, now you have an opportunity to see a foreign correspondent in action.'

'Yes, and that reminds me: I wondered if I could take you down to the docks, to see some of the places that have been bombed.'

'I'm quite capable of going by myself, you know.'

'Yes, but to tell you the truth, my boss has asked me to show you round a bit. I think he reckons it would be good for the war effort.'

'In that case, how can I refuse? When were you thinking of?'

'Would the day after tomorrow suit you?'

'Yes, that will suit me fine. I look forward to seeing you then. Now, what would you like to eat, John?'

CHAPTER EIGHTEEN

Billy spotted Rob weaving his way back towards him through a mass of busy drinkers in the dimly lit public bar at the Huntingdon Arms, a dimpled pint glass of beer in each hand and a cigarette drooping from his lip. The air was heavy with the stink of stale beer, cheap cigarettes and sweat. Rob was making slow progress: he seemed to know everyone in the pub, and was still looking back over one shoulder and exchanging raucous greetings with a man Billy didn't know as he arrived at their small round table.

'There you are,' said his brother. 'Get that down you. It'll make you feel better. A little of what you fancy does you good, eh?'

Rob laughed and sat down. He nipped the remaining

half of his cigarette between his thumb and forefinger and placed it as carefully as he could on the rim of the ashtray, which was already brimming with ash and crushed fag-ends.

'Are you sure it's all right?' said Billy, looking at the beer mug in front of him. 'Supposing someone reports me? What if a copper comes in and catches me drinking under age?'

Rob laughed again. 'Don't worry so much, Billy. For starters, there's not a man in this place would shop anyone to the boys in blue, even if it was Adolf Hitler himself stopping by for a half of mild before closing time. And for another thing, no copper's going to come in here unless he's got the troops out and waiting round the corner. They've had enough cracked heads in the past to know where they're not welcome. Besides, the local bobby'll be round after closing time for a couple of drinks on the house, if you know what I mean, and everything'll be all sweetness and light. That and his bottle of Scotch come Christmas time keeps everyone happy.'

Billy felt reassured. Rob seemed to know so much that he didn't. It was like the good old days, when they were kids: Rob would look after him.

'If you say so,' he said. 'And thanks for this.' He picked up the mug of beer to sip it. It was heavy in his hand, and he didn't want to spill any in front of Rob.

'Not like that,' said Rob. 'Only girls hold it by the handle. You want to do it like this.' He slipped his four fingers through the handle and gripped the side of the mug in his palm, steadying it with his thumb. He raised the glass towards Billy. 'Cheers.'

'Cheers,' said Billy.

Rob took several gulps of beer, set his glass back on the table and spread himself back into his chair. He gazed round the bar as if he owned it.

'That's more like it.'

Billy looked round too. He wasn't used to pubs yet. He knew his mum didn't want him to spend time in places like that, but then as Rob said, that was probably just because she wanted him to stay her little boy. He was getting to be a man now, and a working man deserved his pint. Billy still wasn't sure whether he liked the place as much as Rob seemed to, though. He wouldn't fancy being there if any trouble broke out, he thought. Some of the men looked as though they'd punch you in the face as soon as look you in the eye. Even the bitter taste of the ale was something he was still getting used to. He wondered whether this was typical of the pubs around the docks, or whether it was just one that Rob particularly liked. There were certainly plenty to choose from.

'Cheer up, Billy,' said Rob. 'You've got a face like a wet weekend. What's on your mind?'

'It's Mum,' said Billy. 'I'm worried about her. Ever since Dad—'

His voice broke off. He still found it difficult to say the word.

'Died, Billy. Since Dad died,' said Rob. 'You've got to face it, Billy, and so has she.'

'But she's changed. It's like she's died too. She's not the same; she's not Mum any more.'

'She needs time, Billy.'

'But it's not fair. What's she ever done to deserve all that?'

'Nothing's fair, Billy. The whole world's in a mess. It'll never change until the workers are in control. Till then, the class struggle goes on.'

'The what?'

'It's a war, Billy. Not this war with Germany: that's just the death throes of imperialism. I mean the war between the working class and the ruling class. You can't be on both sides, Billy. There's only one side for people like us, and that's the workers. You've seen what it's like, haven't you? The people who run the world, they're not workers; they're born into the ruling class and they own everything. Even that Churchill: calls himself a mister, but his dad was a lord and his grandad was a duke or something. Talk about born with a silver spoon in your mouth. People like Mum and Dad are just victims of the capitalist ruling class. You and me too. The rich get richer and the poor get poorer, and that's how it'll stay until the workers own the means of production.'

'The what?' said Billy again. He didn't know whether it was the beer or Rob that was making him feel baffled.

'Billy, don't you know anything? Who owns all the factories? Who owns these docks? Who owns your shop? It's the rich, isn't it? You might get a few quid a week for working at Sainsbury's, but who gets all the profits? Mr

Sainsbury, of course. With all the shops he's got, he's stinking rich. You won't find him dropping in for a pint in a place like this, nor doing an honest day's work for that matter. He's probably been out all day shooting birds on his country estate or something. And where did he get those shops from? Did he earn them? No: he got them from his dad, and from his dad before him.'

'But it's good working for Sainsbury's. They treat us well. It's not like the old days – we get pensions, and we get paid when we're off sick. It's much better than ordinary shops.'

'Yes, but that's just it, isn't it? They improve your working conditions a bit from time to time, but that's just to keep you quiet, so you won't rise up. That's the trouble with the Labour Party.'

'But I thought they were good. Mum and Dad said they've always voted Labour.'

'Labour's no good. They're never going to change things properly. They're like you: they think all we need to do is get better terms and conditions for the workers. They're never going to get rid of the ruling class. Only the Communist Party can do that. Labour are just bourgeois, like all the other parties.'

Another word Billy had never heard before. His head was beginning to spin. Rob might just as well be speaking Chinese.

'So when's all this going to happen, Rob?' He was surprised at the way his own voice sounded. He was finding it difficult to get his words out straight.

174

'You'll see,' said Rob, leaning forward over his half-empty beer mug and lowering his voice. 'We're going to make them sit up. You stick with me, Billy, and we'll make a bit of history.'

CHAPTER NINETEEN

Jago wondered how many generations of CID officers had sat at this typewriter before him. The body was scarred with scratches, and the keys were rimmed with grime. He regarded himself as a fairly competent typist, but the keys on this machine had an uncanny habit of jamming: perhaps they just weren't used to a police officer who could manage more than ten words per minute. Resigned to his fate, he pulled the page he'd just completed out of the machine and loaded it with another three sheets of foolscap paper interleaved with two sheets of carbon paper for the required copies. His plans for the day had changed when DDI Soper had called him in for what seemed to Jago a long and unnecessary meeting but which was no doubt deemed of great value to his boss. Such meetings were part of the job, of course, and to be endured, but what was vexing about this one was that he was now required to write what seemed to him an equally long and unnecessary report. He had sent Cradock out to visit Albert Johnson's friend Bob Gray and then to check back through Villiers' cases at the magistrates' court in case they threw up anything of interest. So now it was just him and the typewriter.

His mind felt sluggish, reluctant to cooperate with the task in hand. He gazed out of the CID office window in search of inspiration. Outside, the sky was agreeably free of planes and cloud, and Jago was pleased to be back on his home ground. Dining at the Savoy the previous evening had been an interesting experience, but he had come away thinking he'd be just as happy in Cooke's pie and mash shop in Stratford High Street any day. He wondered what Miss Appleton would make of jellied eels. He was still wary of calling her Dorothy, even in his own mind. She seemed happy enough to be on first-name terms, but then she was American. To him it felt rather forward, and he had a lingering apprehension that getting too friendly with a woman could lead to misunderstandings – something he could do without at his time of life.

But now was not the time to start thinking about such things: he dragged his mind back and resumed his typing. It was already past lunchtime and he hadn't eaten, but perhaps a hungry stomach would make him work faster. The sooner this little job was done, the better.

He was on his third page and beginning to consider at least the possibility of a cup of tea when he heard the air-raid siren sounding the alert: raid imminent.

A familiar apprehension stirred within him. He could see it coming. That feeling in the stomach, the freezing sensation that had ambushed him so cripplingly in the last few days since the heavy raids had started. He replayed the film of those moments in his mind and heard his own voice speaking in his head, as if to a stranger. *If you carry on like that you'll soon be no use to anyone. You've got to fight it, if only for Cradock's sake. You haven't come through two years of slaughter just to curl up and die now. You need to get a grip on yourself.*

The voice stopped and he looked round, half expecting to find himself standing there. 'Get a grip,' he muttered to himself. His automatic reaction on hearing the siren was still to take cover, but he decided to defy instinct. This time he would go outside and watch the raid instead. He liked what Roosevelt had said at his first inauguration: *The only thing we have to fear is fear itself.* It was time to tell his fear where to get off.

He went down to the front entrance and stepped outside to look.

On West Ham Lane, people were scurrying for the nearest shelter. Most faces suggested the alert was nothing more than an irritating interruption to their afternoon arrangements. Others had a look of matter-of-fact resignation. But in some he could see panic, eyes that betrayed their fear. *These are the ones who aren't used to it yet*, he thought. *Or perhaps they're the ones who've already seen loved ones killed, bodies blown apart. Or the ones like me, who've seen so much of it that they'll never get used to it.*

He took up a position just outside the police station, ready to duck back behind the protective sandbags if the bombs got too close. High in the clear sky he could see the raiders approaching. There must have been about a hundred of them: dark specks against blue, growing larger. Puffs of smoke from exploding anti-aircraft shells began to appear all around them. The firing was much more intense than it had been during Saturday's raids: someone must have decided to bring more guns in. Cradock might find the extra noise comforting, he thought, but it didn't seem to be having much effect on the advancing bombers.

He heard explosions coming from the south and guessed that once again the enemy crews would be releasing a torrent of high explosives on the docks. The planes droned on, but then to his relief they began to pull away towards the east. It seemed they were not intent on bombing the north of the borough today. But he pictured in his mind the people living in Canning Town and Silvertown, cheek by jowl with the docks, in those flimsy, vermin-infested slums. The relief that he felt at being spared another assault from the air was sobered by his knowledge of what they would be suffering instead of him. He silently gave thanks to fate that he did not have to live there.

A familiar figure came into view a little way down the street, trying to maintain his dignity as he half walked, half ran along the pavement. It was Cradock.

'Sorry I'm late, sir; I got held up. There was a problem with the buses, so I had to walk all the way to Gray's place and back to the court. I'd just finished when the sirens started and they said I could shelter there, but I wasn't sure whether I should or not. I know uniform are supposed to stay at their posts and only take cover if there's an actual raid, but it's not quite the same for a DC who's been out on a visit, is it? I mean, I haven't got a post to stay at, have I? Anyway, I decided I'd just carry on back here.'

Jago found himself smiling. In some ways Cradock was like a puppy, he thought. Willing and enthusiastic, but just needing to be taken in hand and trained. The young constable's chatter brought him out of himself and restored a sense of everyday normality. He realised something else: the feelings that had gripped him when the air-raid siren sounded had gone.

'Good man,' he said. 'Let's get inside, and you can tell me how it all went. When you've got your breath back we'll go and see Cooper, but I think we should see if we can rustle up a cup of tea first.'

He stepped back in through the station door, followed by Cradock. What he had been thinking in Cradock's absence would remain his secret, but Jago decided the cup of tea would have an additional, private significance. He felt he had a small victory to celebrate.

* * *

180

The all-clear siren was sounding as Cradock handed Jago a cup of tea and took a seat in the CID office with his own.

'Sorry, guv'nor – no biscuits left. Must be the war, I suppose.'

'Never mind,' said Jago. 'I haven't had any lunch, so I won't miss a biscuit. Did you manage to get any?'

Cradock's expression suggested the mention of lunch had brought back a painful memory.

'I did manage to grab a sandwich on the way, but I'm still starving.'

'OK, we'll make sure you get something to eat before we go in search of Mr Cooper. It might be a good idea to get our strength up before we think of tangling with the likes of him.' Jago took a sip of his tea. 'So, tell me how you got on with your enquiries.'

'Well, I found that Gray character at home. He was a bit the worse for wear, if you know what I mean, and his flat was a tip. You could smell the drink on his breath, and his clothes looked like they'd been slept in. All in all, I came away thinking the idea of him and Johnson polishing off a bottle of Scotch in his shelter on Saturday night is quite plausible.'

'So he confirmed Johnson was with him?'

'Yes, he said they were together in the shelter between the times Johnson gave us.'

'Well done. So that would seem to take Johnson out of the picture for the time of death, if he's telling the truth. I have to say, though, that it sounds as though Gray might leave something to be desired as a witness. And what about the court: did you find out anything interesting?'

'I did. It seems Robert Carson appeared before Mr Villiers at the magistrates' court in January. He'd thrown a punch at a supervisor at work and was charged with assault. He was found guilty and fined five pounds, but was lucky not to get sent down for two months. Apparently he lost his job as a result.'

'Interesting. So what do you make of that?' said Jago.

'Well, it means Carson might have had a grudge against him. But surely not enough to want to kill him?'

'I agree. But on the other hand, why did he lie to us about knowing Villiers?'

'There must have been a reason,' said Cradock, 'but I'm blowed if I know what it was. Would a man like him forget the name of the magistrate who'd nearly put him away? Maybe there was something else going on between him and Villiers that meant he didn't want to let on. Or maybe he was just scared when we came round, and it was the first thing that came into his head.'

'Good work, Peter. Now, I suggest we finish this cup of tea and then we go and get something to eat in the canteen.'

Jago had managed to drink half his cup of tea when there was a knock at the door. Sergeant Tompkins came in.

'Sorry to interrupt you, sir, but I thought you'd like to know – it's about that Mrs Carson you've been talking to.'

'What is it?'

'She's tried to kill herself, sir. Seems her neighbour called round to check how she was and got no answer. She could smell gas so called us, and we sent PC Stannard round. He broke in and found her: it was a gas fire job.'

'Could it have been an accident?'

'Doesn't look like it, sir. He says she was laid down all comfy with a cushion for her head to rest on. That's what they do when they mean it, isn't it?'

'Yes. But she's alive?'

'Yes, sir. Close call, though. They've got her in Queen Mary's now, and they say they'll keep her in for a day or two.'

'Thanks,' said Jago, and turned to Cradock.

'Get your coat on,' he said. 'We'd better find out what's made her do this before we see Cooper. Let's go.'

CHAPTER TWENTY

Jago and Cradock left the station a little after five o'clock and headed north up West Ham Lane towards Queen Mary's Hospital. It wasn't much more than a hundred yards' walk, and the weather was fine enough to make Jago uncomfortably warm in his coat. The street was quiet, with just a handful of women venturing out after the all-clear signal to shop for groceries, but the way ahead was partly blocked by a pair of heavily built, maternal-looking women who were standing in the middle of the pavement and talking to each other, each with a shopping basket over her arm.

The two detectives were still some distance away when a man approaching from the other direction, looking lost in thought, bumped into the woman who was closer to the kerb. She remained unmoved, feet planted solidly on the paving stones, but he stumbled and fell into the road. He quickly got back to his feet, picking up the package and gas mask case he had been carrying, which both now looked as crumpled as his suit. The woman gave him a disdainful glance and continued her conversation. Jago smiled to himself. East End women, he thought: not easily moved.

The man stepped round her, straight into the policemen's path. He had a distracted air, his mind apparently elsewhere.

'Talk of the devil,' said Cradock, gesturing towards him. 'Look who it is.'

The man stopped.

'Mr Johnson,' said Jago, 'what a surprise to bump into you, as it were. What brings you here?'

'One of our employees is in the hospital. I've just been to visit her.'

'Would that be Mrs Carson?'

'Yes. How did you know?' He answered his own question immediately: 'But of course, you're the police. I suppose it's your job to know.'

'That's right.'

'I'm pleased to say she's doing well. They say she'll be out soon. But have you seen what's happened up there? The hospital – it got a direct hit in the raid on Saturday. They told me it's the first hospital in London to be hit by a bomb. It's really been smashed about. Two wards have been destroyed, apparently, and six patients and

185

two nurses were killed. Nurses, of all people: where's the justice in that?'

Johnson looked from one man to the other, as if expecting an answer, but they said nothing. He continued speaking.

'I suppose you know Mrs Carson seems to have tried to take her own life. I didn't ask her why, because I don't think it's any of my business, but young Mr Villiers asked me to look in on her on behalf of the company. She's one of our cleaners, so I don't know her well, but she's still an employee. I suppose you'll be going to find out why she did it.'

'We're going to have a few words with Mrs Carson, yes,' said Jago. 'We won't detain you.'

'I'll bid you good day, then, gentlemen,' said Johnson.

'Goodbye,' said Cradock. He chuckled. 'And mind how you go, Mr Johnson: you never know who you might run into. You can't be too careful with women like that hanging around and posing a danger to traffic. You looked as if you'd walked into a tree.'

Johnson gave him a blank look and went on his way.

'We're here to serve the public, Peter, not entertain them,' said Jago. 'A little refined wit may be acceptable, but not slapstick. I think they expect a little more decorum from us. Don't you?'

'Sorry, sir. I said it without thinking.'

'Try not to do that, Detective Constable.'

'Yes, sir.'

* * *

They found Irene Carson sitting up in bed in a hospital nightgown, with a white crocheted shawl round her shoulders. Her face was pale and she glanced nervously from side to side, wondering what her neighbours would make of the two men who strode purposefully to her bedside. A nurse brought a couple of screens to give them some token privacy.

'How are you doing, Mrs Carson?' said Jago.

She looked down into her lap, avoiding their eyes, and spoke quietly.

'Not so bad, thank you. They say I'll be out tomorrow. I'm sorry to cause so much trouble, especially at a time like this. The nurses are wonderful, but you've probably heard a couple of them were killed in the air raid the other day. A whole wing was blown up.'

'Yes, we saw that on the way in. Now then, Mrs Carson, there's no need to worry. We just want to ask you a few questions.'

'But I'm going to be in trouble, aren't I? I tried to kill myself, and that's against the law, isn't it? I don't want to go to prison. We've got enough trouble in the family already, and how would my boys cope without me? Please say I won't go to prison, Mr Jago. Please.'

She looked up at him now, and he could see the tears forming in her eyes.

'The law does treat attempted suicide as a misdemeanour, Mrs Carson, but it's rare for someone in your position to be charged these days. Only one person in the whole of London was prosecuted for it last year, so I don't think you have anything to worry about at this stage, and I'm sure your boys will look after you.'

'Oh, thank you,' she said. 'That's such a weight off my mind. I keep thinking about prison, and I don't think I could bear it.'

'But tell me, Mrs Carson: what made you do this?'

'I've been thinking about that too while I've been in here. I didn't know what I was doing, really. It was because of losing my husband.' She wiped her eyes with a handkerchief as the tears returned. 'I can't see how I can live without him.'

She pulled the shawl more closely around her and primped her hair.

'But I shall have to, shan't I? Soldier on like everyone else. There's plenty that have lost more than me. War's an evil business, and I just have to accept that.'

'When we visited you on Monday you said something that struck me,' said Jago. 'You were talking about people who are profiting illegally from the war – you said people like that deserve everything they get. Do you remember?'

'Yes, I do.'

'We're still investigating the death of Mr Villiers, and I wonder: do you have any reason to believe that he might have been involved in anything like that? Illegal activity, I mean.'

'I'm sorry, but I wouldn't know anything about that. I'm only a cleaner, you know.'

'But you work at the press. Have you ever seen or

heard anything that would suggest he was?'

She thought for a few seconds, then nodded slowly.

'Yes, now you mention it, there was one thing. I was cleaning the offices as usual one evening, and I was going to go in and do his, but I could hear he was on the phone so I waited outside the door. He can't have known I was there, because he was speaking quite loud, and I heard him say something funny. He said, "How many do you want?" which was quite normal, I suppose, but then he said, "You realise I could go to gaol for this? You need to be damn sure this can't be traced back to me." That's all I heard, but it made me think he was up to no good. And after that he was saying, "We'll print the whole lot tonight. No one will know," and that sounded suspicious to me too. Like he was doing something in secret that he shouldn't have been.'

Jago made no response to what she was saying, but she noticed that Cradock was writing it all in his notebook.

'Here! You're not going to get me in trouble, are you? I can't afford to lose my job as well.'

'No, Mrs Carson,' said Jago. 'I just need to ask you one or two more questions.'

'All right, then,' she said. She looked apprehensive.

'You said the other day that you didn't know Mr Villiers well, and I quite understand that, but did you ever have any direct dealings with him – personal dealings?'

'What do you mean?'

'I mean did you ever feel that he was, as it were, taking an interest in you?'

'What are you getting at?'

189

'Did he ever seem to be trying to get to know you better?'

'Right, I think I'm getting your drift. If you must know, yes, he did, and as far as I'm concerned he was being a bit more than friendly. He made advances to me, Mr Jago; trying it on, he was. Dirty old goat. I told him where to get off.'

'Please excuse me, Mrs Carson, but I have to ask this,' said Jago. 'Did your relationship ever become more, er, intimate?'

'How dare you! Certainly not: I'm a married woman.' She gave a sob. 'Or I was then. I had nothing more to do with him after that; steered clear whenever he came in sight.'

'Can you tell me where you were last Saturday evening?'

'I wasn't with him, if that's what you're thinking.'

'No, it's simply a routine question.'

'That was when the big raid was on, wasn't it? I was down the shelter in my back garden thinking Armageddon had come, like everyone else.'

'Can anyone confirm that?'

'No. My Billy had to go and do his ARP duty, so he was out all night. Robert was out with his mates somewhere and didn't say where, but he said they got caught out in the raid and spent the night in a public shelter. He didn't get home till the next morning.'

'Thank you. Now just one last question. When you overheard Mr Villiers on the phone, did you hear any names mentioned?'

She closed her eyes to think.

'Now you come to mention it, yes, I did. What he actually said was, "Look here, Cooper." Yes, that was it: Cooper. He said, "Look here, Cooper. You need to be damn sure this can't be traced back to me."'

CHAPTER TWENTY-ONE

There was a new woman serving food in the West Ham police station canteen. She gave Jago a cheery smile as she slopped a ladle of beef stew onto his plate, then added a substantial helping of mashed potatoes and carrots. She wiped a little stray gravy from the edge of the plate with a cloth and handed him his food.

'There you are, dear. That should keep the wolf from the door.'

Jago murmured his thanks and moved on to get some cutlery. He suspected the cooks must have been briefed by the top brass to pile on the stodge. Most of the men were working even longer turns than usual now that the air raids had been stepped up, so if they got the chance to eat at the station they'd be glad of a solid, filling meal to keep them going. He noticed that the dessert on offer today was suet pudding and custard. It was past six o'clock now, and he was feeling decidedly hungry, but even so he reckoned if he risked a helping of that he'd have trouble staying awake.

His mind went back to his early years as a uniformed constable on the beat. In those days he'd had to make do with whatever sandwiches he could conceal about his person. Once those were finished, there was no knowing when you'd next eat. The thought of those cold and hungry late turns, and especially the nights, still made him appreciate the unpretentious fare that the station offered. Judging by the enthusiasm of his colleague across the table, Cradock had similar memories, perhaps all the more vivid for being recent. The detective constable was attacking his food like a trencherman.

Cradock disposed of another forkful of food, then wiped his mouth with the back of his hand and spoke.

'So, Mrs Carson, sir. Do you believe her?'

'I don't believe anyone until the judge passes his sentence,' said Jago. 'And even then I have my doubts.'

'She looked distressed, and she sounded plausible.'

'Yes, but you don't have to be distressed to look it, do you? It's what actresses do six nights a week if the part demands it. The fact that she looked upset and sounded it too doesn't mean she was giving us the truth.'

'Too true,' said Cradock. 'When did her boy say she got that telegram about her husband's ship being sunk?'

'That was Saturday afternoon.'

'Right. So she'd have been in a right old state, a bit off her head probably, and that was the day Villiers got murdered. She could have done it herself, couldn't she? She says she was in her shelter all night, but she's got no witnesses. He'd been making passes at her, but supposing he'd gone a bit further than that? What if she wanted to get revenge and tried blackmailing him? Or there again, she told us what she'd heard him say to Cooper on the phone. What if she tried to blackmail him after that? She probably needs the money: her old man wouldn't have earned much at sea, and now he's gone, so even that's stopped. Maybe she tried but Villiers wouldn't play ball; maybe it turned nasty. Supposing she got into a rage and killed him? She had reason to want to get even with Villiers, and if she was unhinged enough to try to do away with herself, she could have been unhinged enough to kill him.'

'I'm not sure she was as unhinged as you suppose. I got the impression at the hospital that she was simply a frightened and desperate woman.'

'All right. How about this, then?' Cradock leant one elbow on the table and poked his fork forward into the air, his brow creased in concentrated thought. 'Supposing she told Mrs Villiers what her husband was trying to get up to with one of his cleaners? That Mrs Villiers looks like butter wouldn't melt in her mouth, but supposing she killed her husband? It wouldn't be the first time a woman did it. You know: revenge for his philandering. It's a powerful motive, revenge. Or she and that Edward could have done it, the two of them together. They might have been very pleased to be rid of him and get their own hands on the money for a change.'

'Possibly, possibly,' said Jago with a sigh. 'But while you're at it, Peter, remember that unlike revenge, beef stew is not a dish best served cold.'

'Beg your pardon, sir?'

'Nothing. Carry on, but don't let your lunch get cold.'

Jago thought there was a great deal too much supposition in Cradock's argument, but he was encouraged at least to see the boy trying to think things through for himself. It was fifteen long years, hard years too, since Jago had been a young detective, learning how to think and not just take everything at face value. Those 'What if?' questions were still as important today as they had been then, and it was good that Cradock was asking them. But he needed to learn that every hypothesis had to be challenged at the earliest opportunity and demolished without mercy, to clear the ground for the rare 'What if?' that might take them a step closer to the truth.

Cradock continued with his reasoning, now chewing again as he spoke.

'And another thing. When we were at Mrs Carson's house she said people on the fiddle deserve everything they get. Now, if she thought Villiers was on the fiddle, that he was one of the people who stayed at home getting rich on illegal profits while her husband got blown up at sea, she'd have had plenty of reason to hate him. She'd have had two reasons to kill him.'

'But how would she have known Villiers would be down at Cooper's place?'

'Maybe she found out who Cooper was. Maybe her boys found out. Maybe all three of them were in it together, or her Robert at least. He's certainly got no time for people like Villiers, and like I said, maybe it wasn't just about him losing his job on account of being fined five pounds by the magistrate – maybe there was more to it than that. He's got no alibi, either. Maybe he killed Villiers. And what about that Billy of hers? It's a bit of a coincidence that he turned up at the scene. We know the warden found the body, but who's to say Billy wasn't there earlier? He could have killed Villiers and then seen the warden coming, so pretended to be just passing.'

Jago shook his head.

'No, we know what time it was when Billy left the ARP post and when he arrived at the scene where the body was. It's about right for the journey, but there wouldn't have been time to murder someone too. And besides, why would Villiers have been sitting around in his van waiting to be murdered?'

'What about Johnson, then?' said Cradock. 'Maybe he was the one who told Mrs Carson about it. She heard Villiers mention Cooper's name on the phone, so then maybe she asked Johnson who this Cooper was, and he told her about what was going on.'

'No, that won't work,' said Jago. 'Johnson didn't know enough to tell her. Don't forget, he says he didn't know the person Villiers was meeting. We know it was Cooper, but Johnson's never mentioned that name to us, and we haven't told him either. And he says he didn't know what Villiers was delivering down there, so how could he have told Mrs Carson?'

Cradock paused for thought, stoking his mouth with food. He chewed, swallowed, and continued.

'I don't know, but I can't believe Johnson knows as little as he says. Mrs Carson says she overheard Villiers on the phone saying he was going to print something in the night. People keep telling us he didn't know much about how to print, so if it turns out he was actually printing something on the side that no one was supposed to know about, how could he have done that on his own?'

'Unless it's not true that he didn't know much about printing.'

'Yes, or unless someone who does know all about printing helped him. Enter our Mr Johnson, I'd say. I'm sure he's more mixed up in this than he lets on. Maybe it was him who did the printing in the night. And even if Villiers didn't tell him who it was for, surely he'd have known when whatever it was left the Invicta premises and was delivered?'

'I haven't been counting, Peter, but I have been listening, and there are too many maybes in all that. You could be right with any one of those explanations, but at the moment it's all conjecture. We need some hard evidence. The most important thing we've found out today is what Mrs Carson said about Villiers mentioning Cooper's name on the phone. Johnson's already told us he thought Villiers might be up to something a bit irregular, but now if she's telling the truth – and don't forget there are no other witnesses, so we can't be sure – if she's telling the truth it definitely ties Villiers and Cooper together in what looks like some illegal printing job. And I don't think either of us would be surprised if that was what Villiers was delivering to Cooper the night he was killed.'

'What could it have been?'

'Could be anything, couldn't it? From passports to dirty postcards. Anything that someone can sell for a fat profit if the law doesn't find out – that's what I reckon. I doubt whether it would be anything as sophisticated as passports though, in a place that size. But whatever it was, there's beginning to be a bit of a nasty smell around Mr Villiers, and every trail we follow seems to lead back to Cooper. Maybe he and Villiers had some disagreement over the deal.'

'Maybe, sir?'

'I'm allowed one or two. Now, when Johnson left the place in Whitwell Road on Saturday night to walk home, Villiers was still inside the building with Cooper, so as we've said, that makes Cooper the last person to see him alive, as far as we know. Cooper says he didn't leave with Villiers in the van, but I don't trust him. We know he's been lying, because he denied knowing Villiers the first time you asked him, so he could have gone in the van with Villiers and then either made him stop or taken his chance when they stopped for some other reason. As you said, he's a nasty piece of work, and who knows what he might be capable of? Let's go and find friend Cooper now and see what he has to say.'

Jago pushed his empty plate to one side and noticed a look of disappointment, even perhaps pleading, in Cradock's eyes.

'No, Peter,' he said. 'Your suet pudding and custard will have to wait.'

The sun had already slipped down behind the buildings on West Ham Lane when Jago and Cradock set off in the car for Cooper's house with Jago at the wheel.

He was apprehensive. Cooper might prove to be quite a handful.

'Watch out in case he tries anything on,' he said when they arrived. 'Let's go.'

They walked up to the front door, side by side. Cradock knocked on it.

They had only a short wait before the door opened, but instead of Cooper they saw a woman. She looked thirtyish, thought Jago, or perhaps a bit younger with a hard life behind her. She had fair hair and was wearing a golden brown cotton dress. Her clean and tidy fingernails intimated that she lived in some material comfort, but there was little in her eyes to suggest confidence.

'Mrs Cooper?' said Cradock.

'Yes,' she replied.

'I'm Detective Constable Cradock and this is Detective Inspector Jago, West Ham police. We'd like to speak to your husband.'

'He's not here.'

'Can you tell us where he is?'

'He's at his place, his yard, Whitwell Road.'

Not a great talker, thought Jago.

'What does he use it for?' he said.

'No idea,' said Mrs Cooper. 'All I know is he uses it for his business. I never go down there. He's the only one who's got keys to it. Probably better for me not to know, anyway.'

'What do you mean by that?'

'Nothing. It's his business, not mine.'

She was still standing on the doorstep. It was clear that she had no intention of inviting them in. Jago wondered what she was hiding, what went on within these walls. Whatever it was, everything about her suggested that it wasn't a model of domestic harmony.

'Do you know when he'll be back?' said Cradock.

'No, he didn't say.'

'How long has he been out?'

'He went out before that raid started. I tried phoning him there but the line's out: the whole system seems to have broken down since these air raids started. If you want to speak to him you'll have to go and find him. Can I go now?'

Cradock glanced at Jago, who nodded.

'Yes,' said Cradock. 'I know where it is. That'll be all.'

Before he could say anything else she had stepped back into the hallway and closed the door.

By the time they got to Whitwell Road it was dark. For once, the night was silent too: Jago hoped perhaps the Germans had done their work for the day and would not return before daylight. Cradock pointed out where Cooper had his store, and Jago parked the car by the kerb.

They both kept a wary eye out as they approached the building. Cradock knocked on the front door, but, as before, no one came. They walked the few paces to the double doors that gave access to the yard. Cradock pushed one of them gently, and to his surprise it creaked open.

They stepped into the yard. Everything was as it had been on Cradock's previous visit, except that now a dark shape loomed to his right. He shone his hand lamp onto it carefully. A dozen or more wooden crates and tea chests were stacked in an untidy pile along one side of the yard.

'That's new, sir,' he murmured to Jago. 'A delivery of some kind?'

'We can look at that later,' said Jago. 'We need to find Cooper first. And watch your step: if he's the unpleasant character you say he is, he could be a bit of a handful.'

A few small windows in the main building overlooked

the yard. No lights were visible, and on the ground floor the men could see that the blackout curtains had not been drawn.

'That might explain why no one came to the door, sir,' whispered Cradock, pointing to the windows. 'It looks like there's no one in.' There was something about this gloomy enclosed space that made him instinctively keep his voice down.

He swung his lamp slowly round to take in the rest of the yard before them. Its weak beam cast a small pool of light onto a single-storey brick structure with a low slate roof. It was built against the far perimeter wall and ran the full width of the yard. There was a door at the right-hand end.

They crossed the yard to the door, and Jago knocked. Again, no answer. He turned the doorknob slowly, to make no noise, and leant his shoulder gently against it. No movement: it was locked.

He put a finger to his lips to signal quiet and motioned to Cradock to check the two windows farther down the front wall of the building with his lamp.

Cradock noticed that here too the blackout curtains on the inside of the windows had not been closed. He shone his lamp through the first window. No sign of anything untoward. He shone it through the second one. The same. He angled the beam down and played it across the floor, then gasped. This time he forgot to whisper.

'Come over here, sir. What do you make of this?'

Jago strode over and took the lamp from him, adjusting it to give him a view inside the room. He saw storage racks, a cabinet, and what looked like the end of a table. And on the floor, protruding from behind the cabinet, a pair of booted feet.

CHAPTER TWENTY-TWO

'If I don't get out of this house I shall scream,' said Muriel. She pulled a delicate white handkerchief from the handbag positioned beside her on the sofa and dabbed at the corners of her eyes. 'You don't know what it's been like. I've been a prisoner here for twenty-one years. That's half my life.'

'But now you're free. You can do whatever you want.'

She looked at him, her face a picture of anguish.

'That's what I keep telling myself, but I can't. It's just words. Inside I know I'm still in prison. Nothing's changed. Even though I've been told I can go, even though I've been released, I've got so used to the place I can't bear to walk out of the door. I'm scared, Arthur. I don't know what to do.'

Arthur Villiers felt an unaccustomed anxiety. Muriel's tears were unsettling, and he wasn't sure how best he should respond. On his own territory he was confident. He had commanded men, led them into battle, even into death. He had completed a successful career as a solicitor. But for most of his adult life his dealings face-to-face with women had been confined to the formality of his office, where he was protected by the authority of his desk and the power of the language of law. In informal settings women made him feel uneasy – even Muriel. During the last war he had had to write many letters to women – to the wives, mothers, and fiancées of dead soldiers – but those women were far away and out of sight. Here with Muriel he was in a frightening no man's land of emotion, with no bearings to go by.

He knelt before the sofa, took both her hands in his and scanned her face for clues as to what he should say.

'You won't do anything irresponsible, will you?'

'Irresponsible?' He could hear the bitterness in her laugh. 'I've been responsible since I was an eleven-year-old Girl Guide. I've only done one irresponsible thing in my life, and that was marrying Charles. You know, I sometimes think I should have gone on the stage – if they gave out Oscars for most dutiful wife I'd have been nominated years ago.' She took her hands out of his. 'I've wasted my life, you know.'

'But what about Edward? You've brought up a fine young son.'

She laughed again and cast a glance towards the ceiling.

'Yes, I've done my duty by Edward too. I've been a responsible mother. But I don't know him as a mother should know her son. There are too many secrets in this family, Arthur. Edward has secrets and he thinks I don't know. I have secrets and I play a game with him, and I'm scared that he might see the mask fall. I'm due another Oscar, for dutiful mother.'

'It's not your fault; you're not to blame. You and Edward are both the victims in this: it's all my brother's doing. But he's not here any more; he can't control you now. Your life is your own: you're free to be yourself.' He looked into her eyes. 'If only I could make you see.'

'If only,' said Muriel. 'There are enough "if onlys" in my life already. It's too late, Arthur. I'm not sure that I know who I am any more. I dreamt of being free for all those years, but now I don't even know what it means.'

She paused.

'The police have said they think Charles was murdered.'

'Murdered? I thought you said they were talking about suicide,' said Arthur.

'They raised the possibility on Sunday, and I said the idea was absurd, but now they seem to have made up their minds. I'm frightened, Arthur. They're very suspicious about everything, and I don't know what they might dig up. I just want them to go away and leave you and me and Edward alone.'

'But you've nothing to fear. There's nothing they could find that would compromise you in any way.'

Muriel looked at him with fearful eyes.

'But they might think that I—no, I can't bear to think about it. Oh, Arthur, take me away from here. You're the only one who can help me, the only one I can talk to.'

He moved to sit beside her on the sofa.

'Are you mad?' he said. 'What could be more incriminating than that? If you disappear now, they'll think you did it, and if I disappear too they'll think we were in it together. Besides, where would you go? We're living on an island ringed with barbed wire in every direction, and you can't go a mile down the road without your identity card. Stay here, and let me protect you.'

'Oh, Arthur,' she said again. She leant her head against his shoulder and clung to him.

CHAPTER TWENTY-THREE

Jago paused for a moment to make sure there was no sign of movement in the feet, then handed the lamp back to Cradock.

'We'll have to break in,' he said. 'You go in through that window.'

'But it's private property,' said Cradock. 'Shouldn't we get the owner's consent?'

'The owner's out and his wife doesn't know where. And besides, that looks like someone who's ill or injured, so it's our duty to go in and attend to him – or her. Now carry on.'

The windows were small, and Cradock could see no sign of a latch on the inside. It looked as though they weren't made for opening. Surveying the surrounding area with his lamp, he saw a broom leaning against the wall. He took it in both hands and struck the handle end forcibly against the top right-hand corner of the window. There was a smash of glass and then silence again.

'Shall I climb in, then, sir?' he said.

Jago studied the sill. Now that air raids were coming on a regular basis, and flinging himself to the ground seemed to have become part of his daily routine, he had taken to wearing old clothes while on duty. For someone who took pains to be smart it was a sacrifice, but it made sense. Even so, he thought, he wasn't going to wreck a serviceable coat and a pair of comfortable old flannels wriggling about over broken glass when a younger and more agile man was available to do that for him.

'Yes,' he said. 'Nip round to that door and open it for me. It looked like a Yale lock from the outside, so we may be in luck.'

Cradock clambered up into the space where the window had been and dropped inside. After a quick sweep of the room with his lamp he disappeared in the direction of the door and opened it. Jago went in, closing it behind him. They made their way down a corridor.

'The blackout curtains haven't been drawn here either,' said Cradock. 'I suppose that could mean no one was planning to use this building tonight.'

'Or?' said Jago.

'Or that whoever those feet belong to has been lying there since before it got dark.'

'Indeed. Now, close those curtains in case anyone

comes along and sees a light in here. We don't want that Cooper or any of his pals giving us a nasty surprise.'

They reached the room where Cradock had forced his entry. Jago took the lamp and shone it on the pair of feet, then followed the line of the body up to the head. It was a man, lying awkwardly on his back. Blood glistened in the lamplight. He seemed to have been stabbed several times in the chest. Jago crouched down and studied the face. It was frozen in the contortions of pain, and the eyes were staring fixedly ahead.

'Hang on a minute,' he said. 'I've seen this chummy before.' He thought for a moment, trying to place the man. 'Yes, Rita's cafe. That's where it was. He was there on Saturday, before we went to the football. Do you remember him?'

'I didn't get a look at his face then, sir. But I do know who he is.'

'You know his name? How's that?'

'I was talking to him only yesterday. It's Cooper, sir. Frederick Cooper.'

'Well I never,' said Jago. 'I thought he looked up to no good when I saw him at the cafe. He's not going to be giving us any trouble now, though, is he?' He got to his feet and dusted off his trousers. 'Have a look through his pockets and see if you can find anything.'

Cradock knelt on the floor and put his hand into each of Cooper's pockets.

'Just a wallet in his jacket, sir.'

He opened it and checked the contents.

'Thirty-two pounds in pound notes and about fifteen bob in loose change, sir. Nothing else in it. And a bunch of keys in his trouser pocket.'

He started to get up but stopped.

'Actually, sir, I think there's something underneath him.'

He took hold of a small piece of string that was protruding from beneath Cooper's body and tugged gently, but it would not move. He carefully lifted Cooper's body a little on one side and saw beneath it a partially crushed brown cardboard box attached to the string.

'Looks like he's fallen on his gas mask, sir.'

Jago peered down over Cradock's shoulder.

'Or possibly his killer's. A man like Cooper will have put up a fight if he had half a chance, so it could have come off either of them.'

'I've just remembered, sir. When I came to open the door to you there was a coat and hat hanging on the back of the door, and a gas mask case too. At the time I assumed they were Cooper's and I thought nothing more of it. I didn't want to keep you waiting outside.'

They went to the door.

'A good-quality coat,' said Jago. 'With a Burberry label inside. They're not cheap.' He took the gas mask case down from the door and examined it. 'And this isn't just your common or garden government-issue cardboard box. It looks like a leather carrying case. Both of these would suit a wide boy like Cooper. We'll have to ask his wife about them, but it looks as though he hung these here on his way in. In which case the one on the floor could be his killer's. I'll take that with us. And bring the wallet and keys with you too. Now let's get back to that body and have a look round. And see if you can find a weapon: he's been stabbed, but there's no sign of anything it might have been done with.'

The two men examined the room as best they could with the limited light they had available. What had looked like a table when viewed from outside the window was now revealed to be a kind of workbench running for about twelve feet along the wall. A large Underwood typewriter occupied one end, while the other was empty except for a neat stack of six small cardboard boxes. Jago opened one.

'Interesting,' he said. 'Look at these.'

He pulled out a handful of buff-coloured cards and showed them to Cradock.

'Identity cards,' said the detective constable. 'That certainly can't be legal. Not in a dive like this. Stolen, do you think?'

'That or fakes,' said Jago. 'Either way, worth a lot in the right hands. We'll take a few of these away with us and then get the rest transported to the station.' He slipped the cards into an envelope and put them in his pocket. 'So our Mr Cooper was indeed up to no good. I wonder whether this was the "stationery" that Villiers was printing for him and keeping so quiet about. Perhaps there was a delivery on Saturday night after all. It makes sense. There'd certainly be less risk for Cooper if he could get someone to print them for him rather than steal them. The government doesn't exactly leave them lying around for people to help themselves. And a man like him would probably have all the contacts for forging the stamps and suchlike, and for selling them too.'

'Yes, I don't suppose he'd be planning to flog them in Queen's Road Market.'

There was a brief silence as Cradock thought.

'But that complicates things a bit, doesn't it, sir?' he said, turning to Jago. 'I mean, if we were right and it really was Cooper who killed Villiers, that would mean now our murderer's been murdered.'

'Very good, Peter,' said Jago. 'Those who live by the sword shall perish by the sword. It wouldn't be the first time it's happened. But the question remains, as you so rightly say: if Cooper did murder Villiers, who's killed Cooper, and why?'

'Could it be revenge?' said Cradock.

'You're very keen on revenge, aren't you?' said Jago. 'There are other reasons why people kill each other, you know.'

'Yes, I know, sir, but surely it could be? You know, someone close to Villiers, perhaps, who knew Cooper had killed him and wanted to settle the score?'

'Someone in the family? It's possible. And I must admit it's only recently that Cooper has displaced them in my suspicions. But if the rest of the family had their own various reasons for wanting Villiers dead, why would they want to take revenge if someone else turned up and saved them the trouble?'

Cradock had come to the end of his reasoning skills for the time being.

'Search me,' he said.

'Well, the first thing we need to do is get the police surgeon to take a look before another air raid starts. See if there's a phone in here somewhere that works, and if you can't find one, leg it down the road to the nearest phone box or police pillar that hasn't been blown to pieces and call the station.'

'Righto, sir.'

Cradock began to search the room for a telephone. He was about to move on into the corridor when a whooshing sound, like a sudden gust of wind, filled the air. It was followed immediately by a fierce noise of crackling and spitting.

'Fire, sir!' he shouted.

Smoke began to billow into the room.

'Quick! Come over here and help me get this body to the door,' said Jago.

'I think that's where the fire's coming from, sir: we can't go that way. Do you think it's an incendiary bomb?'

'No, I don't. There's been no noise out there. No sirens yet, no planes. It sounded more like petrol going up. I just hope Cooper hasn't got any more in here. Now come and help me. I'm not going to lose a second body in a week.'

Jago knew there was no hope of saving his coat this time. He quickly pulled it off and folded it in half, then draped it over the bottom of the window frame, knocking out the remaining fragments of glass as he did.

'You first,' he shouted to Cradock.

The younger man climbed out through the window. Jago hauled the body up and planted its head and shoulders in the opening, and together they pushed and pulled it through. Jago was coughing as the smoke got to him.

'Give me a hand,' he said. 'Quick.'

Cradock took one of Jago's hands as the inspector scrambled onto the windowsill, and half dragged him out. They both collapsed onto the cobbled yard and breathed the cool air deeply.

Jago struggled to his feet and grabbed his coat from the sill.

'We need to get him away from the building. Come on!'

They dragged the body clear to what Jago thought was a safe distance and stopped for breath again. Cradock began to wander away.

'Where are you going, man?' said Jago.

'Just over here, guv'nor. Look: that's a bit strange.'

'What is?'

'These crates, sir. They seem to have fallen down while we were in there. They were all stacked up when we arrived. I didn't hear anything, though; it must have happened after that fire started.'

Jago joined him.

'Give me that lamp.'

He took another couple of steps forward and shone the lamp into the space behind the crates.

'Well, well,' he said. 'What have we here?'

In the dim pool of light before him he saw a figure dressed in dungarees and a woollen hat crouching among the fallen crates. But no face: whoever it was turned quickly away. Like a child playing hide-and-seek who thinks if it closes its eyes no one will see it, thought Jago. There was a second figure lying motionless on the ground: a young-looking man, heavily built. Blood was seeping from his hairline and down onto his cheek. He began to stir, clutching his head.

'What's this, then?' said Jago. 'What happened to your friend?'

'He's not my friend. I think he was knocked out by one of these boxes,' said the would-be invisible man, turning round but not looking up.

The voice that Jago heard was not what he had been expecting.

'You're a woman,' he said.

'Of course I'm a woman.'

Jago was immediately conscious that his comment must have sounded inane, but given her presence at the scene of the fire he was in no mood for polite apologies.

'And what are you doing here?'

'None of your business.'

'If I were to invite you to accompany me to the police station to continue this conversation, would that make it my business?'

'Police?' she said. 'Oh God.'

She pulled the hat off and shook out her hair.

Cradock gasped.

'It's her, sir.'

'Who?'

'Mrs Hodgson. You remember: there was that man who got roughed up in the cemetery. This is his wife. I met her Monday evening. What on earth's she doing here?'

Before Jago could speak, he heard wellington boots slapping hurriedly across the cobblestones in their direction. The warden stopped beside them. He looked first at the fire, then at Cradock.

'Oh, it's you again. You're that constable who was asking about the van here, aren't you? What's all this about? We've had enough fires round here from the Germans, without people starting their own. Have you reported it yet?'

Jago stepped forward.

'I'm Detective Inspector Jago. We've got a dead body here and this is a police investigation. We need your assistance.'

'Fair enough,' said the warden. 'Whatever you say. As long as the Luftwaffe doesn't turn up again.'

'Listen, we've only just got out of that building, so please find a telephone and call the fire brigade as quickly as you can. And ring the police: tell them Detective Inspector Jago says get the police surgeon down here as soon as possible.'

'Will do,' said the warden, and strode away into the darkness.

'Peter,' said Jago, 'I want you to stay here and wait for the doctor.'

'Yes, sir.'

Jago turned the lamp back onto the couple on the ground.

'And as for you two, I'm arresting you on suspicion of setting fire to these premises. You are not obliged to say anything, but anything you say may be given in evidence.'

The young man was sitting up now, rubbing his head, but still had not said anything. Jago studied him for a moment and then turned to Cradock.

'Well,' he said quietly, 'I may not have had the pleasure of meeting Mrs Hodgson before, but this young man I do recognise: it's rabbit-face.'

CHAPTER TWENTY-FOUR

'I remind you that you are still under caution.'

Jago contemplated the expression of the woman sitting before him in the interview room at West Ham police station. In the car she had maintained that she knew nothing about Cooper and declined to explain why she had been on his premises, but as soon as she'd crossed the threshold of the station her air of confidence had evaporated. He'd kept her waiting until Cradock returned and told him the police surgeon's verdict: estimated time of death between 4 and 5 p.m. Now she was slumped on the chair, her face despondent. She looked as if she were fighting back tears.

'I'm a law-abiding citizen,' she said. 'My husband is a civil servant.'

'That's as may be, Mrs Hodgson, but I want to know this: did you kill Frederick Cooper?'

'No, I've never met him. Why on earth would I want to kill someone I don't know?'

'Why would you want to go creeping around his property after dark, either? That's not everyone's idea of law-abiding. Now look, Mrs Hodgson, it's late and I'm tired. I've got a dead body, and the only other people on the scene are you and that young man. You can either tell me what happened or we can spend the rest of the night here until you do.'

She sighed, then sat up straighter on her chair and looked at him.

'All right. It's true that I've never met Cooper, but I've seen him and I know who he is. Who he was, rather. It's my husband who knows him, although he wishes their paths had never crossed. Sidney works for the Ministry of Labour and National Service, at the Labour Exchange.'

She paused. It seemed to Jago that she thought he would take these words as primary evidence of her husband's probity.

'He's a good man, Inspector, but he's not very strong, and somehow he got tangled up with Cooper. I think it was something to do with money. Sidney doesn't earn as much as he'd like to, and I think he's felt for a long time that he's letting me down. Perhaps that's why he let himself be bullied into doing it.'

'Doing what, Mrs Hodgson? He wasn't stealing national identity cards, was he?'

She looked puzzled.

'No, I don't think so.'

'Then what was it?'

'It was something to do with call-up papers. Cooper would give my husband certain names, and when their call-up papers came through, Sidney had to lose them.'

'Lose them?'

'Make sure they were never delivered to the person in question, so they wouldn't get called up for the forces. I believe all sorts of papers get lost in the civil service, and no one ever does anything about it. I assume people were paying Cooper to ensure they or their loved ones could avoid conscription. He paid Sidney a small sum to see to it that the papers disappeared. That was Sidney's big mistake, of course. Once he'd taken the money, Cooper could blackmail him, and so he had to do whatever he was told.'

'Or face the consequences.'

'Exactly, and facing consequences is not one of my husband's strengths. He tried to get out of it, but he was trapped.'

'It was Cooper who beat up your husband in the cemetery?'

'Yes, that's what Sidney said.'

'So how did you end up at Cooper's premises tonight? He was a dangerous man, by all accounts.'

'You may think women are the weaker sex, Inspector, but we're not. That man was destroying my husband's

221

life and our marriage. I was not prepared to stand by and watch it happen.'

Jago was inclined to believe this. *I've probably seen more strong women than you've had hot dinners*, he thought to himself. He remembered the street fights he'd run into when he was a young constable in uniform, the big women with arms like hams who'd been thrown out of a pub and slogged it out with fists in the street until one of them went down. They didn't seem to make women like that any more. He doubted whether Mrs Hodgson had ever visited streets like that.

'You weren't just going to stand by. So what did you do?'

'I decided the best way to deal with a blackmailer was to give him a dose of his own medicine.'

'Fight fire with fire?'

She gave him a cold look.

'If necessary, yes.'

'So then what?'

'I wrote him a letter, anonymously of course, to the effect that I knew what he was up to with the call-up papers, and if he didn't stop he'd suffer for it.'

'I trust you didn't include your address for his reply.'

'Of course not. I gave him a deadline and waited to see whether he would stop putting pressure on Sidney. That way I'd know whether he was taking notice. If he didn't, I'd take some action that would make him realise the threat was real.'

'And did he stop?'

'No, he carried on in exactly the same way.'

'So you took that action tonight. You murdered him.'

'No, I've told you already: I didn't do that.'

'What did you do?'

'I found out about his place and decided to start a little fire. I put some petrol in one of my preserving jars and brought it with me. I reckoned it wouldn't take much to get it going, as long as I put it on a door or something else made of wood.'

'That was a very foolhardy thing to do.'

'I know that now, but at the time I didn't have many options at my disposal.'

'And where does that other fellow come into it – the one who was with you?'

'Where is he? What have you done with him?'

'Don't you worry about him. We've put a dressing on him and now he's having a little chat with my colleague. Tell me about him.'

'There's not a lot to say, really. He's Edgar, Edgar Simpson. It's nothing to do with him, really. He's a clerk who works with my husband, and he'd got mixed up with Cooper too – something to do with gambling, I believe. I needed someone else with me in case anything went wrong, and I couldn't risk bringing Sidney. So I enlisted Edgar. It wasn't difficult to persuade him. I was quite surprised at how willing he was. But then as soon as the fire was going we saw you two climbing out, and the fool ran off – straight into that pile of boxes. He brought them crashing down on us and knocked himself out. I would have done better to work on my own.'

Jago was beginning to believe her.

'But it didn't occur to you there might be someone in the building you were about to set fire to? You didn't knock on the door?'

'How could I knock on the door? Supposing Cooper or one of his cronies had come to open it? What would I have said? "Good evening, I'm Mrs Hodgson. I've just come round to see if I can borrow a cup of sugar"? No, I had to take a chance on that. I reckoned a man like him would probably be out drinking in a pub at that time of the evening, and if he was in, well, he'd have to take his chances.'

'What time did you arrive at Cooper's premises?' said Jago.

'About ten minutes before you and your colleague unfortunately found us.'

'And can you account for your movements before that?'

'Yes, I was at a WVS meeting in Kensington all day. I got home just before six o'clock, made our supper, we ate, and then I got changed and came down here.'

'Can anyone vouch for your being at that meeting?'

'Yes, about two dozen WVS members. No one left until the meeting finished, which was at four-thirty. And while we're on the subject, I think you'll find that Mr Simpson was at work all day at the Labour Exchange, as was my husband.'

'In that case, that will be all. I think you're the one who's taken a few too many chances this evening, Mrs Hodgson. Arson is a serious offence.'

'Wait a minute. Isn't this a little ridiculous? The Germans have been dropping incendiary bombs all over West Ham, and every other building around the docks has been blown up or burnt down, but you want to send me to court for one little fire?'

'Mrs Hodgson, if it were within my power to go up there and arrest the Luftwaffe on suspicion of offences under the Malicious Damage Act 1861, that's what I would do, but unfortunately I cannot. Here on the ground, however, setting fire to buildings is a felony within the meaning of that Act, so you will be charged. You can count yourself lucky not to be charged with murder too.'

CHAPTER TWENTY-FIVE

'Right,' said Jago, 'now we must go and break the bad news to Cooper's wife – if bad news is what it is.' He looked at his watch. 'Past my bedtime. Let's hope it's not past hers – or yours.'

'Don't worry, sir, I'm fine: plenty of energy left,' Cradock replied. 'Oh, by the way, sir, I meant to ask you – why did you say "It's rabbit-face" when you saw that Edgar Simpson fellow? Did you know him already?'

'No, I didn't know him. At least, I didn't know his name and I'd never spoken to him, but I'd seen him once. It was when we were at Rita's cafe last Saturday afternoon. He was the man with Cooper. He looked pretty scared, and now we know why. If Mrs Hodgson's right and he'd got mixed up with Cooper's little racket too, that would explain why they were together there and why he looked like a scared rabbit. People like him aren't cut out for negotiating deals with criminals, and he'd probably realised too late that he'd bitten off more than he could chew. What did he say when you interviewed him?'

'Basically it seems he fancies himself as a card player but picked the wrong people to play with. He got sucked into Cooper's circle when he found himself getting into debt with people who weren't inclined to wait for their money. He's not giving any names, of course: too afraid. Apart from that, he's all politeness; says he realises he's made mistakes and learnt his lessons. Says he'll be a reformed character from now on.'

'I wonder. Sometimes that's easier said than done.'

'Yes, fair words butter no turnips, as my mother used to say.'

'Parsnips, Peter.'

'What's that, sir?'

'Parsnips. You don't butter turnips, you butter parsnips. Nobody butters turnips. Your mother was wrong, or you weren't listening carefully.'

'Oh, I see. Sorry, sir.'

'So what else did Simpson say?'

'Nothing of interest, really. It seems Mrs Hodgson was the brains of the operation. He says she provided the petrol and he just did what he was told. His intention was simply to do what she wanted and then get out of it as soon as he could, which is what he seems to have done – or tried to, anyway.'

'Very good,' said Jago. 'Come along, then. The sooner we get this done, the sooner I can get reacquainted with my bed.'

'We'll need to ask you to come to the mortuary to identify the body,' said Jago, sitting in the Coopers' comfortable living room. 'But we've no doubt it's him.'

She had taken the news very calmly. Surprisingly calmly, for a woman being told that her husband had met a violent death. There was no weeping, no sign of grief. Jago had pressed her.

'This must be a shock for you. Do you know of any reason why someone might want to kill your husband?'

Her face had been blank.

'There are so many people getting killed these days, Inspector. Good people. People who've never done any harm to anyone. That's what's shocking.'

'And your husband?'

'All I'm saying is I'm not surprised he's come to a sticky end. He wasn't a nice man, not the man I thought he was when I married him. But we all make mistakes, I suppose. He was mixed up in lots of dodgy business – you know, a bit of this, a bit of that, none of it strictly above board. He was clever, though: knew how to cover his tracks. Never had any trouble with the law, as far as I know. We've certainly never had your lot at the door before. I don't know exactly what he got up to, but I reckon he was always sailing close to the wind. I wouldn't have minded, but he could get violent too. It didn't pay to cross him.'

'Was he ever violent towards you?'

'I could tell you stories, believe you me. But yes, he knocked me about a few times. Seemed to enjoy it too. I'd be lying if I told you I'll be shedding tears now he's gone. You can't help thinking the world'll be a better place without some people. What more can I say?'

It had been Jago's duty on many occasions to break the news of a death to husbands, wives, parents, even children, but he had rarely come across a woman who took it in her stride in such a matter-of-fact way. If anything, she looked relieved. But if what she was saying about her husband was true, it was perhaps not surprising.

'Tell me more about your husband,' he said. 'What was his background?'

'Well, he was local. Not actually born here, but he's lived in Plaistow all his life. His mother – Lily, she was called . . .'

She hesitated, then continued.

'She moved here when he was a baby. She was from south of the river originally, and she'd had a tough time growing up. I don't think it got any better when she married, either.'

'Is that why Mrs Cooper moved here?'

'I think so. I think she liked it better here. Of course, she wasn't Mrs Cooper then; she was still Lily Cordwell when she moved here with the baby.'

'So she was an unmarried mother, then. Is that why she moved?'

Her expression lightened for a moment, and she laughed.

'No, you've got the wrong end of the stick there, Inspector. It was the other way round. She was married all right when she had the baby: she was Mrs Lily Cordwell. She lived over in Custom House, by the docks. That's where her husband was from. But when she moved here she started using her maiden name again – and that was Cooper. Of course, she kept her wedding ring on and called herself Mrs, so everyone called her Mrs Cooper.'

'Do you know why she didn't want to use her husband's name?'

'Not really, no. She died quite a few years ago and never told me what it was all about. I've always assumed it was some funny business with her husband, else why would she go back to her old name? I never met him, though. He died in the Great War, and I think it was then that she moved to Plaistow for a new start. She got herself work as a barmaid at the Coach and Horses. I suppose someone looked after the baby while she was working, but she didn't earn much. It must have been a struggle for her to make ends meet.'

'So your husband had a difficult upbringing?'

'Well, I didn't know him when he was growing up, but I imagine it was hard for him. He used to say he'd had to fight for everything he had, and I suppose that's what turned him nasty.'

'What was his education?'

'He told me he went to North Street School, but he

didn't like it. Left when he was fourteen and went to work as a barrow boy, selling fruit and veg. He made a bit of money at that, and then set himself up on the market, trading things that would make him a bit more money. I was seventeen when I met him. Real charmer, he was. Well, not to everyone, maybe, but he certainly charmed me.'

She fell silent, and for a moment Jago thought he could see a hint of tenderness in her eyes. But it was gone as quickly as it came.

'Anyway, it was only after we got hitched that I found out what he was really up to. I was pretty sure some of the stuff he was flogging wasn't strictly kosher, if you know what I mean. Fallen off the back of a lorry, more like.'

'So you're saying he was dealing in stolen goods?'

'Well, I wouldn't like to say. I mean, I couldn't prove it. It just seemed to me a bit suspicious that he could get hold of all this stuff so cheap. He made enough money to buy this house and he always seemed to have plenty of cash, but I never had any idea how he got it. He didn't seem to keep any books, either, so Lord knows if he ever paid any taxes.'

Jago was beginning to form quite a detailed picture of Cooper in his mind, and was surprised that the man appeared to have had no criminal convictions. He must have been a clever operator, he thought, or perhaps just very lucky – until tonight.

'Is there anything else you've noticed of late that you would regard as suspicious?' he said.

'No, not really. There was just one thing today that was a bit odd. I saw a man outside on the street, a fat little bloke. I didn't know him, but he seemed to be hanging around. I did wonder at the time whether it might be something to do with Fred, but until you asked I'd thought no more of it.'

'I see. I was thinking more of anything else suspicious in your husband's business dealings – people he met, something he might have said, for example. Anything at all that might shed light on how he was making this money you mentioned. You're not required by the law to disclose anything he may have told you during your marriage, but if you're willing to tell me about anything relevant that you may recall, I would be grateful.'

She shrugged her shoulders.

'It's no skin off my nose, Inspector. He's dead now, and he can't get me, and there's no children to be shamed by him. He was a bad man, and I don't care who knows it.'

'Did he ever mention anything about dealing in documents of any kind?'

'What kind of documents?'

'I'm thinking of official documents – things like fake identity cards, for example.'

She shook her head slowly.

'No. Never heard him mention anything like that. But like I said, he didn't take me into his confidence.'

She stared into the fireplace in thought for a few moments, then looked up.

'It would make sense, though.'

'What do you mean?'

'It's just something he said the other day. I was saying how terrible it is to be having this war, but he said something like if you play your cards right there's money to be made out of it. I said we're all supposed to be doing our duty, not making money, and he said not everyone thinks the same way about duty. He said people would pay good money to dodge their duty, and there were some nice little rackets going on to make sure they could. He said he had no plans to be a soldier himself, either.'

'Did he say what these rackets were?'

'No, but I suppose it must've been something to do with dodging the call-up, don't you think?'

'Quite possibly,' said Jago.

He stood up, and was followed by Cradock.

'Before we go,' he said, 'did your husband ever mention any names in connection with his business activities?'

'His rackets, you mean.'

'If you like, yes. Names of people he might have had dealings with.'

'No. Like I said, he never let on about anything like that. Kept it all to himself.'

She got out of her chair.

'There is one thing, though. Come with me.'

Jago and Cradock followed her out into the hallway. She led them to a small room at the back of the house.

'This is what my husband liked to call his study. I saw

him in here once or twice writing in a book, but if ever I came in he'd put it in there and lock it in that old thing. Then he'd give me one of his looks, and I knew it'd be more than my life's worth to try and have a look.'

She pointed into the far corner of the room, where Jago recognised a mid-Victorian mahogany roll-top bureau.

'A fine piece,' he said.

'Old junk, if you ask me,' she said. 'I like something a bit more modern. But anyway, I reckon there's some secrets in there. It's bound to be locked, but you can force it for all I care.'

'I don't think that'll be necessary, Mrs Cooper,' said Jago. 'DC Cradock, have you got those keys on you?'

Cradock took an envelope from his pocket and took out Cooper's bunch of keys.

'Here they are, sir.'

'See if one of them fits that bureau. It'll be one of the smaller ones.'

Cradock tried three keys without success, but the fourth produced a quiet click and he was able to roll up the lid of the bureau.

'There it is,' said Mrs Cooper. 'It's that black one on the right-hand side.'

Jago reached into one of the vertical pigeonholes set into the upper part of the bureau and lifted out a small leather-bound notebook. He flipped through the pages and then handed it to Cradock.

'Looks like a lot of notes in there. You can take a look through it tomorrow.'

'Yes, sir,' said Cradock, putting the book into his pocket.

Jago turned to Mrs Cooper.

'Thank you for your help, Mrs Cooper. We'll be off now, and we shall have to take this notebook with us.'

'You take it,' she said, 'and if it helps you to track down a few more crooks, that's fine by me. I don't even want to look. I don't want to know what he did. It might seem a wicked thing to say, but I'm glad to be rid of him. I think maybe I'm starting to feel like his mum did about her old man: now he's gone, I want to start all over again.'

CHAPTER TWENTY-SIX

'What kind of police car is this?' said Dorothy, standing back and examining the vehicle from end to end. She had emerged from Plaistow Tube station on Thursday afternoon to be met by Jago, who walked her the short distance round the corner to where he had parked. 'I thought you'd have something black with a bell on it.'

'No such luck, I'm afraid. The Metropolitan Police doesn't have enough cars to go round at the best of times, still less in wartime, so people like me have to use their own.'

'How cute. No one can say this country isn't original. I just came about a dozen stops on the District Line, with a map that says it's an underground railway, but half of it wasn't underground at all: it was just like a regular train.'

'And now a police car that's just what you'd call a regular car. Did you see the damage at West Ham as you came through?'

'Yes, the train didn't stop. They said the station was closed because of the bombing. When did that happen?'

'I think that was part of the Saturday night business.'

'I like the way you say that. It was the biggest raid of the war, for goodness' sake. That's something else that's weird about you people: what you say isn't always what you mean.'

'Yes, but in the nicest possible way, of course. It's probably something you should bear in mind.'

Jago opened the low-cut nearside front door for her and she eased herself into the worn leather seat. The car was a four-seat sports tourer, finished in dark green.

'Sorry there's not much room for your feet,' he said.

'Are you implying that I have big feet?'

'Not at all: even size twos would be a bit cramped down there. I think there must have been competition for space between the gearbox and the passenger's feet, and the designer decided the gearbox was more important.'

'I'm sure I'll be fine. If it gets too tight, I'll stand up. I see there's no roof to get in the way.'

'I thought I'd put it down so you could have a better view,' said Jago. 'I'm not too sure about all that cloud up there, but we should be fine if the rain holds off. If it doesn't, you can have the pleasure of being inducted into the mysteries of getting the roof up on this beast. It's a devil of a job.'

'Thank you. So what is this beast, as you call it?'

'It's a Riley Lynx. I bought it second-hand the year before last. Now I'm in the same position as everyone else with a car these days: just hoping it'll last the war out.'

'I love it,' said Dorothy. 'It's so British.'

'What's that supposed to mean?'

'I mean it's understated: it's not a show-off kind of car, but it looks like it could do the job. It's not too big, but it can take four people; it's not a racing car, but I guess it can go fast enough.'

She peered at the chrome instrument panel in the centre of the wooden dashboard.

'It says eighty miles per hour. Can it really do that?'

'Seventy at the most, I should think,' said Jago. 'Not that there's much call for that round here.'

'You see: that's exactly what I mean. American cars are big and brash, but yours have class. Mind you, I can't see Jimmy Cagney careering round Chicago in a Riley whatchamacallit: for one thing the running board doesn't look strong enough to carry me, never mind a gangster with a tommy gun.'

'There's not much call for them round here, either,' said Jago.

He slipped in behind the wheel and started the engine, then pulled out onto Plaistow Road and headed south.

'An afternoon's drive with Detective Inspector John Jago. What could be finer than that?' said Dorothy. She turned to him with a smile. 'Your name – it's unusual. I've never met anyone called Jago before. Is it foreign?'

'No,' he laughed, 'it's from Cornwall – although there are plenty of people down there who think England's a foreign country. All my people were Cornish, going way back, but in 1866 a bank in London collapsed and thousands of people in Cornwall lost their jobs. My grandfather was one of them, and he moved up to London for work. Since then we've been Londoners.'

'Nothing to do with Iago, as in Shakespeare?'

'No, and I don't think Iago would have made a very good policeman anyway.'

She studied his face, her eyebrows raised.

'You know your Shakespeare, then? Most cops I know in the States wouldn't know *Othello* from *Gold Diggers of 1937*.'

'I've seen the play, that's all. My dad took me. He loved the theatre – he even tried to make a living from it.'

'Your father was an actor?'

'No, he sang. He worked the halls, but never made much money out of it.'

'Worked the halls?'

'The music halls. He was still dreaming of being a success when he died. It was hard for my mum. She managed to keep me in school until I was sixteen, but then I had to leave and go to work. After that, my education was whatever I could manage for myself: books from the public library and newspapers.'

'So you didn't give up on newspapers completely?'

'I still can't resist them. I'm trying to persuade my detective constable to open one occasionally. We don't get to see the *Boston Post*, of course. Is Boston where you're from?'

'Born and bred.'

'What's it like?'

'Well, it's a big city and it's got a harbour. I love it.'

He smiled to himself: he liked her style. There was something pleasant about her voice too. He began to think about it, trying to pin down what it was in the sound of her speaking that appealed to him, but found his thoughts drifting instead to the past. He saw a face, a woman's face, with a tender smile, captured for ever like a photograph. It was the face he always saw.

The fresh flow of air over his right arm as he signalled and turned left into Beckton Road brought Jago back to the present.

'I'm going to take you through some of the back streets of Canning Town to the Royal Victoria Dock,' he said, keeping his eyes ahead on the wide, tree-lined street, now pockmarked by bomb damage. 'And then we'll go on to Silvertown. You remember me saying there are some difficult areas in this borough? Well, you'll see some of them this afternoon. The people down here have had a rough time these last few days. You probably know there were about a hundred bombers over here yesterday afternoon.'

'Yes, I do,' said Dorothy. 'I've already been to Silvertown. What chance did they have, sandwiched between the docks and the river? I saw whole rows of houses blown down, people with suitcases and bundles, children carrying pillows, trying to get away.'

Jago glanced round to look at her, his face registering his surprise.

'But I've told you, you shouldn't go wandering round in places like this on your own. It's dangerous. We're in the middle of a war here. People were killed on these streets only twenty-four hours ago. My boss is expecting me to look after you.'

'Is he indeed? I can assure you I don't need looking after.'

Jago felt frustrated. They seemed to be slipping back into the same argument they'd had before. He tried to suppress the note of irritation that was creeping into his voice, but failed.

'I just don't want you coming to harm.'

'You think I've never been near danger before?' said Dorothy.

'Not danger like this. Not where people are dropping bombs on you and trying to kill you.'

'I'm afraid you've got me wrong again. You need to know something about me. I came to Europe in 1934 to work as a freelance journalist. Since then I've been in Spain, Finland, Poland, Czechoslovakia, you name it. You've heard of Guernica?'

'Of course: the Spanish Civil War. The place Hitler bombed for Franco. People say it was a practice run for everything he's done since.'

'Well, I've been there. I saw what they did, and I can tell you it looked a lot like this. Some people would say

Guernica was no place for a woman, but my job is to go where war is. I was in Czechoslovakia when the Nazis marched in, Poland when they carved it up with the Russians, Finland when the USSR invaded. That's what you do when you're a foreign correspondent. You go looking for trouble. The last place I was before I came to London was France, back in June, and I only got out of Paris because an English reporter from your *Daily Mirror* gave me a lift out in his car as the Germans were moving in. So you see, there is honour among journalists – and I do know a thing or two about war.'

Jago was silent. He felt he had been put in his place, and deservedly so. He was annoyed with himself for making assumptions about this woman. He would make amends.

Dorothy reached over to the back seat for her brown leather shoulder bag as Jago edged down a narrow side street. Four boys kicking a can around in an energetic game of football stood back to let the car pass. She pulled out a folded newspaper.

'I've got something here I wanted to ask you about,' she said.

He glanced to his left to see what she was holding.

'Fine, as long as you don't open that thing up – I'll never be able to see where I'm going if you start reading the paper.'

'Don't worry, I've got it folded to the right page already. It was just something I saw in *The Times* this morning. The headline caught my eye – it was more dramatic than usual. It says "Refugees killed in bombed school: babies found in wreckage". It sounds pretty bad.'

She braced her hand against the dashboard to keep the paper steady as the car rumbled over a patch of uneven cobbles. 'It says here a school in the East End was wrecked by a bomb on Monday night. It also says it's feared that a large number of men, women and children lost their lives. Do you know where that was?'

'I do. Would you like to see it?'

'Say, that's more like it. You know where it was because you're a policeman, right?'

'Anyone who reads that and lives round here will know where it was. That's the way it works with our newspapers these days. They're not allowed to say where anything happens, but the people who live there obviously know and can put two and two together. Everyone in this area knows what happened. It was a terrible thing. The school's just a stone's throw from here, in Agate Street.'

'It says about five hundred homeless people were in it. That suggests a lot of people around here have been bombed out of their homes.'

'Yes. It wasn't a school any more, of course. The authorities had turned it into a rest centre, so it was probably crammed full of people, and when a place like that takes a direct hit they don't stand a chance. Men, women, children – it makes no difference.'

He became aware that he was gripping the steering

wheel tightly. He relaxed his hands and took a turning to the right.

'Almost there now. You know, I think one of the worst things about these air raids is that they're totally indiscriminate. Our hospital near the police station was bombed on Saturday too. I was walking up there yesterday to visit someone in connection with the case I'm investigating and I met a man who said two nurses had been killed. "Where's the justice in that?" he said, and I couldn't answer him. I met nurses in the last war, in the casualty clearing stations and hospitals in France, and they were like angels. Where's the justice in nurses being killed?'

Before Dorothy could answer, Jago had stopped the car in Agate Street. He sat in silence for a moment or two, then reached across to the handbrake lever.

'Pardon me,' he said, and pulled it back. It stood only an inch or two from her right knee.

'Here we are.'

He opened his door and quickly doubled round the back of the car to open the passenger door for Dorothy, but she was already halfway out before he got there.

'No need to help me out,' she said. 'I'm used to finding my own way in and out of cars.'

He caught her eye, and she smiled.

'It's not that I don't appreciate your acting like a gentleman,' she said. 'Just saving you the trouble, nothing more.'

* * *

They approached the site. Before they could get close, a uniformed police constable stopped them.

'No public access, sir,' he said, then recognised Jago. 'Sorry, sir, I didn't realise it was you. We've been ordered to keep people out. They reckon there might be a couple of hundred dead here.'

He lifted the rope that was strung across the street to cordon it off and let them through. They passed a couple of wrecked houses and turned a corner. Before them stood a gaping concrete framework – all that was left of the bombed school. In front of it was a crater in the ground that Dorothy guessed was all of twenty feet deep, surrounded by lurching heaps of smashed masonry and timber. It looked as though the rescue parties had now gone, leaving only workmen who were quietly shifting the debris and loading it into lorries for removal. There was a strange desolation over the scene.

Jago noticed that Dorothy was scribbling in a notebook. She paused to take in more of the scene and turned to him.

'This is why I write,' she said. 'I know I may not be able to describe everything I've seen, and I certainly won't be allowed to show a photograph, but in my own way I can tell the world what's happening here. It's what I've done in all those places I've been to – just do the little bit I can to make sure the truth is told where bad people are doing bad things. Do you know what happened here?'

'This is something else you won't be able to print, but there's a story going round that the people sheltering here were supposed to be taken to a safe place on Monday afternoon. The authorities were organising buses to take them, but they never arrived. It may not be true, but people are saying the bus drivers went to Camden Town instead of Canning Town, by mistake. So when the bomb hit it late that night, they were still here. I don't suppose we'll ever know for sure.'

'So they died because of some simple mix-up?'

'We like to think in this country that we have a talent for muddling through, but the truth is sometimes muddle is all we do, and this is where we end up. I've seen it too many times before. Men dying because someone further up the line has bungled, and now it's women and children dying too. It makes me sick.'

Dorothy watched as he turned and began to walk back towards the car in silence.

CHAPTER TWENTY-SEVEN

'What will you have?' said Jago, motioning Cradock to a chair. 'I've got a quart of Watney's Ale, otherwise it's Scotch.'

'I'll have some Watney's, then, sir,' said Cradock. 'Thanks very much.'

It was eight in the evening, blackout time, and the street outside was silent. So far there had been no sirens, but there was no way of knowing whether the Germans intended to bomb London every night.

Jago poured the beer into a glass and set it on the small table before him. Cradock took in the unfamiliar surroundings of his boss's home. The curtains were drawn, and a standard lamp bathed the living room in a cosy half-light. This was the first time he'd seen the inside of Jago's house, and it wasn't as he had expected.

'Very nice place you've got here, sir. You should see where I live. How do you manage to keep it so neat and tidy?'

'That's easy: I pay someone to do it for me. I can't bear to live in a mess, but this job doesn't leave much time for housework, does it?'

'You can say that again. It doesn't leave much money to buy a house with, either, let alone pay for a housekeeper – not on a DC's pay.'

'That might be an incentive to pass your exam for detective sergeant, then, one of these days.'

Cradock didn't like to think what state his few square feet of the section house might be in by the time that day came. He ran his finger idly along the arm of the chair he was sitting in. Not a speck of dust. The chair was solid and comfortable, made from a dark wood that he could not identify. The brown leather upholstery felt warm and supple, not like the brittle and cracking Rexine that covered the only chair he owned.

'You like old-fashioned furniture, then, sir?' he said. 'Don't find it too gloomy?'

'Gloomy? This is Arts and Crafts,' said Jago. 'The best furniture this country's produced in a hundred years.'

'I like something a bit more modern myself,' said Cradock, 'although I suppose this old stuff goes better with a house like this. If I had the money, I'd get one of those new flats, all light and airy.'

'No, no, they're horrible. All those straight lines and

flat roofs, and those funny-looking curved windows. They look so sterile and regimented, cold and characterless. Give me an old-fashioned English house any day, and old-fashioned English furniture, as you call it.'

'Each to their own, I suppose. That Cooper managed to get himself a nice place, though, didn't he? Can't be much older than me, if that, but he must have a lot more cash to his name than I have.'

'Yes, and look where that's got him. What did you get out of that little book of his?'

'Some very interesting information, sir. Mostly names. It looks like he kept a note of names and payments. Some of it was money going out, but more of it was coming in, presumably from whatever rackets he was working.'

'Names we know?'

'Some of them, yes. That Hodgson is in there, for one. In his case it looks like payments going out, from Cooper to him, which bears out what his wife – Hodgson's wife, that is – was saying about Cooper paying him to make sure people's call-up papers were lost.'

'Anyone else?'

'Yes: Mr Charles Villiers.'

'In or out?'

'With him it seems to be a bit of both. Mostly it's Cooper paying money to him. Now that would suggest we were right about the two of them being mixed up in some illegal printing.'

'And Johnson: is he in there too?'

'Yes, but in his case it seems to be money coming in, not going out. If Johnson was involved in this night-time printing thing and it was for Cooper, you'd think he'd be getting his share too.'

'Unless the money Villiers was getting included a cut for Johnson. I can imagine Villiers preferring it if he was the one who decided what Johnson got, not Cooper. Keeping his employee in his place, if you know what I mean.'

'Yes. So why would Johnson be paying money to Cooper?'

'We'll have to ask Johnson that.'

'There's also a payment from Villiers to Cooper, dated about a month ago, but of course it doesn't say what for.'

'That one we'll have to think about. Is that the lot?'

'No, there's just one more point that seems relevant. It's about those fake identity cards we found at Cooper's place. It looks pretty clear that he was selling them on. There's a list of names and dates, and in every case there are two names. It must be the name of the person he sold it to and the name he'd put on the card. You know: the false name.'

'Yes, yes, I understand. Anyone we know?'

'Just one, as far as I could see,' said Cradock. 'And that was someone else who's got connections. Bob Gray. It looks as though he bought a card, and his real name's Coates.'

'Very interesting. A few more stones for us to turn over. Well done.'

Jago sipped his beer thoughtfully.

'It's all about books and covers, isn't it?'

'Sir?'

'You know: never judge a book by its cover. All these people – the more we find out about them, the more unsavoury they turn out to be. You just never can tell. You meet a man who looks as meek as a lamb, then it turns out he's a wife-beater, or worse. Why's that?'

'Human nature, I suppose.'

'When I was a kid, a man like that would just be someone who did bad things, but now you get these new psychiatrists saying it's all his parents' fault, it's all about his relationship with his father. Any truth in that, do you think?'

'Wouldn't know, sir. My dad died when I was three, so I don't remember him.'

'I'm sorry to hear that.'

'Thank you, sir. It's a bit odd, missing someone you never really knew. But it wasn't unusual in those days. Lots of my friends at school had lost their dads. Mine was at Gallipoli.'

'Another of Mr Churchill's great ideas.'

'A bloodbath, more like it, from what I've heard. So I never really had a father. My mum was amazing, though, the way she coped. Brought me and my two sisters up on her own.'

'And you turned out all right, didn't you? So why is it some men grow up to be wife-beaters, thieves and murderers?'

'Can't say I've ever thought about that. We'd soon be out of a job if they didn't, though, wouldn't we?'

'I suppose there's that to be said for it, although on balance I think I'd be happier to be out of a job if it meant no child would ever be harmed again. But it's in us, isn't it? It's in all of us.'

'What is?'

'The killer, the potential to kill. As likely as not there'll be young German men your age flying over here tonight trying to drop bombs on people in their homes, and young British men flying the other way to do the same.'

Cradock was surprised. Jago seemed to be implying there was no distinction between the actions of the two warring sides.

'But we only bomb strategic targets, don't we?'

'Don't kid yourself. How accurate do you think those bombers are? I've heard people round here say they won't use the public shelters because the roofs make a target for the Germans to aim at. But that can't be right. Those Germans are thousands of feet up in the air just pulling some lever or something while we're shooting at them.'

'They have bomb aimers, though, don't they?'

'Look, they might be able to hit a target as big as Beckton gasworks, but they're not going to be able to make sure the bombs land on a factory instead of on Mrs Bloggs who lives next door. I expect the truth is they've got bombs to drop and they don't much care who they land on.'

'But we wouldn't do that, would we?'

'I can't imagine our bombers are any more accurate than theirs, and the sooner you get rid of your bombs, the sooner you can get home. But that's not my point. What I'm saying is we can all turn into killers. Take me, for instance. I was just an eighteen-year-old boy who wanted to be a newspaper reporter, but the army took me and taught me how to stick a bayonet into another man and kill him. If it wasn't for the war, he and I might have been friends and had a pint together, but now I was in khaki and he was in grey, and that meant I had to use a bayonet on him.'

'And did you? Did you ever have to?'

Jago was silent. The only sound in the room was the ticking of the clock on the mantelpiece.

'Yes,' he said.

Neither man spoke for a while. When Jago resumed the conversation, his voice was more gentle.

'You can thank your lucky stars you missed all that. And that you're in a reserved occupation now, so you won't get called up.'

'People say military service makes a man of you, though, don't they?'

'They do, but it's not as simple as that. I've seen it bring out the best in a man, and the worst. My sergeant risked his life to bring me back when I was wounded. He would have laid his life down to save me. There were lots of men like that – really looked after each other. But there were plenty of others who seemed to enjoy killing. They say we're fighting to save civilisation now, but I dread to think what it'll be like when all this is over and we've got thousands of men coming home trained to kill and no jobs, like it was last time. I don't think our job's going to get any easier when peace comes.'

'So why do we always want to kill each other?'

'It'd be a wise man who knew the answer to that one. I certainly don't. It just seems to be in us, as I said. It's in Hitler, and it's in the docker in Canning Town who murders his wife and kids. It's just something about being human, I suppose. I hate it.'

'At least we can do something about it, though, can't we? Put them behind bars, I mean. Send them to the gallows too, sometimes.'

Jago was struck by the simplicity of Cradock's outlook on life. It seemed quaint, somehow. It reminded him of when he was young.

'Yes. I don't know why you joined the police, but it's why I did. I don't mean I wanted to hang people. I mean I thought I could make things better in some way, help to put things right. I'd spent two years in France seeing what men are capable of doing when someone tells them they're allowed to kill. I'd seen what happened to innocent civilians when they got in the way of that vicious war machine running out of control. When I came back I didn't want to see anyone treated like that again. I wanted to be the person who could protect the weak from the strong, make sure there was peace on the streets, and see to it that thieves and murderers got their comeuppance.'

'Do you still feel like that?'

'Sometimes I think it's all a waste of time, but most of the time yes, I do still feel like that. I don't think Charles Villiers was a man I would have liked, and from the sound of him he probably wouldn't have given me the time of day anyway. But whatever he may or may not have done in his life doesn't give anyone the right to murder him. Only the law can take a man's life, after due process. It makes me angry when someone thinks they have that right. Whoever it was who killed Villiers, I'm going to find out who he is, or who she is. After that, the law can take its course, but I'll know I've done my bit. I'll have taken one killer off the streets.'

Jago fell silent again. Not even fifteen years between them, and yet Cradock seemed like a boy. *When I was in the trenches, he thought, Cradock would only have been five or six. I'm not quite old enough to be his father, but I might as well be, there's such a gulf between his experience and mine.* He remembered being back in England on leave. The busybody civilians whose imagination could not stretch to comprehend the agonies of the front. Wanting to shake them by the throat and make them understand, and yet finding there were no words to describe it. *We all decided not to tell them*, he thought; *perhaps we should have. Now the old slaughter's picked up where we left off.* Cradock and his generation would learn for themselves, grow wise through their own agonies.

Jago sometimes wished he'd been able to marry and have a son, but now he wasn't so sure. Perhaps it was better never to have had one than to have one and lose him.

CHAPTER TWENTY-EIGHT

'Morning, sir,' said Tompkins. 'And how are we today?'

'Morning, Frank. Fair to middling.'

The station sergeant nodded sagely.

'And how's that young lady of yours?'

'Young lady?'

'Yes, sir, that American lady.'

'She's not my young lady. She's a professional acquaintance.'

Tompkins gave another knowing nod.

'I see. Seems quite a confident young lady, if you know what I mean. Bit of a handful, I should think.'

'She's American, that's all. I think they breed them more confident over there. There's nothing wrong with that.'

'Strong women, though, sir – they can be a bit difficult, can't they? Reminds me of those suffragettes we used to have. Remember that Pankhurst woman?'

'Emmeline, or Christabel?'

'No, the other one: Sylvia. She was always down here. Very active in Canning Town, she was, just before the Great War.'

'I was still a schoolboy at the time, Frank.'

'Of course, I was forgetting. Bit of a communist, she was. Fell for the old Russian propaganda, if you ask me. But fair's fair: she wasn't all bad. Those suffragettes opened a place down there to help poor young mums and babies, and she'd be there, regular, handing out free milk and suchlike to the locals. That's what my wife said, any rate. They needed it too. Some of those families were starving.'

'They didn't turn you into a Bolshevik, did they?'

Tompkins drew himself up straight.

'I should blooming well think not, sir. I'm an Englishman.'

Jago laughed.

'Only kidding, Frank. I was thinking just the other day about some of the strong women we used to have around. Do you remember the way those old East End women used to fight?'

'I should say. Scrapped like cats, they did. I remember getting called out to a punch-up once, thirty years ago it must have been. These two old girls were knocking six bells out of each other, pulling each other's hair out by the handful. We had to push one of them all the way to the doctor's on the hand ambulance, and when we got there she wanted to go back for another go.'

'Yes, that's something you don't see now.'

'What, women having punch-ups?'

'No, the hand ambulance.'

'Yes, antiquated contraptions, they were. I think they were pensioned off about the same time I was. Ancient history, them and me both.'

'The good old days, eh, Frank?'

'Don't you believe it. Life was hard then. And I thought once the war was over everything would be fine. What mugs we were.'

'Didn't turn out as we'd hoped, did it?'

'Honestly, I never thought we'd be at war again so soon. Seems like we're right back where we started. And I don't know which is worse – being kicked out of France like we are now, or holding the line like we did then and slogging it out for another four years in the trenches. I'm getting too old, I think. Things don't seem to make sense like they used to. I suppose the older you get, the more you remember that used to be different.'

'The world's changed, Frank. We can't stop it. Everything changes. We even have women voting now, don't we? Or some of them, anyway. What a shock that was.'

Tompkins looked uncertain.

'You wouldn't be taking the mickey, would you, sir?'

'Would I ever do that?' said Jago with a laugh.

'Of course not. Tell you what, though: this might surprise you, but I think those suffragettes were right. I didn't back then, but I do now. Everyone should have a vote. I've heard people say half the men fighting in the British Army in the Great War didn't have a vote. Now that can't be right, can it? Old enough to die for your country but not old enough to vote? It's not logical. Same goes for women, I say. Not die for your country, of course, but have a vote, the same as men.'

'So you're a closet radical, then?'

'No, sir, it's just common sense. I was glad when they got the vote – really I was. I was hoping it would bring a bit of common sense into politics. Mind you, judging by the last year or two, I reckon we've still got a long way to go before that happens. Maybe people like your lady friend are going to change things for the better.'

'I've already told you, she's not my lady friend.'

'Yes, sir, so you did. And a charming young lady she is too.'

Jago found Cradock waiting in the office. The detective constable was seated at his desk, a half-finished mug of tea before him. He quickly folded away a newspaper and jumped to his feet when Jago entered.

'Good morning, sir.'

'Good morning, Peter. I trust you got home safely last night.'

'Yes, thank you, sir. It was quiet for a change. I reckon the Germans must have been having a night off, at least as far as West Ham's concerned. I could hear some bombs going off somewhere up west, though. This morning I heard one had just missed St Paul's. Anyway, the only incident I came across was an old man who'd tripped over the kerb in the blackout and cut his face, but he wasn't badly hurt. All quiet for you too, sir, after I'd gone?'

'Yes. I must say it was nice to have a good sleep for a change. First decent night's sleep I've had for days.'

'So are we going to go and turn over some of those stones, sir?'

'Yes, time for a little digging. I thought we could start with the Hodgsons.'

Mr and Mrs Hodgson were both at home. It was Mrs Hodgson who came to the door.

'Oh, it's you,' she said in a flat voice. 'Come in.'

She led them through to the kitchen. Her husband was sitting in the far right-hand corner, in a spindle-back wooden armchair. His head was down, and only a slight movement of his eyes acknowledged their presence before he resumed staring into his lap.

'The police are here,' she said, then turned back to Jago and Cradock. 'Haven't you had enough? I'm not going to run away, you know – not while I'm on police bail. Surely you've got everything you need by now? There's no need to keep harassing me.'

'Just a few simple questions, Mrs Hodgson,' said Jago, 'then we'll be on our way.'

'I should jolly well hope so. I'm very tired of this whole business.'

'My questions are actually for Mr Hodgson.'

'My husband is not well, Inspector. Just look at him: you can see he's ill. He's off work.'

'This won't take long. You're welcome to stay if you wish to.'

'In my own house? How kind of you.'

A woman of some spirit, thought Jago, albeit misdirected. More than could be said of her husband.

'Mr Hodgson,' he said.

Hodgson raised his head and gave him a nervous look, his hands tight on the arms of the chair.

'I've come to ask you some questions about your dealings with Mr Frederick Cooper.'

Hodgson was silent.

'I want to know about the money you've been taking from him,' Jago continued. 'Tell me about those call-up papers.'

'I can't,' said Hodgson. There was an undertone of fear in his voice.

'Cooper is dead, Mr Hodgson: he can't harm you now. And as far as I know he had no accomplices in his criminal activities, so no one else is going to be coming after you.'

A tear trickled down Hodgson's cheek.

'Pull yourself together, Sidney,' said his wife.

He took a white handkerchief from his trouser pocket and blew his nose, then tried to wipe his eyes discreetly before replacing it in his pocket.

'Very well. What do you want to know?'

'I just want you to tell me what you did with those papers.'

Hodgson tried to catch his wife's eye again, but she looked away. He hesitated, then continued, his voice feeble and his head down.

'It was nothing complicated, and not particularly clever. Every so often Cooper would give me some names of men who were due to be called up. My job was to make sure they disappeared from the system. This might sound ridiculous, but the way the Ministry of Labour works, if your papers are mislaid you officially cease to exist, so you can't be called up.'

'So you were the one who mislaid them.'

'Yes. All I had to do was find each man's Form 442 and destroy it, then Cooper would pay me. A pound for each one – that's what he gave me – although I'm sure he charged them twenty times that. It seemed an easy way to make some extra money at the time, but I didn't know what kind of man he was. By the time I found out, there was no way back.'

'Can you tell me the names of any of the men whose papers you lost?'

'I can tell you them all. I kept a list.'

'That's very thorough of you.'

'Maybe it's just the result of working in the civil service for twenty-four years. You keep records of everything. But it was also because I wanted to be sure he paid me everything he said he would. I didn't trust him.'

'Could you show us that list?'

Hodgson left the room and returned moments later with a piece of paper, which he handed over. Jago and Cradock examined it. Jago pointed to one of the names and spoke quietly to Cradock.

'Could be a coincidence, but interesting all the same, don't you think?'

'What are you saying?' said Hodgson anxiously.

'Never you mind. I'll take this with me,' said Jago. 'You won't be getting any more commissions from Mr Cooper.'

'Good riddance,' said Hodgson. 'He was a vicious man, and there was no reasoning with him. Letting him get his claws into me was the biggest mistake of my life.'

'I understand he had his claws into your colleague Mr Simpson too.'

This time Hodgson's eyes did not move in his wife's direction but stayed fixed on Jago.

'She told you?'

'Yes, and now I'd like you to tell me.'

Hodgson sat down again and stared quietly at the floor as if composing his thoughts before speaking.

'There was nothing I could do. Cooper wanted names of other people he could use in the same way he was using me, and he said he'd pay me for them. Poor Edgar had once confided something in me that he shouldn't have. I knew his secret, and I knew he'd do anything to stop it getting out. He'd been indiscreet, and if anyone found out, he'd be disgraced at work and with his family. I told Cooper, and from then on Edgar was at his mercy, but I was afraid of what Cooper might do to me if I didn't cooperate.'

'What was the nature of that indiscretion?'

'It was personal, what you might call a moral issue, but I can't tell you. Please don't make me. I betrayed him to Cooper, and I can't betray him to you too.'

'Very well. I won't press you further at the moment, but I may need to later if our investigation requires it.'

'I wish I'd never met that man Cooper. He was like a snake: once he'd got hold of a victim he'd never let go. I suppose I'm ruined now, aren't I?'

'That'll be for the magistrates' court to decide,' said Jago. 'But I think you can expect to be on the other side of the counter at the Labour Exchange once they've finished with you. I would imagine your career in the civil service is over.'

Jago and Cradock's next call was on Albert Johnson. They found him at work.

'Good afternoon, Mr Johnson,' said Jago. 'I'm sorry to disturb you again, but we need to ask you a few more questions.'

Johnson was moving towards them round a wooden table, a stack of large sheets of paper draped across his arms. He held them to one side and scanned the surrounding area distractedly.

'It won't take long, will it? You can see I've got my hands full. I've got four jobs to get out before we close this evening and I need to check these proofs.' He turned to Cradock. 'Pass me that loupe, will you?'

Cradock gave a blank look and turned to Jago.

'On the desk behind you,' said Jago. 'That brass thing. It's a magnifying glass.'

'Oh,' said Cradock. He picked it up and passed it to Johnson, who laid the proofs on the table and positioned the loupe on the top sheet. He bent down and peered through it.

'What is it you want to know now?' he said, moving the glass across the page.

Jago indicated to Cradock with a nod that he should ask the questions, then crossed the room and began to peruse a shelf of files.

'Mr Johnson, does the name Cooper mean anything to you?'

Johnson stood up straight, with a thoughtful expression on his face.

'Gary Cooper? I saw him in *Beau Geste* at the Odeon last year.'

'No, a Mr Frederick Cooper, of 467 Barking Road.'

'No, can't say it does. Why do you want to know?'

'When Detective Inspector Jago talked to you about your trip down to Plaistow with Mr Villiers last Saturday evening, you said you had no idea who the premises you visited belonged to. Is that correct?'

'Yes, it was none of my business. If Mr Villiers chose not to tell me, that was his prerogative. I wasn't going to start interrogating him about it.'

Johnson picked up the loupe again and made as if to resume working on his proofs.

'Mr Frederick Cooper was the owner of those premises,' said Cradock.

'Was? You mean he's not now?'

'I mean Mr Cooper is dead, Mr Johnson.'

Johnson froze. He replaced the loupe on the table.

'Dead? What happened to him?'

'He was murdered.'

'The poor blighter,' said Johnson, shaking his head slowly. He took a cigarette from a pack on the table and lit it.

'Mr Johnson,' said Cradock, 'you say you didn't know Cooper, but we have evidence from his wife that confirms he was receiving payments of money from you, and also that he was involved in illegal activities. Can you explain why you were paying money to a criminal you claim you've never heard of?'

Johnson's shoulders sagged. He pulled a chair away from the table and sat down heavily.

'He said it would be our little secret; no one else would ever know about it. And I was fool enough to trust him. I didn't even know he had a wife.'

He looked at the floor in silence for a few moments before speaking again.

'I'm sorry, but I haven't told you the whole truth.'

'So you did know Cooper.'

'Yes, I did. Not well, mind you: he was more of an acquaintance. The fact of the matter is, I bought some cigarettes from him – quite a few, actually. What you might call an informal transaction. It was only two or three times, and it was months ago, but I know I shouldn't have. I didn't ask any questions about where he'd got them. I soon realised it was wrong, and I stopped. I swear I haven't bought any since.'

'How did you get to know him?' said Cradock.

Johnson seemed reluctant to answer. He looked weary, as though he had been carrying a burden for too long. Eventually he spoke, in a quiet voice.

'It was through Mr Villiers. He got me involved in this extra work that no one was supposed to know about.'

'After hours?'

'Yes. He and I would stay on and do some printing in the night, in one of the buildings in the yard where we keep a couple of old presses. I think I said when you came here before that Mr Villiers wasn't actually a printer himself. He told me he wanted me to do some extra jobs for him, print them myself. He made it clear that he wasn't giving me a choice. What could I do? You didn't know him, Detective Constable: he was a powerful man, with lots of connections in important places. He could have made a lot of trouble for me, and I couldn't afford to cross him. So I said yes.'

Jago spoke from the other side of the room.

'So what was it that you were printing?'

Johnson gave a sigh of resignation and turned in his chair to face him.

'They were identity cards. Fake identity cards.'

'And you were supplying them to Cooper?'

'Yes, just small runs. So as not to be conspicuous, I

suppose. But I just did what Mr Villiers told me – I didn't get any more involved than that.'

'What kind of man was Cooper?'

'He was another one like Mr Villiers in a way. A powerful man, the kind of character you don't want to get on the wrong side of. He didn't have all Mr Villiers' airs and graces, of course. Quite the opposite. He seemed a real thug, violent. To be perfectly honest with you, I was afraid of him, did my best to steer clear of him. Fortunately for me, Mr Villiers handled all the business side of things with him. So if you want to know what money passed between them or what Cooper was doing with the cards, I can't help you. I assume he was selling them on, of course. I can't think what else you'd do with fake identity cards, and he seemed like the kind of person who'd have all the necessary contacts.'

'Was Mr Villiers paying you for the night work you were doing?'

'Yes. Not a lot, but he gave me something. He and Cooper could have been making a packet out of it, for all I knew. I was just the poor sucker in the middle who wasn't.'

'I have to go now,' said Jago, 'but I would be grateful if you would give a statement to my colleague.'

'Yes, of course.'

'Thank you. And just one last question: where were you on Wednesday between noon and eight o'clock in the evening?'

'I was here at work, then out visiting some

customers. I remember there was an air raid over the docks in the afternoon on Wednesday and I had to take shelter, which delayed me, but I got home by about seven, and after that it was quiet.'

'Can anyone vouch for your movements?'

'Well, obviously there were other people present when I was here and with the customers, and when the raid was on I was in a public shelter, so somebody there might remember me, but once I got home I was on my own. I am most evenings, really. I don't have much of a social life, Inspector; it's mostly just eat, work and sleep, and even that's not easy these days.'

Jago took the 699 trolleybus to Prince Regent Lane and walked back up the street until he found number 9. It was a small chemist's shop with a drab window display of patent medicines and bottles of coloured liquids. To the right of the window there was a door giving access to the first-floor flat. The dark blue paint on the door was peeling, and the door knocker was blackened by age and neglect. He gave two loud raps on the door and waited. No sound came from within, and the door remained closed. He tried again. After three attempts he gave up and went into the shop. A thin, middle-aged woman with greying hair and a melancholy face stood behind the counter; there were no customers.

'Excuse me,' said Jago. 'I'm looking for Mr Gray, who lives upstairs. He seems to be out, and I wondered whether you might know when I might be able to catch him.'

'I don't think I can help you,' said the woman. She sounded bored. 'He keeps himself to himself, does Mr Gray. I haven't seen much of him lately, and of course with his own front door he comes and goes as he pleases. We let the flat to him, but he looks after himself. Well, I say looks after himself, but I don't think he does really.' She lowered her voice to a conspiratorial tone. 'Bit of a drinker, you see, between you and me. What do you want with him?'

'I'm a police officer. I want to have a word with him.'

'In trouble with the law, is he? Can't say I'm surprised.'

'No, he isn't in trouble. I just need to speak to him. What does he do for a living?'

'Nothing, as far as I can see, Constable.'

'Detective Inspector.'

'Oh, I do beg your pardon, Inspector.'

'It's of no consequence. So he doesn't have a job?'

'Well, I don't know for a fact, but it looks that way to me. He pays his rent, but he hasn't been here long, so it's too early to tell whether he's reliable. He doesn't go out much, from what I've seen, and when I've bumped into him he doesn't seem to have any small talk, if you know what I mean. A bit miserable, a loner. What I call an oddball.'

'Is there a telephone in the flat?'

'No, but we've got one here in the shop.'

'In that case, if you see him, please ask him to give me a call on this number.' He wrote his name and the number of the police station on a scrap of paper and pushed it across the counter to her. 'Or better still, if you see him coming back, give me a call, and then I'll come round to see him.'

'Will do, Inspector. Anything to help the police, especially with a creepy character like that.'

CHAPTER TWENTY-NINE

'This time it's my treat,' said Jago. He had parked his car near Stratford railway station and reached it just moments before Dorothy emerged, and now he was walking her towards the high street. He missed the warmth of the previous weekend, and the sky was greying, but at least it wasn't raining yet. The streets were busy with women doing their Saturday morning shopping, and it was easy to spot the butcher's and grocer's shops because of the queues of women patiently waiting for their turn to go in and buy their rations.

'Your treat? That's very kind of you,' said Dorothy. 'Where are we eating?'

'That'll be my little surprise. First I'll show you the sights of Stratford.'

They turned left into Stratford Broadway, and Dorothy saw in the distance the elegant tower and spire of St John's Church. Standing on its grassy island site, hemmed in on both sides by the busy roadway, the church seemed like a ship sailing calmly ahead – a reminder of peace amidst the frenzy of commerce and the urgent uncertainties of war.

'It's beautiful,' she said. 'How old is it?'

'Only about a hundred years, I think.'

'It looks much older.'

'Just the way they built them, I suppose. If you want a really old church, you have to go down the road to the parish church, All Saints'. That's been there about eight hundred years, I believe.'

'Some other time, perhaps. I think it's going to rain.'

They crossed the road and entered the narrow churchyard that surrounded the building. Dorothy strode over to a large stone column topped with a needle-shaped spire and walked slowly round it.

'Look at this,' she said. She began to read the inscriptions. 'Oh my word. Elizabeth Warne, a widow and gentlewoman, taken at a prayer meeting and burned to death at Stratford-le-Bow in 1555.'

'Yes,' said Jago, walking over to join her. 'It's called the Martyrs' Memorial. I think about twenty of them were burned.'

'It's hard to imagine that kind of thing really happened, isn't it? Just an ordinary woman who believed something other people didn't want her to believe. And it

274

says round here that there were twenty thousand people watching. How cruel those days were.'

'I suppose we've made some kind of progress since then,' said Jago. 'Nowadays most people couldn't care less what anyone else believes. Mind you, there's still plenty that like to gang up on anyone who's a bit different, like the Jews. I've heard people spreading all sorts of malicious tales about them. They say the Jews always go into the public shelters early in the day so they can hog the best places. It's spiteful, but I suppose the fact that people are talking like that shows how this bombing's pushing everyone over the edge. We like to believe we're civilised compared with the past, but I sometimes think it's a very thin veneer. Underneath we're still animals.'

He wasn't sure whether Dorothy was listening. She was still looking at the inscriptions on the monument.

'I wonder whether that woman all those years ago knew her life was at risk,' she said. 'She must have, mustn't she? They all must have known they could be taken and killed at any moment. That's something that hasn't changed much. I remember a woman I saw in Poland, three days after the Germans had invaded. She was sitting alone, crying. She wasn't moving, she wasn't making a sound, but I could see the tears streaming down her face, as if they'd never stop. I couldn't imagine what she might have seen in those three days and what she might be thinking about the future. Her whole world must have been turned upside down.'

275

'And now it's happening all over again here, isn't it?' said Jago.

'Yes, or something very like it. Listen, can we sit down for a moment?'

They walked to the side of the churchyard and sat side by side on a wooden bench. It was shielded from the road by a spreading yew tree, but the noise of the traffic was still close.

'You know,' said Dorothy, 'the first war I covered was the civil war in Spain. Being a journalist meant I was able to visit the front line. I met a British professor out there, name of Haldane.'

'J. B. S. Haldane?'

'That's the one. Is he famous here?'

'Quite well known, yes. Very involved with the communists. He's been in the news recently for telling the government it ought to build deep air-raid shelters, but it hasn't come to anything.'

'Right, well he was out in Spain in 1937, advising the government on antidotes for poison gas, and I ran into him. He took me up to the front – he said in the Great War women weren't allowed within six miles of the front lines, so I ought to be grateful for the privilege. We joined the Republican soldiers in the trenches: some of them looked only sixteen or seventeen. I saw dead bodies lying in no man's land and heard the shells whooshing over our heads. The noise of the machine guns was terrible, and I couldn't imagine how anyone could get used to it.'

'So you've seen more of war than most women.'

'Yes. I know it's nothing compared to what you went through, but I hope you'll see I understand a little bit what it must have been like. I wasn't there for long, but I saw enough to know war is like a kind of unleashing of everything that's evil and mad in the world.'

She fell silent, and Jago noticed she was tracing patterns in the dust on the path with her right foot. It was a while before she continued speaking.

'Before I went to Spain I thought it would be exciting, like a cowboy movie, the goodies against the baddies. And it was exciting, in a way. But when I saw it close up, whichever side I visited, the Republicans or the Nationalists, the left or the right, I found the brutality was pretty much the same. I came across soldiers who'd been maimed and killed, civilians dead in the street, prisoners tried by kangaroo courts and executed. I realised life is cheap in war, and that we're never such fools as when we think we'll live for ever.'

Jago nodded thoughtfully. He would talk about the war from time to time with other men who'd served at the front, like Frank Tompkins, but this was the first time he could remember having such a conversation with a woman who seemed to understand it, even if only in part.

'There were many days in France when I didn't know whether I'd live to see the sun go down,' he said. 'Death was so random and so inevitable that it seemed pointless to care. But then suddenly one day it was all over, the guns had stopped, and everything was quiet. We could all go home and be normal again, if we could remember what normal was. I think every single day since then has been a bonus for me, another day of life instead of death.'

'You must think about those who didn't go home.'

'Every day. The men who'd been my friends through thick and thin, and the boys who arrived fresh at the front and were killed before I'd got to know their names. Now it feels like my duty to take each day as a gift and not to leave to tomorrow what I can do today.'

He was standing beside her, and now turned to face her.

'Look, there's something I want to tell you.'

'Yes?'

'I just want to say I've been wrong about you. I've known it for some time, but I want you to know it too. I jumped to conclusions about you, because you're American and a woman. But I of all people should have judged by the evidence, not by my own preconceptions, and the evidence has proved me wrong.'

He paused, trying to find the right words.

'What I'm trying to say is I'd like us to be friends.'

Dorothy examined his face for a few moments, then replied gently.

'I'd like us to be friends too, John.'

CHAPTER THIRTY

Edward stirred his cup of coffee and placed the spoon carefully back on the white china saucer. The cafe was tucked away in a side street off St Martin's Lane, not far from the Duke of York's Theatre, and on a Saturday morning it was quiet and private. Whenever he had the opportunity to steal away to the West End, this was one of his favourite places, a secret refuge.

'It's like a breath of fresh air for me, you know, coming up here,' he said to the young man sitting opposite him. 'There's something about that horrible office that stifles the soul. It's so . . .' He struggled to find the right word.

'Venal?' said the young man.

'Yes, that's about right. We spend all our time haggling over the price for some miserable printing job, always worried about whether we're making enough money to keep the business going. I suppose someone has to do that, but there's just nothing noble about it. It's all about money, nothing else. It was my father's world, but I shudder at the thought of spending the rest of my life in it. I sometimes wish he'd never sent me to that school. I think it gave me unrealistic aspirations, or even expectations.'

'It did rather train us to rule the world, didn't it?'

'Yes, and maybe that was all right for you, Stephen. You certainly seemed to sail through without a care in the world.'

Stephen gave a hearty, good-natured laugh. Edward flashed a weak smile back to his friend. Stephen was tall and broad-shouldered, with fair hair that was thick and wavy. His open expression and insouciant smile gave an impression of a man at ease with himself. He was wearing an old corduroy jacket over an open-necked blue shirt, but even in this simple attire he seemed effortlessly to exude good taste. Edward thought he looked the picture of confidence. Stephen was the sort of person who always landed on his feet.

'I envy you,' said Edward. 'You always seem so *bien dans ta peau*. Ever since I've known you I've sensed that you're happy to be who you are, and what you are seems to work. I constantly find myself forced to be what other people expect me to be instead of being who I am, and not really wanting to be who I am anyway.'

'My word, that sounds complicated. It's funny, you

know: when we used to do those plays at school I always thought you'd be the one who ended up on the stage for a living, not me.'

'That all seems a long time ago now. I thought everything was possible then, that I could be whoever I wanted to be. I suppose I didn't know what severe constraints a lack of means can place on one's aspirations. And now look at me: stuck in a grubby little office on the wrong side of town, printing leaflets and stationery for other grubby little businesses and watching my life slowly sliding down the drain.'

'You poor chap. It's odd how life works out, isn't it?'

'It's the problem with having a family business. I envy people who don't. At least they have some chance of choosing what to do.'

'Yes. I'm sorry about your father, by the way.'

'That's very kind of you, but don't worry. I think we're over the initial shock now. My mother seems to be coping well, as far as I can tell. I never know quite what's going on in her head, though. It's strange, isn't it? When you're little, you never think about why your parents married each other – they're just your parents, a fixed feature on the landscape. But for years now I've wondered what drew them together.'

'Maybe it was the war,' said Stephen. 'In my mother's case I've always suspected she took the first available man that came along who still had all his limbs. Sounds an awful thing to say, but there was quite a shortage of men by the time the war finished, wasn't there? I think there's a whole generation of us with mothers who would probably have preferred to marry some other chap, only he was dead.'

'I'm sure there's something in that,' said Edward. 'It's not the kind of thing one's mother talks about, though, is it? I must say she certainly hasn't been displaying many signs of grief. But that's a feature of their generation too, I suppose: stiff upper lip and all that.'

'Definitely,' said Stephen. 'But we should be grateful all the same. If they hadn't married our fathers, we wouldn't be here – or we might be here, but we'd be different fellows.' He slapped the table and laughed again, this time even louder than before. Edward glanced round the cafe. Stephen had always been an incorrigible extrovert, but Edward was nervous about attracting attention. He decided to change the subject.

'Anyway, how are things for you these days? Are you keeping in work?'

'Have to, dear boy,' said Stephen. 'If you're out of work in my profession for more than two weeks at a time they're liable to call you up. I've been lucky so far. We all thought we were finished last year when the theatres were closed down, of course, but once the government got its nerve back and allowed us to open, everything improved enormously.'

'But you're not opening during these air raids, are you?'

'No. A purely temporary problem, I hope. Since last weekend I believe the only theatre that's still open is the Criterion at Piccadilly Circus, but that's mainly underground, so it doesn't count. It's been taken over by the BBC for variety broadcasts, which is not exactly my line of work anyway. I'm hoping we'll all be able to open again as soon as this blows over.'

This time it was Edward who laughed.

'Ever the optimist, eh? Do you really think the war will end any time soon?'

'Haven't the faintest idea, old chap,' said Stephen. 'But it's a free country, as they say, so I can think what I like. The whole affair is so damnably miserable that I choose to think it will all be over by Christmas and we'll be frolicking on those broad, sunlit uplands that Churchill talked about in the summer. If I'm wrong, well, I won't have lost anything and I won't have done any harm to anyone else.'

'I wish I could take it all in my stride like that. In my brighter moments I know I would swap my world for yours at the drop of a hat. But then I think I worry too much to live the way you do.'

'But to take a more positive view of the situation, you do at least have what some people call a "proper" job. There must be some advantages in that. Having that elusive thing called a salary, for example.'

Edward sipped the last of his coffee and put the cup down. The cafe was beginning to fill with people now that lunchtime was approaching.

'I suppose I should be grateful,' he said, 'but sometimes I think I'd rather have nothing and be free. The people at work know I've only got the job because

I'm the boss's son. I don't think they take me seriously.'

'I don't think anyone's ever taken me seriously,' said Stephen. 'But then I don't take myself seriously either – nor anyone else for that matter.'

'That's all right for you, but you've had the freedom to choose. Don't you see? All my life my father has tried to control me, to make me be what he wanted me to be. I've had to live a lie.'

'I'm sorry, Edward, I shouldn't be so flippant. I do understand what you're saying.'

'He pushed me and pushed me, about as far as he could. There's only so much a man can take.'

Stephen could see the anguish in Edward's face. He leant forward and lightly touched Edward's arm.

'But he's gone now, Edward.'

Edward looked his friend in the eye and calmed his voice.

'Yes,' he said. 'He's gone. And now I'm going to start making my own choices.'

CHAPTER THIRTY-ONE

A cloud broke in the leaden sky. Soft spots of rain began to fall, marking their landing with dark splatters in the dust at their feet. The breeze picked up, rustling the leaves of the tree at their backs. Dorothy shivered and pulled her light jacket more closely round her. She decided it was time to break the silence between them.

'It's raining,' she said. 'I hope that little car of yours isn't going to get all wet inside.'

'No,' he said, 'the roof's up. I looked at the sky this morning and didn't want to chance it.'

'Is it time to eat yet? I'm getting hungry.'

'Yes. Would you like to go right now?'

'Sure. But you still haven't told me where we're going.'

'Don't worry, it's not far from here. It'll be a cultural

experience. Let's go quickly, before we get wet.'

They rose from the bench and left the churchyard, then walked briskly down the street together, Jago leading the way. Within a few minutes they came to a row of small shops, where he stopped. The shower was already fading, the clouds moving on.

'Here we are,' he said.

'This is it?'

'It's not quite the Savoy, I know, but it's a chance for you to enjoy some authentic London cuisine.'

On the pavement outside the shop there was a stall covered in metal trays, each of which contained a wriggling mass of eels. Dorothy gulped.

'We're not eating those, are we?'

'No,' said Jago. 'Although you can if you want to. What I had in mind was some nice old traditional pie and mash.'

'Mash? Where I come from, that's what farmers feed the cows with.'

'No, it's not as bad as that. Here it means mashed potato.'

'Right. So we're having a pie and some mashed potato. Is that it?'

'Not quite. They serve it with liquor.'

'Is that so? I should point out that I don't normally drink this early in the day, especially with a pie and potatoes.'

Jago laughed.

'I'm sorry. I keep forgetting we speak different

languages. This is not that kind of liquor. It's a green sauce that they make from the juice they get when they stew the eels.'

'The more I hear the worse it gets. I think I'd rather just have a stiff drink.'

'Come on, you can't visit this part of the world and not have pie and mash. Besides, it'll give you something colourful to write about. You'll love it.'

He opened the door, and Dorothy followed him in. Inside, the shop was a long rectangle no more than fifteen feet across, but the mirrors on its white-tiled walls made it feel bigger. To Dorothy's left, two aproned women stood behind a white marble counter, and the rest of the space was filled with fixed tables and straight-backed benches that reminded her of the church pews of her youth. She took in the sight.

'Are you sure? There's sawdust on the floor.'

Jago laughed again.

'That's to make it easier to clear up when the customers have been spitting eel bones out onto the floor.'

'You don't say? Well, that is something I don't think I've seen at the Savoy.'

Jago took her to the counter, where one of the women put a pie onto a white plate, added a big spoonful of mashed potato, then poured onto it a generous ladleful of pale green sauce, speckled with chopped parsley. Jago handed this to Dorothy, then got the same for himself and paid.

'Take a spoon and fork to eat it with,' he said. 'You

won't need a knife. And put on as much salt, pepper and vinegar as you like.'

'You've got to be joking,' said Dorothy.

After a few mouthfuls she seemed to be overcoming her initial aversion to the peculiar-looking liquor.

'Not bad,' she said.

'Is that the best you can say for it?'

'No. The best I can say for it is that it tastes better than it looks, which is probably just as well for you.'

'It's the staple diet round here, you know. Nutritious and filling, and cheap enough for people to afford when they've barely got two ha'pennies to rub together.'

'Well, as you say, it's a cultural experience.'

Jago took a mouthful of pie and chewed it reflectively.

'So, tell me about Boston.'

'What do you want to know?'

'Just what it's like. I've only been out of England once, remember, and that was to live in a hole in the ground in France. I imagine where you come from is very different to England.'

'Not so very different,' said Dorothy. 'Despite what you said, we speak the same language – more or less, I guess I should say – and we share a lot of history with you. I'm sure you know the War of Independence started in Boston, or just down the road. We've even got a Cambridge, just like you, right across the river, and a great university.'

'Harvard?'

'That's right. Named after an Englishman, of course, who studied at your Cambridge.'

'Did you study at Harvard?'

'Oh no.' She laughed in a way that suggested she'd been asked this question before. 'They don't admit women students at Harvard. I was at Radcliffe College: it was set up for girls who were smart enough to pass the Harvard entrance examination but not smart enough to be men.'

'So opportunities for women in the United States are not quite as expansive as you were suggesting when we met on Monday at the police station. Am I right?'

'You've got me there,' said Dorothy, with another gentle laugh.

She watched with curiosity as Jago applied vinegar to his pie.

'What was it like growing up in Boston?' he said.

'I guess I had quite a comfortable childhood. It was certainly a happy one. My dad was a writer, so we always had interesting people visiting the house, and he and my mom had a busy social life. When I was a little girl, probably only about four or five years old, I would see them going out to dinner somewhere in the evening, him in tails and a boiled shirt, and her in a pink satin gown and a wrap with ostrich feathers round her neck.'

'A boiled shirt?'

'Yes, one of those old white cotton shirt fronts. People used to put starch in them to make them stiff, and that meant they had to boil them.'

'Very grand. I don't move in such exalted circles.'

'It was very grand indeed. I used to think they looked like a prince and princess, and that one day I'd grow up and have a life as wonderful and exciting as theirs.'

'And did you?'

'Well, I grew up, but you know, it never works out quite like you imagined. By the time I was old enough to go out for a social life of my own, it was pretty dull. The highlight of the week would be going to the afternoon tea dances at Shepard's Colonial. They called it "afternoon tea concert and dansant".'

'Shepard's Colonial?'

'Shepard's was a big department store on Tremont Street, just across from Boston Common. It only closed about three years ago. It had a restaurant upstairs, called the Colonial. It was a stylish establishment, but tea dances didn't quite match up to the glittering balls I'd dreamt of.'

Dorothy took another mouthful of pie and mash. She had not followed Jago's advice about the salt and pepper and was finding the dish bland, so decided to take the plunge and scattered some across the plate. She drew the line, however, at vinegar. Jago watched her and smiled.

'What was your home like?' he said.

Dorothy found to her surprise that the salt and pepper had improved the flavour, so added some more. She finished her mouthful before speaking.

'We lived in a neighbourhood called Back Bay. It used to be a real bay, but they filled some of it in back in my grandfather's time and built a whole new district of the city, with fine houses and an art museum. We had what we call a row house. I think that's what you call a terraced house, but it was nothing like those little things I've seen around the back streets of West Ham. These are big brownstone places, four or five storeys high, and only pretty wealthy people could afford them.'

'So you're one of those rich young American women who travel the world looking for adventure?'

'Adventure, yes, but rich, no. My parents inherited the house, and some money too, but not a pile. My dad was very determined that I should get out into the world and fend for myself, because he knew he couldn't support me for ever. What he didn't know, of course, was that come 1929, they'd lose almost everything in the Wall Street Crash. They had to sell the house and move into an apartment. The only money I have now is what I earn. My dad never made much from his writing anyway, but he gave me everything he could in life. He brought me up to take an interest in the world beyond Boston, and to care about people who are suffering too, whether it's from poverty or from anything else. And here I am today, a war correspondent.'

'Is he still alive?'

'Yes, he is, and still writing, although not as much as he used to.'

'And your mother?'

'Her too. She's a remarkable woman. She was widowed quite young and had to bring up a child on her own, then she remarried and had me. She didn't work, of course, but she was very educated. The house was full of books for as far back as I can remember, and when I was a little girl I spent all my time reading. I guess that's why I always wanted to be a writer, like my dad.'

'So that part of the dream came true?'

'Yes. I can remember it so clearly. Our house was only a few blocks away from Boston Public Library. My mother used to take me there sometimes. It has a huge staircase, all finished in butterscotch-coloured marble that gets lighter and pinker as it goes up. I used to get a book from the Children's Room, then take it down and sit in one of the marble niches by the staircase reading it until she said it was time to go. Then sometimes we'd go to the Copley Plaza Hotel and get a chocolate ice-cream soda. That library was amazing: the kind of place writers call a temple of learning. I used to spend hours in there.'

'I used to spend hours in my local public library too, after I'd left school,' said Jago. 'It wasn't exactly a temple of learning, but it helped me to plug some of the gaps in my education. The trouble is, the older I've got, the more gaps I've found.'

'Me too.'

Dorothy cut a piece of pie off with her spoon and manoeuvred it carefully through the liquor. She lifted it halfway to her mouth, then stopped.

'I've just remembered. There was something else I wanted to ask you – a gap in my own education. In that newspaper report that I read about your medal I saw it had "MC" after your name. What does that mean?'

'It stands for Military Cross.'

'That's some other kind of medal, right?'

She put the food in her mouth and waited for Jago to answer.

'Yes,' he said. 'It's one I got in the last war.'

He wasn't sure whether to say more, but Dorothy was nodding with apparent interest, so he continued.

'Lots of people got them, and plenty of other people who should have got them didn't. Don't ask me why: I don't know. The whole thing seems to be just a lottery. And typically of this country, you can only get the MC if you're an officer. If you're other ranks you can do exactly the same thing but you'll only get the Military Medal. The MC is reserved for officers and gentlemen.'

'Ah, so you are an English gentleman, after all.'

He looked down at the spoon and fork in his hands and gave a bitter laugh.

'Not a bit of it. I'm what they called in those days "a temporary gentleman".'

'What's that supposed to mean?'

'It means they'd made me an officer but didn't want me to get ideas above my station. When the Great War started you could only be an officer if you were from the upper classes, had been to the right school, had the right accent. Just typical of the British class system. Eventually, so many of them were killed that demand for junior officers began to outstrip supply, so they decided to relax the requirements. That meant people like me, from places like this, who were in the ranks and hadn't made complete fools of themselves could be promoted.

I was selected and sent off to an officer cadet battalion, based in a Cambridge college if you please.'

'That sounds nice.'

'It just made the whole experience more bizarre, really. The maddest thing about it was they didn't just train you to command soldiers; they tried to teach you manners. Basically they were schooling you to be members of the ruling class, but obviously only for the duration. Once the war was over, provided you survived it, you'd be expected to resume the position in the lower orders that your birth and education had destined you for. There were lots like me: the top brass plucked us from the ranks because they thought we had leadership potential and could plug the gaps the Germans had made in the officer class. So I was promoted second lieutenant and expected to die pretty sharpish, but for the joy of it I was classified as a "temporary gentleman".'

'That's so British. I love it. It sounds straight out of Dickens.'

'I'm sure it doesn't happen in America. But quaint though it may seem, that's how I come to have "MC" after my name and not "MM". If I were to use it regularly, it would straight away mark me out as an officer. Many people do, because it's an aid to social advancement.'

'But you don't?'

'No, I don't.'

'Why's that?'

'Because I'm not interested in moving in higher circles. I may have learnt how to use the right knife and fork at a mess dinner, but that's not everything in life. No, that whole experience with the army left me feeling cut off from my roots. I wasn't sure who I was any more. Some of the others who got through the war used their rank to get into a profession or a good job in a big company, but now, looking back, I think that's maybe another reason why I chose to be a policeman: I wanted to walk the streets of West Ham again, not sit in a fancy office in Knightsbridge.'

'Sounds like the war was quite a watershed in your life.'

'That's exactly what it was. You know, everything before it seems like another country now – a place that I can try to visit but can never really return to. Wars leave many kinds of wounds. That was one of mine, but I got off lightly. A fifth of the men on that training course with me were killed before the war was over, and some who survived lost their minds. I got away with a bit of shrapnel and a blighted view of society.'

'So you were wounded too? Physically, I mean?'

'Yes, a lump of shrapnel caught me in the leg.'

'Can you tell me about it?'

'There's not much to tell. We were fighting near Cambrai about a year before the war ended, and I was hit. One of the lucky ones, I suppose. One of my men dragged me back and saved me from bleeding to death out in no man's land. I was taken to hospital and patched up. The padre said it was because of the grace of God that I'd survived, but I think it was just luck. I was unlucky to be hit, but lucky it didn't kill me. How could it be anything else? There's a thousand men out there, shells falling left, right and centre, and a million machine-gun bullets aimed at them. Some of them will be hit and some won't. It's just the luck of the draw.'

'What did you say to the padre?'

'Nothing. If that kind of thinking helped him to cope, that was fine with me. It just didn't mean anything to me.'

'So does that make you an atheist, or an agnostic?'

Jago pondered the question as he worked through his food. He was conscious that he was eating faster than Dorothy, probably because he had no love of cold mashed potato. He rested his cutlery on the plate and replied.

'I'm not sure. All I know is I don't believe there's someone up there all the time steering every bullet, deciding who gets shot and who doesn't. As far as I'm concerned it was just a lot of bullets and a lot of men, and they hit whoever they hit. Why? Do you believe in all that stuff?'

'I guess I'm not sure either,' said Dorothy, 'but for me it's a different kind of not sure. I don't believe God steers every bullet, any more than you do. That would make the universe some kind of weird play where he pulls all the strings and we're the puppets. But at the same time I think there has to be something more, some meaning behind it all. There has to be truth somewhere, otherwise the whole thing's just crazy.'

'Well, at least we're agreed on one thing: the world's a madhouse,' said Jago.

'Yes, and the inmates don't seem to have learnt from their mistakes. Your war was meant to be the war to end war, wasn't it?'

'Yes. Wishful thinking, if you ask me.'

'If you don't mind me asking, how did you cope with it?'

'With the war, you mean? I'm not sure that I did. Everyone had to find their own way of coping, if they could. My way was to try to keep it all in a box, to insulate myself from it. I kept telling myself the fighting, the killing, the mud, all of that was one world, but I had another world to live in too. I made sure I always had a book with me, so I could read and take myself off into that different world.'

'And what world was that?'

'You might think it strange, but I read anything I could get hold of by Jane Austen. I've always loved her writing, but it was mainly because her world was about as far away from the trenches as I could imagine. I used to read her whenever I could, to shut off what was happening around me, to stop it getting deeply into me.'

Dorothy laughed.

'That's an interesting choice. I've heard of soldiers in battle reading the Bible, but not Jane Austen. But then you're not that kind of person, are you?'

'No. I remember before we were shipped out to France someone came and gave us all a tiny New Testament to carry around with us. Probably thought we'd need it out there. I've still got mine, but I've never once read it all the way through. There's only one thing in the Bible that I can remember from school, and that's the only thing in it that makes sense to me.'

'What's that?'

'It's when Pontius Pilate says "What is truth?" That's something I can identify with. Right here and now, England, 1940: what is truth? A great question for a journalist too, don't you think? How much of what you write is true?'

Dorothy's face took on a serious expression.

'What are you getting at? I tell what I see. I report what's really happening. Some people never have a good word to say about newspapers and journalists, but I don't think that's fair. A free press is one of the few bastions of truth in this madhouse world we're talking about. I'm proud to be a journalist. Imagine what it would be like if we only ever heard what the politicians wanted us to know. Look at Nazi Germany or Soviet Russia. Without a free press there's no truth. I write the truth.'

'But to come back to my Roman politician, what is truth? What's the truth about what's happening here in the East End? If you read the papers or watch the newsreels, it's all about chirpy Cockneys emerging from their Anderson shelters for a thumbs up and a nice cup of tea. Is that true, or is that just what the government wants people to see?'

'You think that's all propaganda?'

'That's not what I'm saying. It's just something else I'm not sure about. The reality is that it's not as straightforward as that. Yes, most people are coping, much better than officialdom thought they would before the war. They really are getting on with life despite everything. But they're frightened too. There are people who are going to pieces, getting hysterical in the shelters, losing their grip. That's true too, but it doesn't get in the papers.'

'But that's just common sense, isn't it? I know I'm not allowed to report everything. The papers aren't allowed to show pictures of dead bodies. Your Defence Regulations say I can't write anything that could be useful to an enemy, but I wouldn't want to do that anyway. I want to write the truth as I see it. I look at the big picture here and I see that your people are coping with the bombing, are being amazingly resilient. Not everyone, but the majority, so that's the story I want to tell. My articles won't be a catalogue of every single person's experience or reactions, but that doesn't mean what I write isn't true. And the fact that there are contradictions doesn't mean there's no such thing as truth.'

Dorothy stopped, aware that people in the pie shop were looking at her. She lowered her voice and leant forward over the table.

'I'm sorry. I was getting on my soapbox there. It's just that I feel passionate about my job.'

'Don't apologise. I admire your commitment.'

'Now hold on. Are you doing that British thing where you say something but mean the opposite? I find that really annoying.'

He smiled.

'Not at all – I mean it. And that's the truth.'

Jago finished eating first and watched as Dorothy worked her way through the remainder of her meal.

'I'm impressed,' he said. 'You've eaten the lot. I hope it was worth the effort.'

'It was very nice,' she said, 'and very filling. And I don't think I can move yet. Maybe one day when this war is over you can come to the States and I'll take you to an American diner with American portions and get even with you.'

'We can sit for a while; there's no hurry. Tell me more about your family.'

'There's not a lot to say. I have a half-sister, as I think I told you. She's older than me, and wiser too. And I have one brother. He's younger than me, and maybe a little crazier even than me.'

'What does he do?'

'I'll tell you about him some other time.'

Jago was puzzled.

'Not now?'

'If you don't mind. I'd like you to know about him, but not just yet.'

'May I ask why?'

'Well, it's just that I think it might complicate things.'

'Things?'

'It's to do with that friendship we were talking about in the churchyard. I promise you I will tell you, but not right now.'

Jago was puzzled, but she seemed adamant. Whatever it was, he clearly wasn't going to get it out of her today.

She picked up her handbag from the bench beside her and began rummaging in an inside compartment.

'I'll show you some pictures.'

She pulled out a couple of small photographs and pushed one across the table to him.

'That's my brother. It was taken when he was about seventeen, so he's a bit older than that now, but he still looks much the same.'

Jago studied the picture. Judging by the pale grey tone of his hair it looked as though he was fair, and his face seemed to Jago to be recognisably American: square-jawed, confident and healthy. He was wearing some kind of sports clothing: probably something to do with baseball, he thought, although even if the photo had shown the colours he wouldn't have had a clue which team it represented.

'His name's Sam,' she said.

'And the other one's your sister?'

'Yes, here she is. This one's even older, but I carry it because it's my favourite. It speaks to me of her character.'

Dorothy pushed the other photo across. This one was a little larger and worn at the edges. Jago looked at it, then pulled it closer and stared at it. He opened his mouth as if to speak, but the words died on his lips.

'You OK?' said Dorothy. 'You look like you've seen a ghost.'

Jago could not take his eyes off the picture.

301

'It's not possible,' he said slowly. 'It can't be.'

He fell silent again. The picture showed a young woman in a nurse's uniform. She was standing by a table, but the picture gave no clue to the location. There was a certain formality about her pose, straight-backed and looking straight into the camera, which suggested she was on duty. But what captured his attention in an instant was the gentleness in her eyes and the shy, elusive smile on her lips. It was a smile that he knew, a smile that he could still see when he closed his eyes.

'I don't know what to say,' he murmured. 'I know this face.'

'You know my sister?' said Dorothy. 'You know Eleanor?'

Jago gasped.

'I knew an Eleanor: Eleanor Warren. She was your sister?'

'That's the one,' said Dorothy. 'From my mother's first marriage. Like I said, my half-sister.'

She wasn't even sure that he had heard her. He was gazing intently at the frail image in his hand, slowly lowering it back towards the table. Dorothy said nothing. She could see that his mind was somewhere else, somewhere distant.

CHAPTER THIRTY-TWO

It was after three o'clock by the time they were back out on the street. Dorothy was wary of probing too deeply into the memory the photograph had triggered in Jago's mind. Their conversation had faltered, and she had suggested they might leave. He had quietly concurred.

They stood on the pavement outside the churchyard gate. The sky was clouding over again, and she thought she could smell a thunderstorm brewing in the warm afternoon air. She decided to break the uneasy silence that had descended on them.

'Where to next, then?' she said.

Jago came to himself, as if snapping out of whatever thoughts had been preoccupying him. He looked up at the sky, his head on one side, assessing the weather prospects. When he spoke, Dorothy was pleased to hear his usual bright tone return.

'We could go for a little drive, if you like,' he said, 'see anything else that might interest you in the area. I've got the car just down the road, near the station.'

'The local beauty spots? I've heard Beckton gasworks is very striking.'

He laughed.

'Yes, very popular with the tourists, although we don't get many these days.'

'Come, come! Did you not have some very distinguished visitors only yesterday?'

'Who's that?'

'The King and Queen, of course. They were right here in West Ham yesterday afternoon, seeing the sights.'

'Ah, yes. I heard about it, but I was out and about elsewhere. I don't think they would have needed me, in any case.'

'I was there.'

'Really?'

'Don't sound so surprised. We journalists get summoned to these occasions. When there's some important show like that on, it's the kind of thing your Ministry of Information wants the world to know about, so they round us all up and let us see what's happening. It was meant to be a morale-booster, of course. The King and Queen drove down here after lunch and walked about seeing the bomb damage and meeting some of the people who'd been affected by it.'

'What sort of reception did they get?'

'The crowd loved it, as far as I could tell. Plenty of cheering and so forth. But it may have been a selected audience. I don't know. At any rate, I guess your police colleagues would make sure any bad guys were kept out of sight, right?'

'I expect so. But it won't have done the royals any harm to show their faces round here. There's been some resentment that the bombs are all falling over this way.'

'But they had one land on Buckingham Palace yesterday morning, just before they came over.'

'Yes, but it's hardly the same, is it? Losing a room or two isn't exactly going to leave them homeless.'

'Sure, but it does kind of make them one with the people, doesn't it? All facing the same dangers?'

'Yes, I've no doubt most people here will appreciate that. I think they like the fact that the King and Queen haven't cut and run – haven't fled the country for somewhere safer like Canada. They're staying here to stick it out with the rest of us. Far better for them to take a stroll round the streets of West Ham than to stay at home. It sends a message that we're all in it together, even if that's not how everyone thinks.'

'Well, when all's said and done it makes a great story from my point of view. I'll be writing it up this evening. First, though, I have to attend a press briefing.'

'Where's that?'

'At the Savoy.'

'Is that normal?'

305

'Oh yes. There are so many of us staying there, you see. That hotel's like home from home for the American press. It'll be someone from the Ministry of Information telling all the foreign journalists how the war's going – from your government's point of view, of course.'

'Of course. I hope they tell you something you don't already know.'

Jago was about to ask her more about the briefing, but stopped.

'Excuse me, but there's someone over there that I know. I need to have a quick word with them.'

Before she could answer, he was away, dodging round the traffic as he crossed to the opposite side of the road. Dorothy looked to the point where he was heading and saw a woman in her forties, wearing a brown coat, walking slowly along the pavement. A young man in dark working clothes and cap was sauntering alongside her and appeared to be with her. Dorothy waited, uncertain whether she should follow him if it was to be a private conversation.

Jago strode up to the couple, who stopped when they saw him.

'Mrs Carson,' he said, 'I didn't expect to bump into you. How are you doing now?'

'Inspector Jago, how nice to see you. Not so bad, thank you. You remember my son Robert?'

Jago noticed that the young man was making no show of acknowledging him, but rather stood with his hands in his pockets and an expression on his face that suggested defiance.

'Yes, I do,' said Jago, looking him in the eye. 'In fact there's one or two things I'd like to ask you, young man.'

'Please yourself.'

'When I last saw you I was investigating the death of Mr Charles Villiers and I asked you if you knew him.'

'So?'

'You said you'd never heard of him.'

Robert said nothing.

'But since then I've discovered that you appeared at the magistrates' court in January and Mr Villiers was on the bench. He found you guilty of assault and fined you five pounds. So how is it you've never heard of him?'

'I must have forgotten, mustn't I? It must have slipped my mind.'

'And I also understand you lost your job as a result. Did that slip your mind too?'

Robert shifted awkwardly from one foot to another, his head down. Then he raised his chin and met Jago's gaze.

'All right, I'll be straight with you. I did know who you were talking about and I was in court, but that doesn't mean I've got anything to do with what happened to him last week.'

'If that's so, why did you lie to me about knowing him?'

'You could call it a matter of principle.'

'What's that supposed to mean?'

'It means I've got certain political convictions that don't go down well with the people who run this country. You know as well as I do that there's a political struggle going on here and all over the world, and it will only end when we have a proper communist society. In the meantime, I'm on one side and you're on the other. You've probably got a file on me down at your police station already. You and the rest of the establishment are what's keeping the working class oppressed, so I make it a rule never to tell your sort anything. If you want to know something, you can find it out for yourselves. I'm not going to collaborate with the ruling class. One day things'll change in this country, and then we'll have real justice, but until then I'm having none of it.'

'No one is above the law,' said Jago. 'A man has been murdered, and whatever your politics, I'll not have you obstructing my enquiries.'

Robert softened his stare a little and lowered his voice.

'I'm not a murderer. I don't know who killed that man, but I can tell you this. You should read *The Communist Manifesto*. Karl Marx said the fall of the bourgeoisie and the victory of the proletariat are both inevitable. If you want to know who the bourgeoisie are, it's people like that Villiers: they don't come any more bourgeois than him. It's a law of history that his kind will be swept away, exterminated. It wasn't me who killed him. It was the inevitable historical process of the class struggle.'

Mrs Carson stepped forward, putting herself almost between them.

'You mustn't mind how he carries on, Inspector. He's always been one for ideas and long words. Can't think where he gets it from. He doesn't mean any harm, though.'

Robert turned away in disgust, then leant against the brickwork between two shop fronts, watching them as his mother continued talking.

'He's always been a good boy, you know. And that trouble he had at work, that was just his temper. He's always had a bit of a temper on him. But he's a good boy . . . a good boy.'

She seemed to run out of steam, gave a sigh, and looked helplessly at Jago.

'Are you sure you're all right, Mrs Carson,' he said. 'You look rather tired. You haven't gone back to work too soon, have you?'

'I can't afford to be off work for too long, especially the way things are at the press.'

'The way what things are?'

'Don't you know? I've heard that Mrs Villiers is selling up, getting rid of the whole business. If that happens, I'll be out of a job.'

CHAPTER THIRTY-THREE

Jago remembered that he had left Dorothy behind in his rush to intercept Irene and Robert Carson. He twisted round and saw her still standing, waiting, on the other side of the street. He bade a hurried goodbye to Mrs Carson and dashed back across the road.

'I'm terribly sorry to leave you there,' he said. 'Those two people are connected to the case I'm investigating, and I couldn't let the opportunity slip.'

'That's fine,' said Dorothy. 'I was just enjoying watching the world go by. Shall we go for that little drive now?'

'Yes, but would you mind if we took a slight detour first? That woman I was talking to told me something that came as a bit of a surprise and I need to follow it up. If we fetch the car it won't take long, then we can go and find something interesting for you to see. Maybe All Saints', that old parish church I was telling you about.'

'Sure, no problem.'

'OK, let's go, then.'

They walked briskly back to where Jago had left the car. He took a key from his pocket and unlocked the front passenger door so that Dorothy could get in.

'When you're in, could you do me a small favour and reach across and open the driver's door?'

Dorothy obliged, and he got in behind the wheel.

'Is your lock broken?' she said.

'No, the driver's door doesn't have a lock.'

'That's a little unusual, isn't it?'

'Just a quirk. The manufacturers decided to save a bit of money by using the doors from another model, but they wanted to hang them the other way round, so the driver's door ended up on the passenger side. Hence that's where the lock is.'

'British joke?'

'No, British engineering.'

'How quaint. You would have been better off with my old car, the first one I ever owned. It was a Stutz Bearcat, 1912 model. It had no doors at all. Problem solved.'

'That's America for you: the land of solutions.'

'Mind you, it had no roof either. But they breed us tough over there.'

'Tough, but understanding and patient too?'

She smiled at him.

'Of course. Drive on, Inspector.'

Only a few minutes later they pulled up outside the Villiers family home in Forest Gate.

'I'll have to ask you to stay outside in the car,' said Jago. 'I'm going to be interviewing the woman who lives here about something connected with her husband's murder, so it wouldn't do to have a journalist with me – even a sympathetic American lady journalist.'

'Understanding and patient, that's me,' said Dorothy. 'I'll sit here and start thinking out my story about the King rallying the spirits of his loyal subjects. Just don't be too long, that's all.'

Jago hauled himself out of the car and knocked on Muriel Villiers' front door. He heard footsteps approaching, then the click of the catch, and the door opened. Before him stood Edward Villiers.

'Good afternoon, Mr Villiers. May I come in?'

'Of course,' said Edward.

Jago entered the familiar hallway.

'I was hoping to see your mother. Is she in?'

'No, I'm afraid she isn't,' said Edward.

'Do you know when she'll be back?'

'I'm very sorry, but I don't. In fact, I'd go so far as to say that not only do I not know when she'll be back, I don't know whether she'll *be* back.'

'What do you mean? Has something happened?'

'Well, if I were appearing in a B movie, the phrase I would

probably use is that she appears to have done a bunk.'

'What, run away? How do you know?'

'I can't be certain, of course, but I got home about an hour ago – I've been out in London all day – and noticed there was an unaccustomed mess in various parts of the house. It wasn't as though we'd been burgled, but certain things weren't in the right place. I had been expecting to find my mother in, as she normally is on a Saturday afternoon, but when I called out there was no answer. I went upstairs and looked into her bedroom, and noticed an empty suitcase on the bed. It was one of a matching pair my parents had, and when I checked for the other one, it was missing. The wardrobe door was open, and there was an empty hanger lying on the floor.'

'Let me have a look.'

Jago followed Edward up the stairs and into the main bedroom at the front of the house. The scene was as Edward had described it. He scratched the back of his head as he took in the details.

'It certainly suggests a sudden departure.'

'Yes,' said Edward. 'I mean it all looks rather like a set for a play – all the signs you'd expect to see in such a situation.'

'She hadn't mentioned any plans to go away? To visit anyone?'

'No, and I'm sure she would have told me if she were.'

'Had she said or done anything recently to suggest she might want to leave?'

'No. She has been rather tense recently, on edge, but this is a complete surprise to me.'

'It's been suggested to me that your mother was planning to sell the business. Is that true?'

'Sell the business? There's been no formal announcement, but I do believe she's been considering disposing of it, yes.'

'Let's go downstairs,' said Jago.

Back in the hallway, he tried to discern any sign of concern in Edward's face, but could find none.

'Do you have any reason to be worried about your mother's safety?'

'No, I don't think so. There's nothing that I'm aware of.'

'If she has left, who would she go to?'

'My mother doesn't have friends, Inspector. She didn't have an easy life with my father, as you know, and friends were not something he encouraged. There's only one person I think she was close to, and that's my uncle, Major Villiers.'

Jago glanced across the hallway and saw a telephone on a small table.

'Do you have a telephone number for your uncle?'

'Yes,' said Edward. He opened the address book lying on the table and handed it to him.

Jago dialled the operator and asked for the number. He stared at the wall, tapping his foot on the floor while he waited. Eventually the operator told him the line was engaged. He thanked her and put the phone down, then turned back to Edward.

'Right,' he said. 'Thank you for your assistance. I'd be grateful if you'd let me know if you hear from your mother.'

'Of course, Inspector.'

'In that case, I'll bid you good day.'

Jago opened the front door and strode out towards the car.

Edward stood in the doorway and watched him go, then closed the door and walked slowly back into the living room. He mixed himself a pink gin and smiled.

CHAPTER THIRTY-FOUR

When Jago reached the car, he found Dorothy still sitting in the front seat, writing in a notebook with a silver-coloured pen. She put both into her handbag as he got in beside her.

'I'm sorry,' he said, 'but there's someone else I need to see urgently.'

'Business or pleasure?'

'I'll tell you on the way.'

He started the car and pulled away sharply, jolting Dorothy back in her seat.

'My, you are in a hurry,' she said. 'Does this mean you've decided it's time to show me how fast this thing can go?'

'No, but we may need to go a little faster than usual.'

316

'What's the speed limit around here?'

'There's no limit once we get out of the built-up area, but here in the town there is: thirty miles an hour, and twenty at night now that we have the blackout.'

'Are you allowed to break it?'

'On police business, yes, I am.'

'How exciting. Where are we going?'

'A little town called Brentwood. It's in Essex, the same as here, but further out into the country, about fifteen miles away. Are you sure you don't mind coming with me? It's not exactly what we planned.'

'I'd like to come along for the ride. I've never been to Brentwood, so it's a chance to see another part of the country.'

'OK, and afterwards I'll drive you back to the Savoy. I don't want you to miss your press briefing.'

He drove a short distance west, heading back towards Stratford, then turned right onto Leytonstone Road. The road that stretched ahead of them was long and straight, and lined with small shops and terraced houses. It was almost half past four, but there were still plenty of people out shopping. A couple of times Jago had to brake sharply when pedestrians darted across the road in front of him.

'This isn't very fast,' said Dorothy.

'It's always a bit busy here on a Saturday afternoon, but we're going to head north towards the A12, the Eastern Avenue. It's one of our new arterial roads – only opened about fifteen years ago, although it mainly follows the old Roman road from London to Colchester.'

'Not so new, then, really: more like getting round to improving things after nineteen hundred years?'

'I suppose so. The wheels of government turn slowly here sometimes.'

'But yours turn a bit faster, yes?'

'Once we get onto the A12 they will.'

Jago forced his way through the slow Leytonstone traffic, and eventually they joined the smooth and spacious new road. It seemed almost deserted after the crowded High Road, and he pushed up the speed as rapidly as the car would bear. Dorothy looked across at the speedometer in the middle of the dashboard: the needle was nudging seventy miles an hour. The combined effect of the roaring engine and the flapping fabric roof was already making conversation difficult.

'Sorry about the noise,' Jago shouted.

Dorothy replied at similar volume, undaunted.

'So what's happening in Brentwood?'

'It's to do with the case I'm working on. I told you it was a murder, didn't I?'

'Yes. How's it going?'

'One step forwards, two steps back. We've got two murders now, and I've just heard that the first victim's wife has disappeared too. The only place her son thought she might be was at her brother-in-law's in Brentwood, and when I phoned just now the number was engaged. That means someone's in, and I'm hoping I might catch her there, otherwise I've no idea where to look.'

'OK, no more questions till we get there.'

Jago gripped the wheel tightly to keep the car under control as they hurtled eastwards through the Essex suburbs. Soon the housing began to thin out and they broke into open countryside.

'Are those guns?' said Dorothy, looking out to her left. Jago glanced over her shoulder through the small side-screen window. The road was flanked by farmland, and in the distance there was a patch of higher ground. On top of it he could make out a clutch of eight silhouettes like unsharpened pencils pointing up at the sky.

'That'll be the Chadwell Heath anti-aircraft battery,' he said. 'Part of the London defences. They're supposed to stop the Luftwaffe getting through to where I live. Not a total success so far, I'd say.'

'Why's that?'

'Looking for a very small target in a very big sky, I suppose. What young Cradock would probably call trying to shoot a needle in a haystack. In the last war we reckoned the average was thirty thousand shells to one hit, so we can only hope they're more efficient than that now.'

'Is it worth the effort?'

'They don't seem to hit many planes, but people say if the guns are firing it forces the bombers to stay higher, so they can't drop their bombs so accurately. Not that that's much consolation if one lands on you, of course.'

The car rattled on, and the farmland gave way to the

urban landscape of Romford. Jago was worried. What if Mrs Villiers wasn't there? Or what if she'd been there when he phoned but had already gone? People couldn't move around as easily as they used to these days, but even so, if these two birds had flown it would be a job and a half to catch them.

He was relieved to see the houses come to an end again, with open fields and woods on both sides of the road. They came to a junction.

'This is Gallows Corner,' he said.

'Named for the obvious reason?' said Dorothy.

'Yes, indeed: this is where we used to hang the murderers.'

'And if you find one in Brentwood?'

'Then it'll be the noose, the same as ever. The only difference is that it won't be here on the corner; the public will have to be satisfied with reading about it in the newspapers.'

'Ah, the newspapers again. Where would we be without them?'

Jago parked the car outside the familiar house and strode up the path to the front door. He checked his watch: it was a quarter past five. His mind was running through the possible explanations that Mrs Villiers might produce for her sudden departure. He was braced for a confrontation with the major. An indistinguishable shape appeared through the obscured glass, and then the door opened.

The figure before him was not the one he was looking for.

'Mrs Wilson,' he said. 'Detective Inspector Jago. You may recall I visited Major Villiers earlier in the week.'

'Of course, Inspector. I recognise you. Do come in.'

'Thank you, Mrs Wilson, but I won't beat about the bush: I need to speak to Major Villiers urgently. Can you fetch him, please?'

Mrs Wilson put on a sympathetic face.

'I'm very sorry, Inspector, but he's not here. He left in the car some time ago, with his sister-in-law. I do hope you haven't come far.'

CHAPTER THIRTY-FIVE

Billy sauntered out of Charing Cross Tube station and headed for the Victoria Embankment. The war had made a few changes in his life, and one was that the government had adjusted shop opening hours, so that now they had to stay open till seven o'clock in the evening on Saturdays. Today, though, he'd managed to get an hour off, which he felt was a bit of an achievement. For some reason Rob seemed to have it easier in the docks. Billy would have thought they'd have to work harder down there, but he had the impression his brother got time off whenever he wanted it. Today, for example, he'd got the whole day off. Probably something to do with the unions, he thought. Anyway, Billy was grateful for his hour, because it meant he had a little time to see the sights. He hadn't often been up to the West End, except for the odd day out in the school holidays when he was a boy. Then he and Rob would come and spend all day wandering round the city, seeing the famous landmarks and watching the boats go by on the river.

The sign on the street he was walking down said Villiers Street. That's a coincidence, he thought: that was the name of the bloke Mum worked for – the one who was sitting there dead in that van. Not likely to have been named after him, though, any more than the street Billy knew off Beckton Road called Carson Road was named after himself. The only connection was that Villiers Street looked like a rich street, and Carson Road definitely wasn't.

At the end of the street he found a short flight of steps leading to the Embankment Gardens. He went in, and stopped to take a look at a grand stone arch, with every possible kind of ornate decoration, that looked as though it had been there for hundreds of years. He paused in front of a small plaque. It said this was the watergate that used to stand on the north bank of the Thames. The river was now more than a hundred yards away, because the Victorians had reclaimed the land by some clever engineering. The plaque said the gate was built in 1626 for George Villiers, first Duke of Buckingham. So that was the Villiers the street was named after, thought Billy. He wondered whether Charles Villiers, the one his mum used to clean for, was some relation, a descendant perhaps. He'd certainly been one for putting on airs and graces, by all accounts, and liked to act superior to other people.

Maybe there was something in all that stuff Rob was saying at the pub, he thought. Some people are born rich and stay rich, while everyone else is born poor and stays poor. He'd been brought up by his mum and dad to know his place and respect his betters, but maybe that was just old-fashioned nonsense. Maybe Rob was right, and the world was going to change.

He strolled through the gardens, imagining he owned them. Yes, and pigs might fly, he thought, but then remembered the words Rob was always using: 'Come the revolution'. The way he talked about it, when that happened everything would change. It sounded like heaven on earth. Rob might be right, but today didn't look like a day for that kind of thing. He didn't know much about revolutions, but he knew they happened in places like France and Russia, not in England.

He emerged from the gardens onto the Embankment and crossed the road to the parapet that ran along the side of the river. He leant on the cool stone wall and studied the whirls and eddies in the water below. The river looked as though it was more or less at high tide. The water was a dirty brown colour, with a greasy sheen, and here and there bits of wood and other debris floated by. An unpleasant smell of rotten eggs came off it, as if the water itself were putrid. Surely no fish would survive in a river like this, he thought. People talked about the Thames as something majestic, but actually it was filthy.

To his left he could see the nine arches of Waterloo Bridge, and in the distance a glimpse of the dome of St Paul's rising above the trees that lined the Embankment. He knew the Waterloo crossing was known as 'jumpers' bridge', but he thought you'd have to be pretty desperate to choose jumping into this disgusting water as a way of ending your life. Then he remembered his mum. In an instant he felt guilty: it wasn't right to treat something like that lightly, even if it was only inside your own head. He knew now that life could push the best of people, even someone like his mum, to the edge and even over it.

He was due to meet Rob here soon, but there was time to take a little walk. He set off towards the bridge, passing Cleopatra's Needle. The weathered granite column, covered in baffling Egyptian hieroglyphics, looked completely out of place here on the Thames Embankment in the heart of London – such an ancient relic in such a modern setting. Passing under the bridge he came to Waterloo Pier, the floating police station used by the river police, moored at the side of the river. It consisted of a row of cheap-looking huts mounted on some kind of pontoon. Positioned here below the magnificent eighteenth-century river frontage of Somerset House, it seemed to Billy to look like an obedient dog lying at the feet of its master.

He walked almost as far as HMS *President*, the old Great War ship that was permanently moored here now and used by the navy for training. He spent a while watching battered-looking tugboats towing barges quietly downstream on the far side of the river, then crossed the road to sit on an empty bench on the pavement. Across the river he could see a row of dilapidated old warehouses and wharves, and then the solemn splendour of the Oxo Tower, rising like a twentieth-century rival to Cleopatra's Needle in its uncompromisingly modern art deco style.

Billy ran his eye up and down the solid-looking tower for a moment and wondered what it must have cost to build it and how much money a company like that must have to be able to afford it. That was probably what Rob meant when he talked about the bastions of capitalism, he thought. The things he came out with: anyone would think he'd swallowed a dictionary.

He pulled the folded newspaper out of his jacket pocket. Rob had given it to him this morning and told him to read it before they met up. It was the one Rob was always reading: the *Daily Worker*, yesterday's edition. The front page was all about the Communist Party campaigning for better air-raid shelters for Londoners, and there was a report that on Wednesday evening the staff at Holborn Tube station had abandoned their rule of turning away people who wanted to shelter in the station. It said two thousand people had turned up with blankets and pillows and spent the night there, and the transport staff had even provided emergency chemical toilets for them. He wondered how many: that was a lot of people to share a toilet. Even so, it showed Rob was right. He'd been going on about it for weeks, saying the government ought to let people shelter in the Tube, and now they'd done it. That was probably why he wanted Billy to read it.

Talking of Rob, he thought, it was time to get back to the Embankment Gardens: that was where they were supposed to be meeting. He didn't know what they were going to do together, but with Rob it was bound to be fun. As long as they didn't get caught out in a raid, of course.

CHAPTER THIRTY-SIX

Dorothy walked slowly down the wide staircase. After chasing round Essex in Jago's noisy car she had been glad to return to the opulent tranquillity of the Savoy Hotel in time for a wash and to change her clothes. Compared with some of the accommodation she had experienced on her foreign assignments, the Savoy gave no grounds for complaint. Once you were through the front door, she thought, if it weren't for the sound of the sirens and the occasional distant thud of a bomb, you would hardly know there was a war on. This no doubt explained the presence of so many obviously wealthy people who had chosen to make it their temporary home, some of whom she now knew by sight. Even here, though, the intensity of the past week's bombing seemed to have left many guests feeling vulnerable, especially those on the upper floors. She had witnessed the nightly migration of the well-to-do down to the basement, where guests could shelter in bomb-proof, gas-proof accommodation. Some of them probably reckoned they were having a hard time of it, she thought, obliged to spend the night on camp beds and mattresses, but the freshly laundered bed linen suggested the hotel was not letting its standards slip.

Jago had kept his word and returned her in good time for the press briefing. The elegant meeting room in which it was held had been laid out with comfortably upholstered chairs, and the foreign press corps was well represented, with a particularly large contingent of Americans. Many of them were familiar faces, and some were old and valued friends. She had worked with them in all the hotspots of Europe over the last six years, and now they were together again, sharing old stories and creating new ones.

The briefing was more or less as she had expected it to be: a confident review of how the war was progressing, laced with illustrative stories and facts but strictly controlled. The man from the Ministry of Information did his best, providing figures for the recent air raids, claims of aircraft lost and enemy planes shot down, descriptions of the bombing damage and the morale of the population, but she could not help feeling throughout his talk that there was another story he was not telling. This was no surprise, of course, and nothing new. It was the government's job to control the news, and hers to read between the lines.

Dorothy finished working on her article just before eight o'clock in the evening and decided to wander down to the hotel's American Bar for a drink. It was the focus of her expatriate colleagues' social life, so she was sure to be able to spend a pleasant hour or so there with them. Before she got there, however, the quiet of the corridor was broken by the sound of the air-raid alert. This part of London had experienced nothing like the bombing of the East End yet, but she felt obliged to go down to the shelter. No doubt she would find some of her friends there, and there was a bar quite close to it. She could also pick up an evening paper in the front hall on the way down.

She skipped lightly down the staircase, but as she approached the ground floor she heard something odd.

It was not a sound she had heard before in the hotel. First a single sharp cry reached her, then a harsh clamour of voices. It sounded like a mob of people all talking animatedly at the same time, but it wasn't like the sound of lively chatter at a party. There was something menacing about it, something angry. It was coming from the front hall. She continued to the bottom of the stairs and positioned herself where she could see what was happening. By now some of her fellow journalists had joined her, drawn, no doubt, by the noise, as she had been.

An extraordinary commotion was taking place just inside the hotel's revolving entrance doors. Two things surprised her immediately. The first was the appearance of the people. At this time of the evening she was accustomed to seeing men in evening dress and women in fine gowns and fur stoles making their way into or out of the hotel. But the motley crew she could see across the front hall were dressed in the drab, shabby clothes of the working people she had seen all over the East End. The second was their behaviour. It wasn't the self-possessed, cultured manner of the rich. They were jostling and elbowing their way into the hotel, past the top-hatted doorman, shouting and cursing like costermongers fighting over a pitch.

Dorothy counted several dozen men and women at the heart of the rumpus. Some of the women were carrying blankets and had small children in tow; one or two even had babies in their arms. Once the crowd had established their presence in the front hall, a few began to unfurl banners. It seemed to be some kind of organised protest. She could see that the hotel staff manning the reception desk looked nervous, and the three or four of their colleagues who were exposed on the public side of the desk were looking about anxiously as if in search of help.

One man stepped forward from the mob and began to address the room. His voice had the nasal rasp of the East End accent, which she still found difficult at times, but he seemed to be saying something about shelter –

that the sirens had sounded, these people needed shelter, and the hotel had shelters, so they must be allowed in. This had the makings of an interesting confrontation, thought Dorothy, since as far as she knew, people with shelters were legally obliged to take in visitors during an air raid. She supposed it might depend on whether these people constituted visitors.

From the corner of her eye she saw a few police constables quietly entering from the street. Someone must have called them. So far they were simply watching, not intervening. Another figure joined the proceedings: a tall man in a black tailcoat, with the bearing and manner of a person in charge. Someone from the hotel management, she assumed. He spoke to the leader of the group, but Dorothy was too far away to hear what he was saying. She began to move closer, but before she could hear any more the incident seemed to be over as quickly as it had begun. The manager type was leading the mob away in the direction of the stairs to the basement floors. She slipped across the lobby and stopped one of the staff.

'What did he say to them?' she said.

'I think he invited them to come and have a cup of tea,' said the young man and walked away.

Typical of these British, she thought: *you think there's going to be a riot, but they have a cup of tea instead*. The fascinating story she had begun composing in her head seemed to have evaporated before her eyes. She watched the crowd of protesters ambling towards the stairs. Her eye was caught by the back view of one young man who was walking with an exaggerated swagger. Beside him was an even younger man, a boy really, who was casting an anxious glance around the hall, as if fearful that there might yet be some rough handling by the staff or the police. But they had already gone. His swaggering companion turned round to chivvy him along. She saw his face, and was surprised to realise that she had seen him before.

CHAPTER THIRTY-SEVEN

It had rained overnight, and the pavement was still damp. The air had the fresh smell of a September morning, the warmth of summer slipping away and leaving only the prospect of harsher days to come. As Jago stepped out of his house and walked to his car, he felt tired. He had been up half the night in his Anderson shelter, uncomfortable and wishing he were in his own bed. He wondered what it would be like if the raids were still going on when the cold weather came: those shelters would be freezing.

It was Sunday, but it was set to be another working day. Part of his waking hours in the night had been spent turning over in his mind why Muriel Villiers should have taken it into her head to run away. He needed to track her down and find out exactly what was going on. He had phoned the station this morning and found Cradock already at work. He was pleased: it showed initiative. He had told Cradock to contact the neighbouring constabularies in the first instance and ask them to look out for Muriel and Arthur. They had taken Arthur's car, and the petrol rationing would prevent them travelling too far afield, so they were most likely to be in one of those areas.

Jago would have to go in to the station himself later, but first he needed to pay some calls on a few ARP wardens. He also wanted to speak to Edward Villiers again. His discovery of Muriel's mysterious departure yesterday had prevented him from asking Edward some important questions, but he needed the answers. He intended to get them today.

He arrived at the Villiers' house well after eleven o'clock in the morning – late enough, he imagined, for a man like Edward to be up and about on a Sunday. He had assumed Edward did not attend church: the young man hadn't struck him as the type.

He knocked at the front door, and it was opened by Edward. He was wearing a silk dressing gown and smoking a cigarette, and did not look as though he had been out of bed for long.

'Good morning, Inspector,' he said. 'I didn't expect to see you again so soon.'

'Good morning, Mr Villiers. Pardon me for disturbing you, but I just wanted to bring you up to date with one or two matters in connection with your father's death. It won't take long.'

Edward showed him into the drawing room.

'Take a seat, Detective Inspector. You have my undivided attention.'

'Thank you, but I prefer to stand,' said Jago. 'First I must ask whether you've heard anything more about the whereabouts of your mother. I checked at your uncle's house yesterday, and Mrs Wilson the housekeeper told me that she and your uncle had left together.'

Edward gave a low whistle and looked surprised.

'Well I never. The saucy devils,' he said. 'Do you think they've run off together?'

'All I know is what Mrs Wilson told me.'

'She phoned me last night, you know. My mother, that is. She said she wanted to let me know she was safe, but when I asked her where she was she wouldn't tell me. I did actually ask her if she was with my uncle, and she said no. But she sounded flustered, so my guess is she wasn't telling me the whole truth. I wonder what they see in each other.'

Edward was moving around the room as he spoke. It struck Jago that while the young man's voice sounded calm and self-controlled, his movements suggested that he was on edge.

'I'm anxious to find your mother,' said Jago.

'I'm sure you are,' said Edward. 'It doesn't look very good for her to disappear with her brother-in-law days

336

after her husband is murdered. But there's nothing more I can tell you about it. Her disappearance is every bit as much of a surprise to me as it is to you.'

Jago was not sure what to make of this comment. He did not trust the elegantly attired young man who stood before him.

'I have another question for you, Mr Villiers.'

Edward made a show of giving him his full attention. 'Yes?'

'You once said that you thought your father might have been engaged in what you called "informal enterprise", and you suggested he might have had "murky underworld connections".'

'And?'

'We have reason to believe you were right.'

'How intriguing. So the old man wasn't as straight as a die after all.'

'We believe he may have been involved in some unlawful activities with a man called Frederick Cooper. Do you know him?'

'No, I don't believe I do.'

'Think carefully, Mr Villiers. This is a very serious matter.'

'I'm sure it is, Inspector, but I'm really sure I don't know anyone of that name. Who is this Cooper?'

'The property that your father visited on the night he was killed belonged to Frederick Cooper. As far as we know, Cooper would have been the last person to see your father alive.'

'All very interesting, but what does this have to do with me?'

'We also have evidence that Cooper was taking money from people to ensure they could evade conscription into the armed forces, and that he took money from your father. This was about a month ago, and when we first met, you told me you'd registered for military service a month or so ago but had not been called up.'

Edward's expression had changed. He was now beginning to look wary. He lit a second cigarette as Jago continued.

'We know that people were paying Cooper to make sure their call-up papers were lost in the system. Did your father pay him to do that for you?'

Edward thought for a few moments, then stubbed the cigarette out firmly in an ashtray.

'All right, Inspector, I'll tell you. You have to believe me: it wasn't what I wanted. I wasn't trying to wriggle out of anything. I was happy to serve. If nothing else, it would be a way out of this dead-end job and dead-end family. I actually wanted to get into uniform and be out from under my father's thumb – prove that I could be his equal in some way. To me, joining the forces was my ticket to freedom. He was the one who was against it. He was worried sick – memories of the last war, I imagine. He wanted to keep me out of it. He wouldn't say why, and now I'll never know, but I can only imagine it was all just another part of his controlling my life. He'd made up his mind, and that was the end of it.'

'So he arranged for your papers to be lost?'

'No. There you've got it wrong. I don't know anything about this man Cooper's business with call-up papers, but my father wouldn't have had to do that anyway. I told you I'd registered, but the reason why I wasn't called up was because I was found medically unfit. That's what my father paid for. He got me a green form: a medical discharge certificate. I don't know whether it was forged or stolen, but once I had that there was no question of my being called up.'

This was not what Jago had expected to hear. He was unsure whether Edward was at last telling the truth, or whether this was just another story. If it was, what was it intended to hide?

'It's as simple as that, Inspector,' said Edward. 'I can only assume this Cooper man has a tame doctor eating out of his hand, and that my father obtained the discharge certificate through him, but I don't know any of the details. You'll have to ask Cooper that.'

Jago studied Edward's face carefully as he spoke.

'I'm afraid that won't be possible, Mr Villiers. Frederick Cooper is unfortunately dead.'

Edward showed no sign of surprise.

'I see. I imagine that complicates your investigation. Or perhaps if this man was the rogue you say he was, you're not sorry to see him go.'

'I take the murder of any man very seriously, Mr Villiers.'

'Murder?' said Edward. 'You didn't say he was murdered.' He looked nervously at Jago and backed

339

away slowly. A new thought seemed to dawn on him.

'Wait a minute. Are you trying to suggest that this was something to do with me?'

'Well,' said Jago, 'was it?'

Edward's face showed alarm.

'No,' he said, in a tone of angry disbelief. 'It's preposterous. I didn't even know him. What reason would I have to murder him?'

He waited for a response, but Jago was silent. Edward's voice became louder, more urgent.

'Look, Inspector, you have to believe me. I didn't kill him! And I didn't kill my father either!'

He sat down heavily on the sofa and put his head in his hands. It was the first time Jago had heard the young man's voice betray emotion.

CHAPTER THIRTY-EIGHT

Jago drove to the station. The streets were still quiet, but in the distance he could see scores of planes in the gaps between the clouds, and the smoke of fires curling up into the sky. It looked like a heavy raid somewhere over South London. He pitied the poor blighters who were on the receiving end of the pounding, but it was far enough away for him not to have to abandon his own journey and seek shelter. He parked his car in the yard behind the station and walked in through the front entrance.

He was welcomed by the solid, reassuring presence of Tompkins.

'Messages for you, sir. That lady friend of yours called.'

Jago declined to correct him again: knowing Tompkins, this might be his idea of a joke.

'What did she say?'

'I wrote it down here.' Tompkins picked up a notepad. 'She said there was a communist invasion of the Savoy Hotel last night. No one was hurt, but she was there and saw what happened. A mob stormed the place. She said to tell you that she recognised one of them. It was the young man you met in the street in Stratford yesterday. She said you'd know who she meant. Does this mean the Bolsheviks are coming? Hope it makes more sense to you than it does to me.'

Jago considered the possible significance of the message.

'Yes, thank you, Frank. It makes some sense to me.'

He turned to go, but Tompkins called him back.

'Messages, sir. There's another one. Mr Soper wants to see you.'

'What? On a Sunday morning? What's he doing here?'

'Blowed if I know,' said Tompkins. 'He doesn't confide in me much. Can't think why.'

'Morning, sir,' said Jago. He glanced at the clock on the wall near Soper's desk. 'My goodness, is that the time already? Good afternoon, sir. I didn't expect to see you here today.'

'I didn't expect to be here myself. The fact is, John, I want to know what's happening with this Villiers murder case. I haven't heard from you for days. I came in looking for you yesterday, but I gather you were off gallivanting round Essex with that American woman. And now there's been this other murder, this Cooper fellow. What's going on?'

Jago was more interested in catching up with Cradock. He had the sense that things were coming to a head, and there was no time to lose. He tried to make his report as concise as possible.

'We've had a lot of developments, sir. I've just heard an interesting piece of news as I arrived here today. There's a family who are all connected with the case in one way or another. The mother worked for Villiers and had some trouble with him, and it was her boy who reported the body. It turns out her other son is some kind of communist agitator – he was involved in an incident in the West End last night. We've also discovered he was up before the police court earlier this year, and Villiers was the presiding magistrate. I've spoken to this lad, and he strikes me as a bit of a hothead. Seems to have his head stuffed full of communist ideology – death to the bourgeoisie, and that kind of thing. But having said that, I can't see why anyone would kill Villiers just for being a middle-class businessman and a JP.'

'What else have you got?'

'Well, there's this boy's mother, Mrs Carson. A bit unstable, I'd say. Villiers tried it on with her one evening, apparently, and there might be more that she's not saying. Grounds for revenge, perhaps, but I don't think she's the killing sort. Then there's a fellow called Johnson who worked for Villiers. He's been spinning us a line, and I don't trust him, but he must have made a good living from Villiers, so why bite the hand that fed him?'

'And what about the other murder – Cooper?'

'There was a connection between him and Villiers. They were both involved in the fake identity card business, and Johnson was mixed up in it too, but whether that's why they were both killed I don't know. It's small fry, really. Not the kind of crime that involves killing people.'

'Crime nevertheless.'

'Yes, of course, and Cooper seems to have had a number of irons in the fire as far as crime's concerned.'

'And what about Villiers' wife? You had some suspicions, I recall.'

'She's a bit of a dark horse, that one. The first time I met her I thought butter wouldn't melt in her mouth, but now it seems there's what you might call something of an indiscretion going on between her and her late husband's brother.'

'Indiscretion? What do you mean?'

'I'm not certain yet, but there are indications that she may have run off with him.'

'Absconded? Are you looking for them?'

'Yes. I've had Cradock alert the neighbouring constabularies. It may mean nothing, but we won't know for sure until we've spoken to her. On the face of it, she's not behaving like the perfect widow, but it all seems more like a comic opera than a conspiracy to murder.'

'And what of the son?'

'He's a bit of a puzzle too. His mother said he's got secrets, and I'm not certain I've found out what they all are. Something's going on with him, and it's not straightforward. He tries to cover it, but I get the impression there's some turmoil going on just beneath the surface. I saw him this morning and he got very emotional. There was definitely bad blood between him and his father, and there's more to him than meets the eye. But does that make him a murderer? I'm not convinced.'

'Right,' said Soper, 'that's very helpful. And what's next?'

'Next is a cup of tea.'

Jago got his drink and went in search of Cradock. He found him at work in the CID office.

'You got a statement from Johnson?'

'Yes, sir, it's all in order. How did you get on after you left the press?'

'Not very well. I went to see Gray, but he wasn't there. I spoke to his landlady, but she didn't know where he was. It was unusual, apparently, because she said he doesn't go out much. She didn't have a lot to say about him, except that she reckons he's an oddball and a bit of a drinker.'

'He doesn't sound like a pillar of the community, then.'

'No. And for a man who doesn't get out much, he's a remarkably elusive fellow. I'm getting more and more interested in meeting him.'

'Has anything else come to light?'

'Yes. Robert Carson was involved in some kind of communist demonstration at the Savoy last night.'

'What do you make of that?'

'I'm not sure. I only found out when I got here, and since then I've been in with the DDI. I think as soon as I've finished this cup of tea I need to go out for a little walk by myself and think about things. I won't be long.'

Five minutes later, and after a brief detour via the canteen to get a sandwich, Jago left the station and crossed the road, heading for West Ham Park. It seemed more than a week since he and Cradock had been dodging the shrapnel from the two anti-aircraft guns that stood guard in the middle of the park. Looking back, that Saturday evening now seemed to mark a dividing line: the moment the war had changed. At the strategic level, the newspapers were saying it was the day when the East End of London had become the front line. *For most of us who live here, though*, Jago reflected, *it was the day when we stopped sleeping*. He was beginning to feel the effects of the endless sirens and bombing raids, the constantly interrupted sleep. *What wouldn't I give for a few quiet nights*, he thought.

He strolled through the park, enjoying the serenity of the trees and the lush grass at his feet. It was good to be out in the open air, he thought. But not a good place to be if there was an attack from the air. The only protection available in the park was the trench shelter dug the previous year, and that wasn't an attractive proposition. The ones in Hyde Park might be up to scratch, but West Ham was all marshland and springs. He'd heard of one trench shelter in the borough that got so wet, a fire engine had to come and pump out the water twice a night, and another where small boys sailed their toy boats. He kept the shelter in sight, but hoped he wouldn't need to use it.

He found an empty bench to sit on, where he could think while he ate. The park was quieter than he had expected it would be on a Sunday, but it was lunchtime. Most families would be at home eating together rather than here. It would probably get busier later in the afternoon, if the weather held. The roads skirting the park were quiet too. There were never many people on the streets on a Sunday, of course, as the shops were closed, and only occasionally could he hear any traffic passing. The main sound was that of the birds singing, just the same as ever. They didn't know there was a war on. The openness and colours of the park made a pleasant contrast to the office, but it was also a lonely place. How nice it must be to sit down for a Sunday roast with your children round the table, he thought, instead of sitting here on your own with only a cheese sandwich for company.

He reminded himself that he had a lot to be thankful for. A roof over his head and a job he enjoyed, for instance. He also had the privilege of eating in peace and quiet, with no needs to attend to except his own. There was something to be said for the bachelor life, when all was said and done. It kept things simple. So many men of his acquaintance seemed to regret getting tangled up with women. Or maybe it was the one woman they were tangled up with that they regretted. Who could tell? What you saw of a relationship from the outside wasn't always the whole truth. It was odd that so many people got married professing their undying love, then seemed to spend the rest of their lives fighting.

He saw a squirrel hop across the ground to the foot of a tree and stop to forage in the grass. It snapped into a sitting position, resting on its back legs with tail up and eyes unblinking, and nibbled something from its front paws. Then just as suddenly it was away, bounding up the tree trunk with the food clenched in its teeth. What a simple, uncomplicated existence, thought Jago. That was the trouble with human life: you had to live with your choices. He was content on his own, but perhaps his life would have been better if he'd married. Too late to know now. But then, as they said, what you don't know, you don't miss.

He was glad he'd brought his coat. The sky was clear overhead, but the air was a little chilly. To the south, the docks were covered in cloud, and he wondered if it was going to head north and bring rain. He finished his sandwich and brushed the crumbs off his lap, and was about to turn his thoughts to the previous day's developments when his ears were assailed by the air-raid siren.

To Jago, this harsh intrusion felt like a conspiracy to prevent him enjoying a few moments of peace, and he was a little surprised to find a sense of defiance rising within him. The warning might turn out to be a false alarm, but if not, he would have time to run to the shelter. He decided he would stay put.

It was not long before his ears picked up the sound of aeroplane engines. It reminded him of the buzzing of a swarm of bees, but lower-pitched and slower: a persistent, menacing growl. The planes themselves were not visible, but the sound was coming from the deep banks of cloud that hung over the docks to the south. From somewhere in the same direction came the sound of anti-aircraft fire, muffled by distance.

The first planes emerged from the cloud. There seemed no end to them: more than he had seen together at any time since the first big raid a week ago. There were five groups of bombers, each of about twenty planes, and around them a mass of protecting German fighters – more than he could count. He could see RAF Spitfires and Hurricanes everywhere too, although there seemed to be twice as many German fighters.

It was like the scene he had watched from the pavement outside the police station on Wednesday, albeit on a larger scale. But there was something different. As the planes droned steadily closer, he began to realise what it was. He felt calm. His mind and his body were under control. Four days ago it was only by steeling his will that he had managed to step outside the sandbagged safety of the police station. Today he had simply done it. In that one small decision he had recaptured some vital long-lost ground, and the fear that had paralysed him when the first bombs fell a week ago was gone.

It reminded him of France. Not the shock of first coming under merciless artillery fire, but more that strange indifference to shelling that he had so slowly and painfully acquired through the following two years of active service. It was all more than two decades ago, yet it was still there inside him, in some mysterious place that he could not identify. It was perplexing, but trying to force his mind to unravel its own workings seemed pointless.

What had wounded him more deeply, he wondered: the incessant hammering of the guns at the front or the shocking silence that marked the war's end? He had no answer to his own question, but he felt a surge of energy and relief as it gradually became clear that he could cope. He would never forget, but he would not be for ever haunted by fear.

The noise of the engines was growing louder as the bombers drew closer, and only now did it strike him that he had not heard the sound of exploding bombs. Why was that? The answer was clear in the sky: the thick cloud over the docks must have prevented them dropping their load. He looked up and saw the sky above his head was cloudless – they must be saving their bombs for West Ham instead. As if in confirmation, the anti-aircraft guns in East Ham opened fire with a thunderous roar. Puffs of black smoke smeared the blue sky as their shells burst around the planes.

He clamped his hands over his ears as the guns just across the park joined in. Within seconds, the bombs began to fall. They were still landing some way to the south of the park, but it looked as though they were getting close, just the other side of the railway line. Now it was definitely time to run. He set off as fast as he could, wishing he had brought his tin helmet as he heard shrapnel from the anti-aircraft shells landing on the paths. When he reached the long sloping entrance to the trench shelter he ran down it and threw himself into the narrow refuge. Inside it was stinking, muddy and waterlogged, but by now he didn't care.

CHAPTER THIRTY-NINE

When it got to about half past one Cradock thought he had done enough work to deserve a bite of lunch. It was his habit to come in for a while on Sundays whenever he could, mainly because the cook at the section house didn't work at weekends. Unpaid overtime was part of the job, but the extra hours were well worth it if it meant he could get lunch at the station. The canteen was quiet, and as he walked in he could see PC Stannard alone at a table on the far side of the room. He got his tray of food and walked across to where the uniformed constable was sitting.

'Afternoon, Ray,' he said. 'Mind if I join you?'

'Hello, mate,' said Stannard. 'Make yourself at home.'

'How's tricks?' said Cradock, taking his seat.

'Not too bad today. Just popped in for lunch, have you?'

'Course not. I'm still working on that murder case.'

'Ah, yes. You and DI Jago. How are you getting on with him?'

'So-so, I suppose. He's a funny old stick at times, though.'

'Probably thinks the same of you. Mind you, I expect he can teach you a thing or two.'

Cradock began to eat his lunch. It was meat and two veg – just the way he liked it.

'You're right there,' he said. 'He seems to know everything. Trouble is, sometimes he seems to expect me to know everything too, as if I'd been in the job for twenty years like him. I think he ought to make allowances.'

'Perhaps he is. He probably thinks he's being soft on you. I reckon they had it far worse when he was starting out. The way the old 'uns talk about those days, it makes your toes curl. You should hear the stories Frank Tompkins tells.'

'Yes, I've heard some of Frank's stories. It's like being a kid again and listening to your grandad.'

'So what does that make the DI? Your dad?'

'It feels like that sometimes.'

'Well, you could do far worse. How's the case going? Getting close to an arrest?'

'I can't say I know, really. We don't seem to be getting very far. Which reminds me: have you come across a bloke called Bob Gray?'

Stannard thought for a moment and shook his head.

'No, can't say I have. Why, what's he done?'

'That's what I'd like to find out,' said Cradock. 'He lives down Prince Regent Lane and we've found out he's got himself a false identity card for some reason. It seems his real name's Coates, but we haven't had that from him yet. Do either of those names mean anything to you?'

Stannard shook his head again, his mouth full of food. Cradock continued.

'We need to find out why he's decided to change his identity. DI Jago went looking for him on Friday but didn't find him, so I'm thinking we'll need to go back tomorrow and see whether he'll own up. It must mean he's been up to no good, got something to hide.'

'Not necessarily,' said Stannard. 'Supposing your name was Crippen, or Hitler. You'd want to change it then, wouldn't you? It could be a family thing. Have you checked the records?'

'Yes. There's no record of any convictions for either name round here, but then again we don't know how long he's lived here.'

'Maybe you should ask Frank, then. He's got records back to the year dot in his head. How old's this Gray?'

'Early twenties, I should think.'

'If he's from round these parts, then old Frank might have had a run-in with him when he was a nipper.'

'A clip round the ear, you mean?'

'Yes. Frank's a proper old-time copper, isn't he? Learnt his stuff when they knew how to get the job done. Put your boy Gray in a cell with Frank or one of his mates in those days and they'd soon have found out what you wanted to know. Not like now.'

There had been a time when Cradock would argue with Stannard, but now he tried not to take the bait. Ray was an old pal, and it wasn't worth annoying him by disagreeing. He busied himself by shovelling a forkful of sliced carrot into his mouth and made that his excuse not to speak. He chewed in silence, then nodded slowly.

'Good idea,' he said. 'I'll pick his brains.'

Cradock had fully intended to talk to Sergeant Tompkins, but his plan was cut short by the air-raid siren. When the anti-aircraft guns opened up and he heard the thud of bombs, he grabbed some work and took it down into the basement shelter. At last the all-clear sounded. He climbed the steps back up to the ground floor and made his way to the front desk. Tompkins was standing behind the counter as usual.

'Afternoon, Sarge,' said Cradock. 'You still here?'

'Someone's got to do their duty, lad. We can't have the front door open and the desk unmanned when there's an air raid on, can we?'

'You won't be much use to the public if you're blown to bits, though, will you?'

'That's highly unlikely, unless we get a big one on the roof or straight down the chimney. And if that happens, I don't think any of us'll know much about it. A little bit of noise doesn't bother me. The lads in

Flanders used to say you never hear the shell that kills you, so if you hear it, you're safe.'

Cradock looked at him for a moment with a puzzled expression.

'But how would you know that's true? The only person who could tell you he hadn't heard it would be the one who was killed. So only dead people could prove it was right.'

Tompkins gave him a look of perplexed pity.

'You'll just have to take my word for it, then, Detective Constable. Trust me.'

Cradock was about to ask him about Gray when the phone rang. Tompkins turned away to answer it.

'I'll come back later,' said Cradock, beginning to walk away.

The station sergeant acknowledged him with a wave of the hand and spoke into the mouthpiece.

'I'm sorry. He's not in . . . Can I take a message? . . . Yes, I see . . . I'm expecting him back shortly . . . Yes, yes, of course . . . Would you like me to send a constable round? . . . Hello?'

Tompkins clamped his free hand over the mouthpiece and shouted after Cradock.

'DC Cradock, you'd better come back and speak to this lady.'

Cradock turned round and hurried back to the desk. He put out his hand to take the handset.

'Ah,' said Tompkins. 'Too late. She's hung up.'

'What was that all about?' said Cradock.

'I couldn't get much sense out of her. She wanted to speak to your guv'nor.'

Tompkins' eyes shifted slightly as he looked over Cradock's shoulder, towards the front entrance door.

'Ah, there you are, sir,' he said. 'I was getting worried about you out there in the middle of a raid.'

Cradock followed Tompkins' eyes and saw Jago striding in through the front door, dishevelled but apparently unharmed. *He must have heard all the shells*, he thought.

'I was fine, Frank,' said Jago. 'I was over in the park having a sandwich. I had to use the trench shelter, which wasn't the greatest of pleasures, but nothing fell too near.'

'You've just missed a call, sir,' said Tompkins. 'It sounded urgent. It was a lady called Mrs Cooper. She said she wanted to speak to you.'

'Did she say what it was about?'

'I couldn't get much out of her. She was very agitated. She said someone had phoned her and said she's been giving the police information about her husband's business affairs that she shouldn't have. Whoever it was warned her not to say anything more. That's why she's frightened: she thinks something's going to happen to her. I offered to send a constable round, but she just rang off, as if she hadn't even heard what I was saying.'

'And this was just a few minutes ago?'

'Yes, sir.'

'Right, give me the phone book.'

Tompkins reached under the desk for the telephone directory and handed it to Jago, who quickly found Mrs Cooper's number and called her. He drummed his fingers impatiently on the desk until he heard a woman's voice answer.

'Mrs Cooper?' he said. Cradock and Tompkins listened to his end of the conversation.

'Detective Inspector Jago here. I've just heard that you . . . Yes . . . How can I? . . . I see . . . Yes, I understand . . . Don't worry, we'll be there as soon as we can.'

He slammed the handset back on the telephone's cradle and turned to Cradock.

'Right. Drop whatever you're doing and come with me. This sounds like an emergency.'

CHAPTER FORTY

Jago raced for his car, with Cradock close beside him. It was unlocked, and he slipped in smoothly behind the wheel. As Cradock was getting into the passenger seat, Jago turned the ignition key, retarded the ignition and pushed the starter button. The engine came to life with a throaty roar. He pulled away immediately, changing gear rapidly upwards as the car built up speed.

'What did she say?' said Cradock, raising his voice and gripping the top of the door as the Riley bumped along the road.

Jago kept his eyes fixed to the front and shouted to Cradock without turning his head.

'She was telling me what she'd already told Tompkins,

about someone phoning her and threatening her. Then she said she'd seen two men in her back garden.'

'What – still there?'

'Yes, she said she could see them and she was frightened. Then before I could get any more out of her she screamed and put the phone down. I think she's in danger.'

He braked as the road took a sharp turn to the right, then forced the car back up to speed.

'And this morning, sir – did you find out what you wanted to?'

'Some of it, yes. I saw Edward Villiers. He came clean, up to a point.'

'So did Cooper make sure Edward's call-up papers got lost? Was that the link between Cooper and his dad?'

'No, he said it wasn't like that.'

'But it's there in Cooper's book: money from Villiers.'

'He didn't deny there was a fiddle going on,' said Jago, 'but it was a different fiddle. He says Cooper arranged for a doctor to sign a medical discharge form for him. Says he wanted to join up, but it was his dad who was against it. He said it was his dad's idea and his dad who put Cooper up to it. Not what you'd expect of an officer and gentleman, eh?'

'That doesn't put Edward in the clear, though, does it? Not if he used that form.'

'No. He said he didn't know whether it was forged or stolen, but he obviously knew it was falsified. That young man's still got a lot of explaining to do.'

Jago slowed down behind an elderly van that was lumbering down the street, then with a sharp turn of the wheel he threw the car into the middle of the road to overtake it. He was thankful it was a Sunday afternoon and they weren't running into too much traffic.

'How about you? Have you made any progress?' he said, raising his voice again as he accelerated.

'Not much,' said Cradock. 'I think we need to track down Bob Gray tomorrow – find out why he got that identity card.'

'Agreed.'

'And there's something else that's been bothering me.'

'What's that?'

'It was something Hodgson said on Friday. It didn't tally with what his wife said. When you questioned her, she said Edgar Simpson had got mixed up with Cooper over something to do with gambling, right?'

'Yes, that's right.'

'Which is more or less the same as what Simpson told me. So she said it was gambling, but then her husband said it was because of some moral issue in Simpson's personal life. They can't both be right.'

'Maybe, maybe not,' said Jago. 'We'll need to talk to Simpson tomorrow and see if he's got anything more to say.'

'And another thing: I checked Cooper's book again and there was no mention of Simpson in it. If Cooper did know some secret of Simpson's and was blackmailing him, surely there'd be a record of payments received in it. Cooper seemed to be quite thorough with his records, didn't he? Regular little book-keeper, he was.'

'Yes, but maybe that's the point. That book was all about money. That's usually what blackmailers are after, but not always. Maybe in Simpson's case Cooper wanted payment in kind.'

The car slowed a little as the road rose to cross over the District Line railway that ran from east to west across the borough, then picked up speed again as it went down on the other side. A hundred and fifty yards farther on he turned left into a side street.

'Hold on!' he shouted. He slammed on the brakes. Cradock braced his hands against the dashboard to stop himself flying forward into the windscreen. The car swerved. Ahead of them they saw the smoking ruins of a house.

'I should have thought,' said Jago, banging his fist on the steering wheel. 'I was pretty sure the bombs were coming down on this side of the railway line, and I was right. I should have realised we'd run into trouble getting to Cooper's house.'

A heavy rescue party was shifting wooden joists and rafters from the site and pulling away bricks. Their truck was parked in the road, and there was no way through.

'There must be someone under that lot,' said Cradock.

'Yes, but they don't need help from us. I'm worried about what might be happening to Mrs Cooper. We've got to get there fast.'

He selected reverse gear and flung the car backwards towards the kerb, then forward again to turn it round. It meant taking a longer route, but there was no alternative.

'Come along, you brute,' he said to the car, and headed back at full speed the way they had come until he found a way round the blocked road. His eyes were stinging from the acrid smoke. He had to slow down twice more as they came across firemen fighting blazes where the bombs had fallen, but then suddenly they were through the chaos and into clean air. Four minutes later they were on Barking Road. He parked a little short of Mrs Cooper's house so as not to be visible from it.

He pulled on the handbrake.

'Back garden,' he said. 'We'll go down that alleyway there and see if we can get into her garden – see what's going on.'

The two men dashed down the alleyway and found a path leading along the end of the houses' back gardens. They counted the houses and slowed to a quiet prowl as they reached their target.

Jago eased open a wooden gate and peered in. There was no one in the garden.

'Either they've gone, or they're inside the house,' said Jago. 'Follow me.'

He crept along the garden path. Cradock fell in line behind him, keeping a careful eye out for movement in the bushes. They got as far as the back of the house without seeing anyone. Jago pointed to the back door. The glass by the handle had been smashed. He gently eased the handle down and the door opened without a creak. They were in.

From the kitchen they could hear voices coming from the living room at the front of the house.

'Sounds like two men and one woman,' whispered Cradock.

'Yes,' murmured Jago. 'Let's go and give them a surprise.'

They crept down the hallway and halted by the living-room door. Jago gently turned the handle and stepped into the room.

CHAPTER FORTY-ONE

'My, my,' said Jago. 'What have we here?'

Across the room he could see Mrs Cooper, backed into a corner as if willing the wall to open up and swallow her. The two men with their backs to him whirled round, their faces reflecting a surprise that quickly gave way to wariness. The shorter of the pair began to advance unsteadily across the room, a hip flask in his right hand. Jago glanced back over his shoulder to check: yes, Cradock had already placed himself squarely in front of the closed door. There was no other way out.

He looked each man in the eye in turn and shook his head.

'No. Don't even think about it. You're not going anywhere until I say so. I've got a few questions for you, so I suggest we all take a seat and have a little chat.'

The unsteady man glared at him and slumped awkwardly into an armchair. The other said nothing, but took a chair facing his companion across a low wooden coffee table.

Jago addressed the man with the hip flask first.

'I don't think we've had the pleasure.'

Cradock stepped forward and said into Jago's ear, 'It's Gray, sir.'

'Ah, Mr Gray,' said Jago. 'I've been looking forward to meeting you for some time. I see you've brought your own refreshments.'

Gray looked down at the flask in his hand.

'Just a little drink. No harm in that.'

Jago turned to the other man. 'And how nice to see you again, Mr Johnson. I know that you and Mr Gray are friends, but I didn't know you were acquainted with Mrs Cooper. Perhaps one of you would like to tell me what you're doing here.'

Johnson spoke first.

'Just a social call, Inspector. We were about to leave, weren't we?' He turned to Gray, who nodded.

Mrs Cooper moved forward from the corner of the room for the first time and looked imploringly at Jago.

'It's not true,' she said. 'I don't know these men. They broke into my house. They were threatening me.'

'Is this true?' said Jago, directing his question to the two men. They exchanged a glance, and Johnson answered.

'My friend just wanted to have a word with her, that's all.'

'What do you mean, *I* wanted to?' said Gray.

'You'll have to excuse my friend,' said Johnson to Jago. 'He's had a little too much to drink and he doesn't know what he's saying. Don't take any notice of him.'

Jago turned to Mrs Cooper.

'In what way were they threatening you?'

'They said they wanted my Fred's book, and if I knew what was good for me I'd hand it over.'

'Now that is interesting,' said Jago. 'So, gentlemen, what would your interest in Mr Cooper's little book be, I wonder?' He crossed the room to where Gray was sitting and stood over him. Gray looked up at him, bleary-eyed.

'I've told you, Inspector, the man's drunk,' said Johnson. 'You won't get any sense out of him.'

'We'll see about that,' said Jago. 'Mr Gray, I've come to ask you a few questions about the murder of Frederick Cooper.'

'Who? I've never heard of him. I don't know who you're talking about.'

'Come, Mr Gray, you know perfectly well who he was, and he knew you, didn't he? You can deny it, but he kept a record of his dealings with you, and that record is now in our possession. We know all about your dealings with him, and I'm afraid your time's up.'

'No,' said Gray, his eyes widening in panic. There was a new note of fear in his voice. A memory slipped into Jago's mind: he was a private, in the front line for the first time. The officer blew his whistle to order an advance, and the man beside him collapsed in a kind of delirium, refusing to go over the top. Jago did not want to remember what happened next. He refocused his attention on Gray. Like a cornered dog, he thought.

'No,' Gray was saying, 'I'm not going back. You can't make me. I don't care if you shoot me. I'm not going.'

Now Jago understood.

'I see. So that's what it's all about. You're a deserter, aren't you?'

Gray tried to compose himself.

'No, that's not true. I'm just having a bit more leave than I should, that's all.'

'So much leave that you have to kit yourself out with a false identity card, yes? That won't wash with me. Cooper was blackmailing you, wasn't he? Was he threatening to expose your real identity?'

Gray looked first at Johnson and then back to Jago. He seemed bewildered.

'Yes,' he said angrily. 'He was a money-grubbing swine, that man. They sent me to France. They should have sent him too, let him die in the dirt.'

'And what would have happened if Cooper had exposed you?' said Jago calmly.

'It's obvious, isn't it? I'd have got arrested and sent back, handed over to the army.'

'That's not what you wanted, is it?'

Gray shouted again, his voice slurred and pleading.

'Of course not! Don't you understand? I can't go back.

I can't bear it; I've done enough. I can't take any more.'

He put his elbow on the arm of the chair and gripped his temples with one hand as though trying to control the pain in his head.

Jago continued.

'I suggest you thought the only way to be safe was to get rid of Cooper, so no one would know your secret.'

'No!'

'That you went down to his yard and stabbed him to death.'

'No! It's not true!'

'We've already established you're a liar. Why should we believe you now?'

Gray hauled himself up from the chair and sank to his knees before Johnson.

'Help me,' he pleaded. 'Tell them, Albert, tell them. I'm not a killer!'

Johnson prised Gray's hands off his leg and got out of his chair. He stepped back, away from Gray, and spoke quietly.

'But you are, Bob. You told me yourself.'

'What?' said Gray. He cast his eyes from side to side as though he could not believe what he was hearing.

'Surely you remember. "They've turned me into a killer," you said. "There's no way back now."'

'That's not what I meant! I was talking about killing Germans, not some bloke like Cooper.'

Jago interrupted him with a question for Johnson.

'Is this true?'

'Yes, Inspector, that's what he said.'

'And did you take it to mean that he was talking about Germans?'

'Well, at the time I didn't know who he was referring to. He'd been drinking too. But now that I've heard what you said about him being blackmailed by Cooper, I don't know what to think.'

Gray struggled to his feet and stood facing Johnson.

'But Albert, you're my friend! Help me!'

'I'm sorry, Bob,' said Johnson. 'But it's what you said. Don't you remember? When I came round to your flat?'

Gray took two steps back so that he could face Jago and Cradock while keeping a wary eye on Johnson.

'Look, I swear I don't know anything about Cooper being murdered. I don't know who it was, where it was or when it was.'

'Where were you on Wednesday between noon and eight o'clock in the evening?' said Jago.

'Is that when it happened?'

'Just answer the question.'

Gray backed away cautiously until he was up against the wall, then slid slowly down and slumped on the floor. He looked up at the two policemen, his eyes struggling to focus.

'That's it, isn't it? That's when he was murdered.'

He sat without speaking for a few seconds, lost in thought, then began to laugh, louder and louder. He thumped his hip flask down onto the linoleum.

'I'll tell you where I was. I was in the cells at

Walthamstow police station. One of your pals claimed I was drunk and incapable in a public place. I think that's what you call an alibi, isn't it?'

He gave another bitter laugh, then looked at Johnson and began to sob.

CHAPTER FORTY-TWO

'So, Mr Johnson,' said Jago, 'if what your friend says is true, it would appear that killer or no killer, he did not kill Frederick Cooper. In which case, perhaps it was you who were at Cooper's premises on Wednesday.'

'I wasn't,' said Johnson. 'I've told you before, I was there last Saturday evening with Mr Villiers, but that was the only time I've been there, and I've never been inside.'

'What does being inside have to do with it?'

'Well, I was just assuming. You're asking me if I was at Cooper's place, so that presumably means that's where he was killed, and I'm assuming if anyone did kill him it'd be inside, not out on the street. Don't go reading too much into what I said, Inspector.'

'But you'll remember,' said Jago, 'that originally you

said you hadn't been with Mr Villiers for the whole of that journey, and then you said you had. You said you didn't know who those premises belonged to and you didn't know Cooper, but then it turned out that you did know. So you'll forgive me if I don't take everything you say at face value.'

'All right. But that doesn't alter the fact that I didn't kill Cooper. And I've already told you I was out for whenever it was on Wednesday.'

'You told us on Friday that you'd been in a public air-raid shelter and that someone might remember you, but that's not exactly a cast-iron alibi, is it?'

'Well, I can't help that, can I?'

Jago beckoned Cradock over and handed him a key.

'I need you to get something from the car,' he said. 'Bring me the package on the floor behind the driver's seat.'

Cradock left the room, and Jago turned back to Johnson.

'Perhaps you can help me with something else, then,' he said.

'I'll try,' said Johnson.

'Very well. Do you have your gas mask with you?'

'Yes, I always have it. I was caught out in that raid this afternoon.'

'Then perhaps you could show it to me.'

Johnson crossed the room to where his coat lay in a crumpled heap on the floor and pulled a cardboard gas mask box from under its folds. He returned and handed it to Jago.

Jago opened the box and pulled out the mask. He turned it over in his hands.

'This is in very good condition. It looks brand new.'

'It is,' said Johnson. 'My old one got damaged, so they issued me with a new one. I only got it on Thursday.'

'Could you provide us with the old one?'

Johnson looked puzzled.

'No, I lost it. What's this got to do with anything? What's so interesting about my gas mask?'

'We saw you with one on Wednesday afternoon, when we met you on our way to the hospital. You dropped it in the street. Presumably that was your old one?'

'Yes, that's right.'

'You were quick to get it replaced.'

'Yes. If you'd seen men gassed like I did in the last war, you'd want to make sure you always had a mask with you. I don't trust those Germans any further than I can throw them.'

'And yet you lost it that very day?'

'Yes, but I don't know how – it just got lost somehow.'

'Could someone have stolen it?'

Johnson's voice began to rise in anger.

'No. I tell you I just lost it.'

Cradock came back into the room and gave Jago a package. Jago opened it and handed a gas mask to Johnson.

'Is this your old one?'

Johnson took it from Jago and looked at it warily.

'How am I supposed to know? There are millions of these things. They all look the same.'

'When they're new they do, but this one isn't new. Look at that eye panel: you can see there's a crack in it.

A crack like that would leak and let gas in. You didn't want to take that risk, did you? You can see there that someone's tried to mend it. That was you, wasn't it?'

'No, it's not mine. There must be some mistake.'

'Would it help to jog your memory if I told you we found it in the same room as Cooper's body?'

'No: I wasn't there. I've told you. It's someone else's.'

'Mr Johnson, you were worried when you found this crack, weren't you? You'd seen what gas can do to a man, and you didn't want to take a chance. I'd be the same myself. You followed the correct procedure and reported it to your local air-raid warden.'

Johnson shook his head slowly from side to side but did not speak. He lit a cigarette and began to smoke it in short puffs.

'This morning I visited a number of air-raid wardens,' said Jago. 'They are all responsible for sectors where certain people live – people with whom we've had contact as a result of this case. I asked them if they'd had anyone reporting a damaged gas mask this week. One of them was your local warden. I showed him this mask, and he confirmed it was the one you showed him on Wednesday. He said he'd told you he'd get you a new one and you'd be able to exchange it on Thursday.'

'No, no, it's a mistake.'

'The only mistake is yours, Mr Johnson. You went out on Wednesday night with murder in your mind, but you cared enough about your own skin to try a temporary repair on this mask. Something happened that night that caused you to lose your mask, and the circumstances were such that you had to flee without it. Either that or you were in such an extreme situation that you didn't notice you'd left without it.'

Johnson looked helpless. He seemed to be mouthing words, but his voice was inaudible. Jago continued.

'Those circumstances were that you were killing Cooper in cold blood. You were there, weren't you? You killed him.'

Gray was still sitting on the floor, his back against the wall, but now he seemed to come back to life. He started to laugh.

'It was you, wasn't it?' he said to Johnson, almost shouting. 'They've got you, mate.'

'Shut up, you fool,' said Johnson. 'You're drunk!'

'Ha! I've had a couple of nips, yes, but not so many that I can't tell a liar and traitor when I see one. Get him, Inspector.'

'Well?' said Jago. 'Did you do it?'

Johnson scanned the room, as if looking for help or a way out, but Cradock was again barring the room's only door. He fell silent and sat heavily on a chair, then spoke in a barely audible whisper.

'Yes.'

Jago took the gas mask from Johnson's hands and handed it to Cradock.

'There's something else I want to ask you, and this time I want an honest answer. We have evidence that Cooper was running a racket that involved getting men's call-up papers lost in the system, and one of the names connected with that was a George Johnson. Is he any relation to you?'

Johnson's confident manner had crumpled. He looked defeated, and his voice was again little more than a whisper.

'Yes.'

'What relation is he?'

'Not is: was. He was my son.'

'So he didn't want to be in the armed forces?'

'No, and I didn't want him to be either. That crook Cooper said he could see to it that my George's call-up papers would disappear. Said he had a contact in the ministry who owed him a favour, and he could get it done for me, as long as I paid up.'

'So when you told us that story about paying Cooper for cigarettes, that wasn't true, was it?'

'No.'

'You gave him money to enable your son to avoid military service?'

'Yes, I did. Cooper said he'd fix it, and I paid him, but then he wanted more money – more than I could afford. I thought I could persuade him to leave me alone. After all, I'd paid what he asked. But he double-crossed me, said he needed to make an example to his other clients.'

'Double-crossed you? How?'

'He did the opposite of what he'd said he'd do. He made sure George was put back into the system and didn't even tell me. George got called up, and there was nothing I could do about it. He ended up being sent to France not long before it fell. He was killed on the beach at Dunkirk, waiting to be taken off. Those boys didn't stand a chance. Cooper killed my son, Mr Jago. It may have been a German bullet that took him, but it was Cooper and his greed that put him there.'

'So you decided to take revenge on Cooper.'

'Yes. I killed him, but I don't regret it. He was the scum of the earth. He deserved it.'

Jago turned to Gray, who appeared to have been shocked into silence.

'And do you have any connection with George Johnson?'

'Yes,' said Gray. 'He was my friend, my best friend, and he died beside me on that beach.'

'And it was because of your friendship with his son that Johnson here asked you to provide him with an alibi for the night Villiers died? I advise you to answer truthfully.'

Gray hesitated and exchanged a glance with Johnson.

'Go on,' said Johnson. 'Tell him. It won't make any difference now.'

Gray cleared his throat nervously.

'Yes, you're right. Albert wasn't with me all the time I said he was. He arrived at my house later, about a quarter past nine.'

'Tell us what happened, Johnson,' said Jago.

'Can I have a drink first?'

Jago asked Mrs Cooper to fetch some water. She returned with a jug and poured some into a glass. Johnson sipped it, then put the glass down slowly on the table. The room was silent until he spoke.

'It was in the war,' he said. 'The last war. My mate Tom was with me in the trenches: we were in the Essex Regiment, in the West Ham Pals Battalion. We'd both volunteered in 1915. Both from the same area, though we didn't know each other before the war. I was a bachelor, but he was married with a baby son. It was 1917, and we were in the Arras offensive, the usual bloodbath. We'd been through two years of hell, and we'd become best friends. I always thought Tom was braver than me, but it got to the point where he couldn't cope any more. One day we got the whistle to go over the top and he just stood there in the trench, paralysed, staring straight ahead. He had his hands over his ears and was saying, "The noise, I can't bear the noise." I tried to drag him with me but he wouldn't go. I went over without him. Next day we were back where we'd started, but Tom had been arrested.'

Johnson's voice had begun to shake. He took a sip of water.

'Go on,' said Jago.

'There was a court martial and Tom was sentenced to death for cowardice. We had this officer, a new one and a real swine, always throwing his weight about. He'd just been transferred into the regiment, to our battalion. He put me in the firing party. I was never certain whether he knew I was Tom's friend and did it deliberately or whether it was just one of those things, but it was the same either way. Making us shoot one of our own. It was just . . . I can't find words for it. Just so cruel. We were there to shoot Germans, not our own mates. But he seemed to think nothing of it. Heartless, he was.

'There was one blank round, so none of the six of us would know who'd killed him, but it made no difference to me. I did my best to miss him, and maybe the others did too, because after we'd fired we could see he'd been hit but he wasn't dead. So the captain stepped up and finished him off with his revolver. I felt sick to my guts. I was nothing to that officer – he wasn't the type who cared for the men – and I knew he'd forget my face the next day, but his always stayed in my mind, and his name too.'

'I think I know what that name is,' said Jago quietly, 'but tell me anyway.'

'It was Captain Charles Villiers.'

'So how did you come to be working for him all these years later?'

'After the war I went into the print trade, then one day a couple of years back I saw a photo of a Captain Villiers in the paper and recognised him. It said he was a businessman and a JP, so he'd obviously done all right for himself – not like some of my old mates who ended up busking on one leg. I found out a bit more about him and discovered he owned a print business in West Ham, so I thought I'd see if I could go and work for him. In the summer of 1938 I applied for a job with him, and I was right: he had no idea who I was.'

'And you got the job, presumably?'

'Yes, I did. I'll make no bones about it: my thinking was that if I got on the inside I could find some way of ruining him or exposing him for what he was. Then the war started, and my son was called up and sent off to France, just like I'd been. You already know what happened to my George. I can't describe what I went through. Have you got a son?'

'No,' said Jago.

'Then you can't know what it's like. But it brought back everything else too – everything I'd seen in France, the friends I'd lost there. I knew people had made money out of what we went through back then, and now I could see Villiers doing the same thing, making money out of a war. I'd just had enough. I didn't know what I could do about it, but when I was out with him that night when the big air raids started it suddenly struck me: in all this chaos I've got my chance.'

Johnson paused and took more water. He seemed reluctant to go on.

'You were alone with him, yes?' said Jago.

'Yes. I confronted him, told him he'd murdered my mate. At first he said he didn't know what I was talking about. That just made me even more angry – the fact that he didn't even remember it. When I reminded him of what he'd done to Tom, he just sneered at me in that superior voice of his. Said it wasn't murder, it was due process, it was the law, and anyway he couldn't be expected to remember one coward from so long ago. Just brushed me off like a piece of dirt. It was as if he thought because he'd been an officer I'd just do whatever he said. But I couldn't get that sneer out of my mind. I can still hear it – still see that stuck-up face of his.'

'And what did you do then?'

'I got into a rage and hit him. He knocked his head against the door frame in the van and it stunned him, so I hit him again. I wanted to kill him, and in that moment I decided I'd make it look like suicide. I hadn't planned it that way and I daresay I made a pig's ear of it, but I knew he was the kind of man who thought suicide was a coward's way out. I know it's not like that, and anyway, if anyone was a coward it was him. All bullies are cowards. I wanted it to look like he'd killed himself, to show he was a coward. Maybe that doesn't make sense to you, but like I said, I was in a rage. I didn't care what I did. The first time I had to bayonet a man in the war I threw up, but the second time I didn't. It's what they'd trained us to do.'

'So you cut his wrists to make it look like suicide? What did you use?'

'That old printer's knife of his. The one you showed me when you came to the office. I knew he always carried it in his inside jacket pocket, so I reckoned it would be there, and it was. I got it out while he was still stunned and cut both his wrists. For me it was a kind of justice: I wanted him to know he was dying and not be able to do anything about it. Just like Tom. Then he started coming round. At first he just sat there and looked at the blood, as if he couldn't believe it, then he started shouting and screaming for help. I think maybe I panicked then and just stabbed him in the chest to shut him up. Then he went quiet, and I knew he was dead.'

As Johnson came to the end of his account his words were lost in a succession of quiet sobs.

'I just wanted to show he wasn't the man he pretended to be,' he whispered. 'It was justice, and he deserved it.'

Jago stood directly in front of Johnson and looked him in the eye.

'I am arresting you for the murder of Charles Villiers and—'

Johnson interrupted him, his voice sounding strained.

'Yes, I know, I killed them both. But it was worth it. They killed the two best men I ever knew. There's no justice for the likes of them in this world – it's all just about power and money, and it was power and money that killed my son and my friend. Even if I hang for it, at least I got justice for my George and poor old Tom Cordwell.'

Jago caught his breath. Before he could speak, Cradock blurted out what the detective inspector was thinking.

'But that's—'

They exchanged a shocked look, then Jago spoke again to Johnson.

'Your friend Tom Cordwell: was he married?'

'Yes. She was called Lily. Why?'

'And were there children?'

'Yes, one, a little boy. He was just a baby.'

'And his name?'

'They called him Fred.'

Jago did not think his heart could go out to a man who was a self-confessed double murderer, but it did. How could he tell him? There was no alternative to the cold truth. He spoke as gently as he could.

'I'm sorry to have to tell you this, but Cooper's real name was Fred Cordwell.'

Johnson's face slowly changed. His mouth opened as if to form a word, but he made no sound. His breath came in anguished snatches and his eyes widened into an unfocused, uncomprehending stare. Jago said nothing. For a moment, the faces of young soldiers came before him. Boys barely shaving, new to the front line, seeing their best friend blown apart by a grenade, shot clean through the head by a sniper. He refocused his eyes on Johnson. He knew that face well. It was the face of horror – the unspeakable horror of death. There was no justice in war, and sometimes no justice in peace.

CHAPTER FORTY-THREE

'Morning, Mr Jago,' said Rita. 'I see you've got your nice young assistant with you again.'

'Ah, yes, I don't think I introduced you last time we were here. This is Detective Constable Cradock.'

'Pleased to meet you, Mr Cradock,' said Rita. 'Are you a married man?'

Cradock looked a little alarmed. Seeing him lost for an answer, Jago stepped in for him.

'Now, now, Rita, don't pounce on the poor man like that. It's a bit early in the morning for matchmaking. He hasn't even had his breakfast yet.'

'Just being friendly, Mr Jago. I take an interest in the younger generation. You might be a confirmed bachelor, but it wouldn't do if everyone was, would it? A young man like this should be thinking about settling down.'

'Leave the boy alone – you're embarrassing him. And less of the "confirmed bachelor", if you please. I may be a bachelor, but who says I'm confirmed?'

'Well, if that's a hint, I'll take it.'

'You can take an order for breakfast, that's what you can do,' said Jago.

'All right, then,' Rita sighed. 'What will you be having?' She cast a maternal eye on Cradock. 'You need feeding up, you do.'

Cradock tried to put on a polite smile, but it only made him look more nervous.

'Don't worry. She means well,' said Jago. 'Have what you like. It's my treat today.'

'In that case, I'll have sausage, eggs and bacon,' said Cradock, 'and some fried bread, and a cup of tea, thank you.'

'Right you are,' said Rita. 'Just what you need on a Monday morning. Same for you, Mr Jago?'

'No, I think I'll just have eggs and bacon today, and a cup of tea, of course.'

'That's not enough for a grown man like you. Are you on a diet?'

'No, I'm going out to dinner this evening and I don't want to spoil my appetite.'

'I see. Anyone I know?'

'No comment,' said Jago.

Rita pulled a face and marched off in the direction of the kitchen. Jago watched her go and thought her remarkably cheery, considering the state of the cafe. It wasn't the same place it had been just a few days ago. Since his last visit on Tuesday a bomb had landed across the road and blown out all the windows. The front of the cafe was boarded up now, with just a couple of small panes of glass set into the panels to let in some light. Like many other shopkeepers, she had chalked a 'Business as usual' sign on the outside, but she hadn't tried for the jocular style favoured by some and of course beloved by the photographers and newsreels. Plain and no nonsense, that was the way Rita was, and he admired her for it.

The bomb had damaged a few shops and houses on the other side of the street, but the cinema on the corner had come off worst. One thing, however, had cheered him as he arrived at the cafe that morning. The blast had taken down the wall opposite, and with it the despised red poster that had annoyed him for so long. There was no trace of it. *Well done, Goering*, he thought: *at last you've done us a favour*.

'It's kind of you to treat me to breakfast, guv'nor,' said Cradock. 'Thanks very much.'

'Well, I thought we should celebrate,' said Jago. 'We've caught our killer. You did well.'

'Thank you, sir.'

Cradock felt a glow of pleasure. Hearing those three words at the end of a job from a man as hard to please as Jago was akin to being presented with a gold watch.

Jago's mind was already elsewhere, thinking of

something else that was cause for celebration. After yesterday afternoon's heavy attack the Luftwaffe seemed to have given up for the rest of the day, and as a result he had slept soundly all night. He was also looking forward to a more refined occasion this evening, but he would not be discussing that with Cradock.

Rita arrived with their breakfast and placed it on the table.

'Bon appertee,' she said and departed.

Jago laughed.

'That's a bit posh for a place like this, isn't it?' said Cradock.

'She's just making fun of me,' said Jago. 'She asked me how to say that, and I taught her.'

'French, isn't it?'

'Yes.'

'Edward Villiers kept coming out with foreign stuff when we were talking to him the other day. Was that French too?'

'Yes, it was.'

'A bit hoity-toity, wasn't he, talking like that? I think people like him do it to make you feel inferior, left out. Probably got it from his dad. I didn't understand a word of it myself. Did you, sir?'

'I did, since you ask.'

'You must have gone to a better school than me, then.'

'I doubt it. I learnt it from my mother. She was French.'

'Really, sir? Well I never. I once heard old Frank Tompkins saying there was more to you than meets the

388

eye, but I never would have thought you had a foreign mum. Fancy that.'

'Try to contain your amazement: it's not that unusual. My father simply happened to marry a French woman, and she therefore happened to be my mother.'

'Yes, sir, of course. I didn't mean to be rude.'

'I know you didn't. Now, get on with your breakfast. You don't want it to get cold.'

The two men ate in silence until their plates were almost cleared. Cradock wiped his mouth with the back of his hand and resumed the conversation.

'So, a good result, sir, yes? Everything sorted out, and Johnson and Gray both on their way to court. What do you reckon it'll be for Johnson? The drop?'

'That's a crude term, Peter. You're still talking about a man's life, even if he is a murderer. As for whether he'll hang, you never can tell which way a jury will go: we've all seen some rum verdicts. If you're asking me, though, I'd say his prospects aren't rosy.'

'And what about Gray?'

'I can't see him wriggling out of that business with the alibi for Johnson, and of course he'll be handed over to the army for deserting. Mind you, I'm not so sure they'll want him back in the state he's in, and with a criminal conviction to boot.'

'So he may still get what he wanted when he went AWOL in the first place?'

'If you mean staying out of the army, yes. And talking

of going AWOL, is there any word about Mrs Villiers and the dashing major?'

'Yes, sir. Essex phoned yesterday while we were out at Mrs Cooper's house. It seems they were found staying at a village inn in Theydon Bois.'

'I see. Difficult to keep a low profile in a place as small as that.'

'Yes, and it looks like you were right about the petrol, sir. That's probably about as far as they could get. Apparently the innkeeper thought it was a bit odd – they turned up together looking like a couple and their identity cards said Major Villiers and Mrs Villiers, but the addresses were different. On top of that, he said the man asked for two rooms, but when he said they only had a double available, the woman said they'd take it. Anyway, he didn't do anything about it until yesterday evening, when the local bobby dropped in. The innkeeper mentioned them – probably thought they might be German spies or something – and the bobby recognised the names from our message. But a double room: can you believe it? What a scandal if anyone finds out. I wonder what Edward'll make of it?'

'Well, we're certainly not going to tell him. He can find out for himself, or they can tell him if they want to. But who's to say it's a scandal anyway? I keep telling you not to jump to conclusions. If that was the only room available and they were running out of petrol they may have had no alternative. It's quite possible there was nothing untoward going on at all. In any case, it's none of our business. More to the point, what did our esteemed colleagues in the Essex Constabulary do with the pair of them?'

'They didn't put them in the cells overnight, sir, if that's what you were thinking. Which is probably just as well, considering what we now know about the case. Just told them we'd want to speak to them today and not to go anywhere. Mind you, they'd have had to steal horses to get away, and I don't think they're the kind, really.'

'Right, we'll speak to them, but I think they can sort out their own lives from now on.'

'What about Edward Villiers? We can't just ignore that business with the medical form, even if it was his dad who got it for him. Using a certificate like that with intent to deceive, that'll be an offence, won't it? National Service Act 1939?'

'Correct.'

'So we'll charge him?'

'I expect so. But I wonder what the bench will make of it. If he's telling the truth when he says he wanted to serve, they might wonder where he'll be of most use: in prison or in the forces. Have you ever heard of Lord Penzance?'

'No. Some bigwig in Cornwall?'

'No. He was a judge about sixty years ago; he died before you were born. He said the law is only the handmaid of justice, or ought to be. You can think about what that means later, but I'll be interested to see what the magistrate decides. In a case like this, the law might say convict him, but justice might say let him go and serve his country.'

'I see what you mean, sir. He'd probably be more use to the army than Bob Gray. At least our Edward seems to be sober most of the time.'

'Anything else?'

'Yes, sir. Do we still need to talk to Edgar Simpson about that business of Cooper blackmailing him about his personal life?'

'Yes, we'll do that – find out what really happened. But again, let's not make assumptions about his private life until we know what it was. The fact that he was being blackmailed doesn't necessarily mean he was up to anything illegal.'

Cradock reflected for a moment on what Simpson might have been doing to make himself susceptible to blackmail without breaking any laws, but decided Jago would probably think it inappropriate to speculate. He was almost at the end of his list of questions.

'So that just leaves the Carson family, then, sir.'

'Yes. I went to see them last night. Mrs Carson seems in better spirits now. She says she wants to start again, try to make a new life for herself, although I can't see that being easy. Young Billy's got a new job, though – something to do with munitions at a chemical place in Carpenters Road – so maybe he'll start bringing in more money.'

'And what about that Robert? You said he'd been in a demonstration at the Savoy.'

'Yes, protesting about air-raid shelters, apparently. I've had a chat with him. I thought I ought to explain what sedition is, and I told him to watch his step. He's an excitable lad.'

'Was that reported by a source of yours at the hotel, sir?'

'Never you mind about my source. That's confidential.'

'Of course, sir. Was he nicked?'

'No, I don't think any of them were. From what I've heard it all ended quietly, no harm done. But I've told him not to get too carried away. The last thing his mum needs now is a son in trouble with the law.'

'Do you think he'll manage to stay on the straight and narrow?'

'That remains to be seen, but I think his heart's probably in the right place. It seems these goings-on at the Savoy were a protest – they were saying everyone ought to have access to decent air-raid shelters. When you've seen what's been happening round here in the last few days, I can't say I disagree with them. Same goes for war profiteering: it's a disgrace. I just happen to think the right way to deal with it is through the law, not by having a revolution and stringing people up. But he's a young man, and they get led astray. You ever been led astray, Peter?'

'Not as far as I know, sir.'

'Well, steer clear of religion and politics, that's my advice. Too many people seem to think they can make the world a paradise by killing people. Young Robert seems to have put his money on Joe Stalin, but I personally don't buy it.'

393

'Old Joe seems to be very popular in Russia, though, doesn't he?'

'Depends who you talk to, I suppose. He's certainly got plenty of people in this country with a lot more education and brains than Robert Carson eating out of his hand. Maybe it's wishful thinking: he says Russia's a socialist paradise, and they want to believe it.'

'It could be true, though.'

'Yes, and what's the first rule of detecting? Whatever anyone tells you, assume they're lying. Sad, isn't it? The trouble with our line of work is we see too much of what really goes on in life. What the bullies do to the weaklings, what husbands do to their wives, what vicious old men do to little girls. It's our job to lift up the stones other people don't want to look under. And once you've seen what's underneath, you can't believe the simplistic stuff that the likes of Hitler and Stalin and Mosley come out with. At least I can't. I don't think you can make heaven on earth when you've still got hell in your heart.'

'Not much hope for any of us, then, is there?'

'I'm not sure. There has to be hope, otherwise why would we keep on fighting this war? All I'm saying is if we want something better to come out the other end of it, we've got to be realistic too. At least young Robert has a sense of justice. If he can keep his feet on the ground, maybe he can put it to better use.'

'I suppose so,' said Cradock. He could think of nothing else to say. It was a feeling he was getting used to: in discussions with Jago he always seemed to run out of arguments. *Perhaps I should start reading the newspapers more, or even books*, he thought. *If I can ever find the time.*

'So, I think we've tied up all the loose ends now,' said Jago. 'We should get back to work. I'll go and pay.' He rose from his chair and took a ten-shilling note from his pocket.

'Before we go, sir, there's one other person you haven't mentioned.'

'Who's that?'

'It's someone else you've been dealing with during this case, sir: that American lady. Miss Appleton. Is she a loose end you've tied up too?'

Jago laughed.

'Don't be impertinent, Detective Constable. As far as I'm concerned, she is definitely still a loose end. I shall be questioning her further this evening.'

They walked briskly up West Ham Lane towards the police station. The weather was getting a little chilly, and it was raining. Jago turned up his coat collar and pulled the brim of his hat down over his eyes.

'I hope it stays like this,' he said.

'Why's that, sir?' said Cradock. 'I prefer it dry and sunny.'

'Because I think if it's raining the Germans might not be able to see anything and it might persuade them to stay at home for a change, that's why.'

'They might not want to come back after the pasting

we gave them last night. We shot down a hundred and seventy-five of their planes.'

'Who told you that?'

'No one. It was all over the front page of this morning's paper – I saw it in the newsagent's on my way in.'

'How do you know it's true?'

Even as the words came to his lips, Cradock sensed he was on thin ice.

'Well, it's in the paper. And it must be what the government says.'

'So therefore it's true,' said Jago. 'Have you ever thought the only difference between you and Robert Carson could be that the propaganda you believe comes from different sources?'

'You think the number's false?'

'I'm saying I'm not sure, and that's not just because I'm not in a position to count them for myself; it's because I prefer not to take everything I'm told at face value. They're certainly not going to underestimate the number, are they?'

'I still reckon we shot down more of theirs than they got of ours,' said Cradock.

'That sounds a more plausible position,' said Jago. 'I agree with you.'

They entered the station to find Soper in conversation with Tompkins. The DDI turned round and extended a hand to Jago.

'I've just been hearing about the Villiers and Cooper cases. Well done, John.' He glanced over Jago's shoulder. 'And you too, Constable.'

He hesitated as if unsure what to say next, then with a nod he turned away and strode off.

'Well,' said Tompkins, 'that didn't take too long, did it? I expect you're relieved you didn't have to stand here for ten minutes having your detective skills praised to the rafters. That sort of thing can get a bit embarrassing, can't it?'

'To labour and not to ask for any reward, save that of knowing that we do thy will, that's us,' said Jago. 'That's what they taught me at school. You know we only do this job for pleasure, Frank.'

'Some of us love it so much we even come out of retirement to go the extra mile when we could be digging our allotment instead. Not like the younger generation.' He peered at Cradock over the top of his glasses.

'I don't know why you're looking at me like that,' said Cradock indignantly.

'Don't worry, lad,' said Tompkins. 'I'm only having you on. I'm sure you love the job just as much as I do.'

'Right,' said Jago. 'If we're all so keen, I suggest we get on with our work.'

CHAPTER FORTY-FOUR

Jago was taking a chance. His blue pinstripe suit had survived its previous outing, but another evening on the streets of London at the mercy of the Luftwaffe could easily spell its doom. In matters of suits he believed in paying for quality. He'd once been surprised to see Soper coming out of the Fifty Shilling Tailors on the corner of Angel Lane – not something anyone would ever catch him doing. But if quality had to be paid for, quality had to last. With four suits in his wardrobe, three for work and the other for best, he was keen to avoid losing one. He hoped he would not end the evening throwing himself onto a carpet of broken glass to dodge a bomb blast.

Before leaving the house, he had ironed his white shirt twice and chosen a tie in blue and grey stripes which he thought tasteful and hoped would pass muster. They would surely throw him out of the Savoy if he wore anything that didn't. Standing alone in the front hall of the hotel, he wondered whether he looked like a policeman. He glanced down to check that his shoes were clean and then straightened his back: not quite standing to attention but definitely not at ease.

He chided himself inwardly for being intimidated by the place. He had every right to be there: he was the guest of a resident. As he waited, a succession of patrician figures passed through – regular patrons of the establishment, presumably, and clearly at home amidst its splendours. Where on the scale of social acceptability would they place him, in comparison with Saturday evening's communist intruders? He couldn't help feeling some of them might not make much of a distinction. Judging by his wartime experience of the army's officer class, he suspected they would be likely to lump him in together with everyone else in the country who hadn't been to the same school as them.

Dorothy came into view – a composed figure descending the wide staircase and walking towards him across the hall. Unlike himself, she was not wearing the same outfit as last time: she looked elegantly understated in a grey, long-sleeved silk dress with collar and belt, and a white fur wrap round her shoulders. He had not seen her dressed like this before, but then these didn't look like working clothes. He also realised, in a moment of awkward self-consciousness, that he was admiring her hair. He could not have named the style, but it was something about the way it framed her face that he liked.

He cleared his throat and hoped he had not been staring. He raised a hand in greeting as Dorothy approached.

'Hi,' she said. 'You made it. How nice to see you.'

'The pleasure's mine,' he said. 'And no riots tonight, I see.'

She laughed.

'Yes, so far so good. We should be able to have a quiet evening, raids permitting, but let's not waste any time, just in case they decide to pay us a visit. Shall we go have something to eat? The Savoy Grill is highly recommended. It's just through that door.'

They walked side by side towards the entrance to the Grill on the far side of the hall.

'I feel a bit awkward,' said Jago. 'This is twice in a week you've treated me to a meal here, and all I've offered in return is lunch in a pie shop. It doesn't seem very gentlemanly, expecting you to rough it like that.'

'But you forget,' said Dorothy. 'You were helping me to gain valuable colour for my writing by introducing me to local culture. And when I entertain you here, it's all in the line of business and I can claim it on what some of my less scrupulous colleagues call the "swindle sheet". So there's nothing to feel awkward about.'

'I see,' said Jago. He paused when they reached the doorway, then spoke again.

'I feel rather underdressed, not wearing a dinner suit. I hope you don't mind. It's just that I don't own one:

400

there's not much need for one where I live. I don't want to show you up.'

'I don't think there's any danger of that,' said Dorothy. 'You know, I think these air raids are changing things. Even in this last week I've noticed not so many men are wearing dinner coats or tails here in the evenings. A lot of them have switched to business suits. Maybe at last they think being comfortable is more important than sticking to the old formalities. Whatever the reason, don't you worry: you'll look just as good as anyone else here.'

They entered the Grill and were shown to a table for two. It was immaculately presented, with a heavy white cloth, an array of silver cutlery, and white linen napkins folded into crowns. They both ordered Scottish salmon *bonne femme*, accompanied by a bottle of Sauvignon Blanc.

'How's your investigation going?' said Dorothy.

'Very well. All over bar the shouting, I'd say.'

'Meaning?'

'Meaning I have a man sitting in the cells at West Ham police station who's confessed to two murders. He'll be appearing in the magistrates' court tomorrow, and I expect he'll be committed for trial.'

'So justice will be done?'

'I think so. But it was a tragic case in a way. The man had been terribly wronged and wanted justice, but the trouble was he didn't know the whole truth, so the result was an equal injustice, if not worse.'

The wine waiter arrived and poured a little of the white

wine into Jago's glass, waiting for his approval. Jago imagined the man could probably tell just by looking that what he knew about wine could be written on the back of a postage stamp, but he complied with the ritual and nodded his assent. The waiter poured them each a glass. As a second man headed across the room towards them with their food, Dorothy resumed the conversation.

'You're saying we can't have perfect justice without perfect truth?'

'No, I'm not saying that. If I could achieve perfect anything in my job, believe me I would, but it's not like that. The way I'd put it is we can't have real justice without complete truth. The man in my case killed two men because of what he saw as injustices they'd done, on the basis of what he knew. He had no right to take the law into his own hands, but leaving that to one side, it would seem that if he'd had possession of the complete truth he would only have killed one. The problem is, how do we ever know if we've got the complete truth? It's impossible.'

'So let's compromise: the more truth we have, the more justice?'

'That's more like it. As I see it, the whole world seems to be run on half-truths and downright lies these days, and that's probably why we don't see much justice.'

'We're on the same side, then. You're getting justice for those people who were murdered, because you went for the truth first.'

'In that case,' said Jago, raising his glass, 'I propose a toast: to the truth, and may we both find it.'

Dorothy echoed the toast, and Jago replenished their glasses.

'That's enough philosophy for one evening,' said Dorothy. 'Maybe we should be thinking about doing this salmon justice.'

They began to eat. As Jago savoured the fish melting in his mouth, he wondered again what his companion must have thought of the pie and mash.

'I expect your boss is pleased that you've got to the bottom of it all?' said Dorothy.

'I suppose he is,' said Jago, forcing himself back to the subject of work. 'He hasn't said much about it, but on the other hand he hasn't complained about anything either, so that's a good sign. He and I go back a long way together, and we've never really seen eye to eye on much. To be honest, if I did the job to please him, I'd be disappointed. But I don't: I do it for myself, and if I think I've done a good job, that's enough for me.'

'You're pleased, then?'

'I'm always pleased to finish a case. I don't like leaving things unresolved.'

Jago heard his own words echo in his head as though someone else had said them, and he felt agitated. They reminded him of the question that he had brought with him and that had been troubling his mind all evening. The unresolved question. He knew he would have to ask it, but not yet. For now, he would keep the conversation on the same track while he thought of how to bring it up.

'How's your own work been going?' he said.

'It's been good. And on Saturday, of course, I didn't have to go looking for the story: it came to me, which was very convenient. An eyewitness account of an interesting event, and I didn't even have to leave the hotel. I hope that young man that I recognised didn't get into trouble, though. You got my message?'

'Yes, I got your message, and thanks for letting me know. I went to see him and had a quiet word. I hope that'll help him keep out of trouble in the future.'

'Good. I was concerned about him, and about his mother too, after seeing them out together. These ideologies get such a grip on people. I saw it on both sides in Spain, the communists and the fascists, and when I see those rallies the Nazis have, it makes me shudder.'

'That's why we have to fight this war,' said Jago. 'You can't do a deal with people like that.'

He knew this was the point in their conversation where he should ask his question, but before he could speak the waiter arrived to take their dessert orders. They studied the menu and made their choices: a fruit salad for Dorothy and a more substantial apple crumble and ice cream for himself.

As soon as the waiter had gone, Jago took a deep breath. He knew he could not put it off any longer.

'Dorothy,' he said, 'there's something I need to ask you.'

'Fire away.'

'It's about the war, the last war.'

'OK. What is it?'

'It's difficult for me to talk about. I'm not quite sure what to say, but it's really important to me, so please bear with me.'

'You can say whatever you like; I won't mind.'

'Thank you. The thing is, it's to do with your sister. When you showed me that photograph of her on Saturday I was shocked. You could probably tell.'

'Well, yes. Like I said, you looked like you'd seen a ghost.'

'I had, in a way. I hadn't seen that face since 1918, and I'd never imagined I would. I couldn't believe I was looking at her again after all these years.'

'You said you knew my sister. Did you meet her?'

'Yes: it was when I was wounded, towards the end of 1917. They got me to a casualty clearing station, which probably saved my life, and then I was evacuated to a British base hospital near the French coast. They called it a hospital, but actually it was a huge camp of huts and tents, about a mile long and half a mile wide, with twelve thousand beds. Anyway, there were some American nurses there, and one of them was your sister.'

'That sounds right: I know she was in a place like that. She went over there in 1917, just after America declared war on Germany. A team of volunteer doctors and nurses from Boston went to France to work in a base hospital on the coast, near Le Touquet. I remember before they went they set up a hospital on Boston Common to show everyone what it would look like, and my parents took me to see it. Then just a few days later, I think, we saw Eleanor off on the train from South Station with the rest of the unit. All the local papers had pictures of them going: it was quite a big thing in the city.'

'It was a big thing for me too. I arrived just before Christmas, and it was like waking up in a different world. Those nurses really made an effort to make it special for us – we had presents, Christmas dinner with plum pudding, and even Christmas trees in the wards.'

'That sounds like Eleanor – she always wanted to do more, do better.'

'I'm not sure how reliable my memory is of arriving there,' said Jago, hesitating, 'but—well, it's always seemed to me that your sister was the first person I saw when I woke on my first morning.'

He paused. Dorothy could tell that he was struggling to control his voice. To his relief, the waiter arrived with their desserts. Jago took the opportunity to compose himself, then continued.

'Just two days before that I'd been under continuous shelling and machine-gun fire at the front, and now I woke up in a place that was clean and light and peaceful. I don't believe in heaven, but that's where I thought I was. I saw your sister standing by my bed looking down at me, and I thought I was seeing an angel.'

Dorothy smiled.

'I can vouch for the fact that she wasn't an angel,' she said. 'But when I was a little girl she was everything I wanted to be. Seeing my big sister go off to Europe on an adventure like that had a big influence on me. Just look at what I'm doing today. It sounds like she made quite an impression on you. Did you ever tell her?'

'It's one of the greatest regrets of my life that I didn't. I knew too many stories of men in hospitals falling in love with their nurses and I didn't want to make a fool of myself. Even more, I didn't want to embarrass her. In the end it was taken out of my hands: before I could find a way to say what I felt, I was moved out. They got you back into active service as quickly as they could in those days. I never saw her again.'

'Didn't you write?'

'I suppose I could have written to her at the hospital, but I thought if I couldn't say it face-to-face, how could I do it in a letter? I was afraid she wouldn't understand. You see, I knew what I felt, but I had no idea whether she held any affection for me or whether she was simply being kind. Then when the war ended I assumed she'd gone back to America, so there was no way of contacting her. I just got on with life.'

'But you carried a torch for her, right?'

'Oh yes. I thought I saw something in her that I'd not seen in any other woman, and that stayed with me. I sometimes think in a way I've been looking for her ever since, but always with the fear that she might not have been all I imagined her to be. After all, she was a nurse and I was her patient. Perhaps I've just wasted the last twenty years. You probably think I'm a fool.'

'No, I don't. How could I? You loved my sister.'

'Please just tell me, then, what happened to Eleanor after she left France.'

'OK, but eat your dessert. You haven't touched it.'

Jago had forgotten the dessert, and now had little appetite for it. He took half a spoonful.

'It's quite a simple story,' said Dorothy. 'She came back to Boston and nursed at the Massachusetts General Hospital. She was there for about fifteen years.'

'Did she marry?'

'Not during that time, no. But in 1937 she went out to Spain as a volunteer nurse.'

'She was there the same time as you?'

'We did overlap for a short while, but we were in different parts of the country. I only met up with her once before I got transferred to cover the German takeover in Austria, and then Czechoslovakia. It was just after I left that she wrote to me to say she'd met someone.'

'I see,' said Jago. 'So how does the story end?'

'He was a writer, an American. They married and moved back to the States.'

'And she's happy?'

'Oh yes, she's very happy. But I guess that's maybe not what you wanted to hear.'

'No, I'm truly pleased for her. She deserves all the happiness in the world. I'm glad she found someone who could give her that.'

'How does that leave you feeling after all this time?'

Jago poked at the remainder of his dessert with his spoon while he reflected on what he had heard.

'I think,' he said slowly, 'it makes me feel released from something I've been carrying for a very long time and that's become heavier year by year. It's regret, I suppose, and regret isn't good for you. I think now perhaps it can become just a good memory. A door has been closed, and I can no longer keep nudging it open in my mind. I suppose what it means is I feel free.'

'Free to find your own happiness, perhaps?'

'Yes, perhaps.'

Dorothy said something about having to go powder her nose and left him alone with his thoughts for a few minutes. He finished his dessert more out of duty than of pleasure. It had not been the easiest of conversations, but knowing what had become of Eleanor had finally laid something to rest in him. It also made him feel closer to Dorothy.

She returned to their table and took her seat.

'Would you like a coffee?' said Jago.

'Yes, I would,' she replied. 'But then I think I'll have to call it a day: I've got a lot to do tomorrow and I can't afford to be sleepy.' She looked into his eyes. 'But it's not that I want to run away. Thank you for this evening.'

'It's me who should be thanking you.'

'No, really, I mean it. You can't know how much I've enjoyed this time.'

'So have I,' said Jago. 'I'm sorry I've been a bit serious, but it's meant a lot to me to get the answer to my question at last.'

'I'm glad I could help. Any more questions before we go?'

Jago's face relaxed and his frown disappeared. His voice was lighter when he spoke.

'Well, actually, yes, there is. I've just remembered: it's only a little thing. When we were here on Tuesday you saw that actor Leslie Howard having dinner and you were about to say something, but then you said you didn't want to bore me. What did you mean?'

Dorothy lifted her glass and tilted it a little towards her, then gazed into the pale gold of the wine and blushed. She looked up at him and smiled.

'I was just going to say that you remind me of him, and I think he's rather sweet.'

Jago made no reply. In the brief silence between them, they heard the ominous wail of the siren drifting eerily across the rooftops.

ACKNOWLEDGEMENTS

In 2012 I went to the London Olympics. The games took place in Stratford, once part of the Essex County Borough of West Ham, where this book is set. Sitting with my wife in the stadium waiting for the women's heptathlon to start, I worked out that we were only a few dozen yards from my father's old workplace, in Carpenters Road, now buried under the Olympic Park. Later we walked past Stratford Town Hall. In the Blitz of 1940 he was on its roof, doing fire-watching duty as a seventeen-year-old Home Guard volunteer, responsible for spotting and extinguishing any incendiary bombs that might land on it. As we emerged from the Olympic stadium into the twenty-first-century shops and traffic it was difficult to believe those days had really happened.

In writing this book I've been depicting a world that is still vividly present in our cultural memory and yet irretrievably lost to the past. Some would say the transformation of the East End of London in the post-war years is a tragedy; others would say it's a triumph – the truth is no doubt a mix of the two.

For those like me, born in the decade after 1945, the war was part of the background to our lives, but as remote as anything that happens in the world before we enter it. When I was a schoolboy, all our dads had been 'in the war' in one way or another, so there was nothing unusual about it. Most, like mine, who went on to serve in a reconnaissance regiment in the Italy campaign, didn't talk about it much: I think they wanted something better for their children.

The little they did say, however, was eye-opening. My mother's description of seeing the sky red over London from the fires on the first night of the Blitz is as vivid in my imagination now as it was when I was nine years old.

Sadly, the people I would most like to thank for their contribution to this book – my parents – are no longer here, but I can at least record my thanks and admiration for the part they played in those dramatic days, and for leaving a little of it in me.

This book is fiction, but the time and the location where it takes place are real. I would like to thank Richard Durack and Jenni Munro-Collins of the Heritage and Archives Team at Stratford Library for their help in exploring the rich resources held by the library's excellent local history centre, and also John and Muriel Moore for their stories of the old days.

I am grateful to the Friends of the Metropolitan Police Historical Collection and to the Metropolitan Police Heritage Centre for their assistance on factual aspects of policing in West Ham in 1940. I am also indebted to Retired Superintendent Roy Ingleton, Retired Chief Superintendent Robert Bartlett and Retired Detective Chief Inspector Mike Gurton for kindly allowing me to draw on their experience and knowledge in creatively portraying the life of a detective in those days. Any inaccuracies are due to my ignorance or to the artistic licence necessary in fiction.

I am grateful to Richard White for introducing me to his Riley Lynx, and to my friends Rudy and Sara Mitchell in Boston, Massachusetts, for their help with the American dimensions of the story.

As this new edition is published, I would like to thank Tony Collins and Jess Gladwell and their colleagues at Lion Hudson who helped to bring DI John Jago to life, my agent, Broo Doherty, and all at Allison & Busby for opening this exciting new chapter for the Blitz Detective. A big thank you to my dear family and to so many friends for their constant interest and encouragement along the way. And lastly, my love and thanks to my wife, Margaret, who has been as always my most patient and perceptive support through all the long hours and days it has taken to make this book a reality.

DON'T MISS THE BLITZ DETECTIVE'S
NEXT CASE

THE CANNING TOWN MURDER

September, 1940. As the Blitz takes its nightly toll on London and Hitler prepares his invasion fleet just across the Channel in occupied France, Britain is full of talk about enemy agents. Suspicion is at an all time high and no one is sure who can be trusted.

In Canning Town, rescue workers are unsettled when they return to a damaged street and discover a body that shouldn't be there. When closer examination of the corpse reveals death by strangling, Detective Inspector John Jago is called upon to investigate. But few seem to really care about the woman's death – not even her family. As Jago digs deeper he starts to uncover a trail of deception, betrayal, and romantic entanglements . . .

MIKE HOLLOW was born in West Ham, on the eastern edge of London, and grew up in Romford, Essex. He studied Russian and French at the University of Cambridge and then worked for the BBC and later Tearfund. In 2002 he went freelance as a copywriter, journalist, editor and translator, but now gives all his time to writing the Blitz Detective books.

blitzdetective.com   *@MikeHollowBlitz*